Tough Love

ROSEWOOD RANCH SERIES

ALEXANDRA BANKS

WILLOW HOUSE Publishing

For more information, or to book an event, contact:

alexandrabanksauthor@gmail.com

Book design by Alexandra Banks

Cover design by Alexandra Banks

ISBN (ebook): 978-1-7635496-2-3

ISBN (paperback): 978-1-7635946-3-0

First Edition: July 2024

For every reader who wants to run off into the mountains and live with a gorgeous cowboy with a Stetson and a horse…

This one's for you.

Author's Note

TW –

Death of an animal/s.

Mature, explicit intimate scenes.

Coarse language.

The location and topographies of the places in this story have been fictionalized. They may not accurately represent actual location and terrain.

P.S The playlist is in the back!!

TOUGH
LOVE

2016
Pre-Olympic Show Jumping Qualifiers

Jewls prances under seat, as nervous as I am. All one thousand pounds of bay mare, lit and ready to go. We have been together every day for five years. I trust her. She trusts me. I shorten the reins and scope the course quickly, one last time. The water jump will be our pinch point before the sharp turn to the triple.

"And our final rider of the day, nineteen-year-old Adeline Howard, with her mare, Jewel of the Nile. This magnificent duo has taken the competition by storm this year, folks, *the* combination to watch today." The commentator talks us up, like I haven't worked for over a decade to come this far. The early mornings, the broken bones. The losses, some more heart-wrenching than others.

Last rider out is a big deal. In show jumping, they always save the best for last. I squash down the imposter syndrome that has been creeping its way up ever since I saw the order list. That little voice in my head that tells me this isn't real, I'm not that good, and soon everyone is going to see it.

The horn blows, blasting through my ears.

I shift forward in the saddle, the only cue Jewls needs, and she takes off toward the first jump. I hold my breath.

"And they're off!"

We power for the jump, and I pace her back a little, pulling back on the reins. We sail over the top rail.

Clear.

I force myself to breathe, pacing my own body as I do hers. Her half-Arabian bloodline pushes her faster than we need some days. The stadium lights are glaring. The crowd waits with bated breath. Only murmurs poke through the heavy silence as they wait for Jewls and I to either fly or fall. This round determines who goes to the Olympics. The next few minutes define other riders' fates, not only mine.

The next jump is across the damp sand arena, the double. She pops her head. I shorten her stride.

"Steady, girl."

I'm up out of the saddle as she takes off for the top rail. We sail over and she lands, square. *Good girl.*

I pat her neck, and we take off toward the third set. Then the next and the next. The only sounds are her hooves, her breathing, my soft words. I glance at the giant red digital clock. Shit, we are behind time. I give Jewls her head, and she picks up the pace. We have run these courses together hundreds of times. She knows every move I make. Knows when we are good and when we're not.

Four jumps left. We soar toward the hedge. Up and over, her back legs trail through the hedge. She flinches. Okay, not a big deal. We will steady the lead up to the next one. Another double.

Jewls moves underneath me; her stride is jerky. Something's not right.

I push her forward.

She takes the first set of the double. We land off-kilter, and she makes for the second, too early. We clip the top rail. The crowd gasps. If it falls, we won't have the points to come in first. I steady her, leaning back to slow her down. I shorten the reins again. The water jump is next.

Jewls tosses her head. Her dark eye flicks to mine.

I glance at the clock. Another second too slow.

My gut sinks.

I push her ahead. A strangled whinny leaves with her breath, but she bursts toward the water. I set the pace and loosen the reins as she launches over the blue plastic wave at the start of the jump. The water on the other side glistens. Jewls tenses midair. I brace for a hard landing.

But she hits the ground with a solid stride. I turn her for the hairpin, and she tosses her head again.

"It's okay, girl. Easy."

She nickers, snorting a breath.

Something has her riled up. Her tail flings side to side, erratically.

One last jump.

The triple.

I give her more rein, and we pick up pace. Every stride now, she grunts a breath. Sand flies out from under her back feet. I shorten her stride and push out of the saddle. She launches at the poles, but her body flails sideways. Blood and spit fling from her muzzle.

What the hell?!

"Jewls!"

I tighten my legs around her. She smashes into the poles. They clatter to the ground as we tumble through them and toward the ground. Her head plows into the sand. I lurch forward. My foot is stuck in the right stirrup as she rolls. My back slams into the sand. Air rushes from my lungs. My head bounces, rattling in the helmet.

The lights of the stadium ceiling flood my vision. Silence presses down.

Then screams and shouting grow, echoing around me. Jewls jerks and rolls, still pinning me to the ground. My hip bone cracks. Pain floods my body, consuming it whole. Ringing in my ears drowns the crowd's frantic roar. A shallow breath burns its way into my lungs. Pain lances through my ribs. My body is fuzzy, my right leg numb.

Then Jewls stills.

I snap my head to the side, searching for movement.

Something thuds. The pole from the double has fallen to the ground.

Limp, Jewls lays on top of me, unmoving.

No!!

"Jewls!"

Tears burn my eyes and roll down my cheeks. A shadow appears overhead.

Men file in around Jewls and me. Hands steady my neck.

"Addy! Oh no!" Mom's voice slips through the ruckus. Her hand touches my cheek. Five men lift and roll Jewls from my crushed leg and hip. Fire courses through every inch of flesh and vein. My foot drops from the hung-up stirrup.

Darkness.

Beep.

Beep.

Beep.

Whoosh. Whir.

Soft voices.

Tight blankets and warmth.

I force my eyes open . . . and the world spins.

"Mom?" I choke.

She stands by the hospital room door with a man in a white coat.

"Adeline was lucky to get out of that accident, Mrs. Howard. Her injuries could have been far worse. If the horse had rolled over her completely, she wouldn't be here."

I swallow.

Jewls.

Emotion closes over my throat. I grip the blanket at my sides, and something stings in my right wrist. I lift it. An IV.

"Your daughter is young. She could make a full recovery with the right physical therapy. But I doubt she will have a show-jumping career from this point onward."

The white room and bar windows of the hospital room close in on me.

Footsteps clack toward where they stand in the doorway. Dad appears. His face is twisted, sadness lining his eyes. He shakes his head.

"Oh Jesus, she is going to be so devastated, Logan."

Dad pulls Mom into a hug, and her shoulders shake.

"The horse?" the doctor asks, but he looks down at his clipboard.

Dad stares at him. "Snake bite. She was gone before we even got Addy out from under her."

"How the hell does that happen?" Mom pushes out of Dad's arms.

"It was in the bloody hedge jump. The course builders figure it came in for the water and hid in the hedge. Addy and Jewel were the last ones over that jump. It would have been good and riled up after twenty-odd horses disturbed it. Was a taipan."

"At least it was quick." Mom's words are barely there.

I knew something was up with Jewls, and I pushed her anyway. My chin wobbles and tears burn down my cheeks. My poor girl. She trusted me, and I didn't listen.

Mom sighs, folding her arms over her chest. "The doctor was saying Addy will need physical therapy to get back on her feet. No more jumping."

"So, we funnel all of our efforts into vet school for her." Dad's words are kind, hopeful.

I slam my hands over my face.

How can they be thinking about me still becoming a vet after this? Sobs wrack my body. I struggle to pull air to my lungs. Mom's hands land on mine a moment later. I sit up and she folds me into her. Her hands stroke my hair, the way they always have since I was a little girl when I'm upset. "I'm so sorry, Addy."

Dad's splayed, warm hand rubs my back. I know I should be glad I'm okay. I have seen things go so wrong for other show jumpers in the ten years I have been doing this. Much worse than a messed-up hip. But I can't breathe.

Jewls is gone.

The day I met her, she changed my life. She chose me.

Just walked on over and rubbed her dark muzzle into my arm. We were so much more than a girl and her horse.

She had my back for five years. And I let her down.

I was so obsessed with making time, I didn't pay enough attention to her. This is all my fault.

My heart shatters.

Chapter One

HUDSON

Almost eight years later . . .
Summer 2024

Charlie trots beside my paint gelding, nose to the ground, tail up. As if he is tracking the herd of pregnant mares ahead of us through the flowing grass on the hilly peak. He's shorter than the grass and disappears now and then, the swaying sea of stalks swallowing him whole. I chew on one such stalk I plucked before we set out for home.

The wind is up today, buffeting against the brim of my Stetson, and the gelding tosses his head, mane flopping over his patchy neck. The sun warms my tanned arms. There's a solid line where the light blue t-shirt ends and the sunburnt skin starts. Mountains flank us on either side. Snow-capped and blue, and they darken as the clouds drift overhead.

Our pace is steady, despite the fact that my father will be pacing the barn as he waits. Nothing is ever fast enough or done well enough for Harrison Rawlins. The oversized, full bellies of my mares sway ahead. We are taking it slow; they will be foaling in a few months. The ranch will need new blood in a few years.

Charlie barks, taking off after a rabbit, his ragged terrier instincts kicking in.

I slide my sunglasses down a little as he darts around the grass, white with patches of tan long-haired pup appearing now and then. I chuckle, enjoying the serenity of the quiet ride home. I know that the moment I'm off this horse, the old man is going to want to get right into breaking in.

And while I love that part of raising ranch horses, and the challenge that comes with every new filly and colt, I hate playing by the old man's rules. But since I will always be the dutiful son, the only one out of the four of us that is still here *and* invested in the ranch, I do.

Not too many people would dare talk back to Pa. It's his way or the highway. Which for the middle of nowhere, mid-Montana, that's saying something. My three younger brothers found a work-around for the old man's condescending and continuous demands. One joined the army, one decided to be utterly uninteresting and work in ranching, happy to be left alone. One moved to New York and got a human resources degree. Sold his soul to the devil, if you ask Harry. They have balls, my little brothers, I'll give them that.

We round the last of the hilly terrain and start the descent toward the homestead. The house my father built spans the big yard. Big windows and a wraparound porch complete the multi-gable home with twin chimneys. Charlie takes up his place beside the horse—he has the drill down pat.

The homestead is flanked by smaller paddocks for the working horses. The two large red barns sit behind the homestead, with old oaks dotted around the area. Ma's favorite spot, the southernmost oak, shelters a long wooden table for Sunday lunches and other occasions.

Reed's fancy truck is in the driveway still. Must have had a big night. Reed Rawlins, youngest of the four of us, and the only one of my brothers to still live at home with us, despite his waning interest in ranch life.

When we reach the holding paddock the mares will stay in for the next few months, I ride in behind them until the last of the mares has filed in. I turn the gelding, maneuvering him sideways to shut the gate. Charlie slips under the wooden railing and trots around the herd, as if inspecting the goods.

I whistle and he races back. I push the gelding into a lope down the long, fenced laneway between the foaling paddock and the barn and sit back in the saddle. The steady lope of the gelding reminds me why I do this every day. The effortless movement of man and beast—my favorite part of the job.

When I slow to a halt, Pa waits, his arms slung across the top rail. Charlie races past my old man and jumps away when Harry reaches out to pat him. Charlie has never liked anyone but me. Reed jokes about Charlie's aversion to the old man, says the dog is a good judge of character. He's probably onto something; Harry Rawlins is a hard man. Hard to work with, hard to live with. Expectations are impossibly high when it comes to our father.

"Damn dog got social anxiety, Hudson?" Pa asks. His words are gravelly.

"He's picky. Don't take it personal."

"Any trouble with the mares?"

"Nope, all good and steady. Looking ready for November foaling."

"Good. Keep an eye on them. Don't want to lose any when the weather starts to cool down. You ready for this colt? I ain't gettin' any younger, son."

He nods to the yearling in the pen he leans on. The young'un walks in circles, sniffing the ground, trotting, and prancing.

"Sure, give me a minute to turn out the gelding."

"Make it quick. Larry's waiting and wants to see how the little upstart gets on."

"Yes, sir."

I walk the gelding to the barn and unsaddle him. Swapping out his bridle for a halter, I take him to the concrete pad by the side of the barn and hose him off. Unclipping the lead, I turn him out into his yard. He wanders away, content to graze, and I make my way back to the round yard. Pa has the young'un already in the center, halter on with a long lead. I climb through the rail and walk to where they stand.

The colt nickers as I take the lead from Pa.

"Send him 'round, then bring him in."

I click my tongue and toss the end of the lead toward his rump. The colt takes off around the pen, following the rail as I hold him in the center. He is doing well. For just over a week of working together, he has picked up most things fast.

"Fast learner," Pa says, now outside the round yard again.

"Yep."

"Keep him goin', don't let him turn lazy." He pushes off the rail and walks back to the house. Always has the last word, Pa. Always.

Steadying the colt, I tug the lead, coaxing him in. When he stops inches from where I stand, he rubs his face on my shirt. "Yeah, I know, buddy. He's a mean old man. Lucky for you, you're stuck with me."

Charlie trots back over from wherever he's been. No doubt herding Ma's chickens behind the eastern barn. He's going to get his ass whooped one day, when she catches him. My stomach grumbles. I rub the colt's face and remove the lead. I work the colt until the top of the hour. With a broken pipe to mend this morning and ten miles of fencing to start on, I call it quits. But first, Ma's cooking is callin' my name.

Charlie follows as I walk to the gate that leads to the colt's paddock. I open it and he walks through before I shut it behind him. I hear her nicker before I find her. Silver. The mare I learned to ride on. Ancient, as far as any horse goes. But she's special. Too old now, I keep her in the paddock closest to the homestead. Having been promised a cushy retirement, that's what she got. She worked hard, my girl. Owes me nothing.

Charlie sits, watching Silver take her time getting to the fence. I rub her forehead. "Hey, girl. You alright today?"

Charlie has been my constant companion for the last five years. I brought him home from a shelter in the city, the day after my heart was broke in two. I was twenty-nine, thought I had life handled. Sworn off women since then. Settling down is something I am supposed to want, but once bitten, twice shy. It's going to take one hell of a woman to convince me to hand over my heart again.

Charlie is right behind me when I push through the back door and make my way to the kitchen. Ma is rolling out dough for something that will be delicious, no doubt. She glances up from her work as I drop into my chair at the table. The kitchen is enormous, a testament to her constant cooking. And I figure she loves doing it, since she is always cooking up something—literally.

"Huddy, how are the girls?"

"Good, Ma. All settled in."

"See your father? He wanted to take a look at that colt."

"Yup. Done that, too."

Dusting off her hands, she plucks a couple of freshly baked cookies from a cooling rack and pours a cup of coffee before rounding the counter and dropping both in front of me on the table. Leaning against the table, she folds her arms over her chest. "Your brother was out again last night. You should have gone along, too."

"Not interested. Reed's the ladies' man, Ma."

She shakes her head at me and sighs. "Only want you to be happy. Next weekend, tag along. You don't have to stay as long as Reed, but go out, hang with your friends, meet some new people."

"By *new people*, you mean women."

She raises both hands, palms up, with the most inno-cent 'I don't know' face. *Nice try, Ma.* "Did I say that? Come on, Hudson, thirty-four is well and truly the age to be settled. I'm not getting any younger, and this old lady wants grandbabies, you hear me?"

I roll my eyes at her and sip the coffee. Sharp, bitter and hot. The way I like it. "You should have this conversa-tion with the ladies' man instead, then."

As if summoned by Lucifer himself, Reed walks around the corner, hand running through his blond bedhead, bare-chested in boxers. "What did I do this time?"

"Nothing yet, little brother."

Pushing out of the chair, I pluck a cookie from the plate and shove it into my mouth, heading for the door. Fences don't build themselves, and the day is only going to get hotter. "Working on the northern fence line today. See you out there in an hour, Reed."

He grunts and sinks into a dining chair.

"I'm serious, lover boy. Or I'll send Charlie back for you."

"Alright, I'll be there, tyrant. Don't send that cranky mutt anywhere near me."

"Thanks for the coffee, Ma," I say.

"Anytime, my love. Think about what I said, will you?"

I grumble a half-answer and walk through the back door. I'll think about it—maybe for ten seconds. Hudson Rawlins and women is a bad idea. It will end the same way it did with Jemma. Her wanting something I can't give. Me with a broken heart.

I snatch my phone from my pocket and check the battery life.

I'm not anticipating anything to go sideways, but fencing can be a sneaky trade. One wrong move on taut wire can have it slip and fling back to slice you open. I still have the scar on my wrist from back when I was seventeen to prove it. I try not to make that mistake too often, but you can never be too careful. Jumping into my banged-up old Chevy, I head to the barn.

Hooking up the fencing trailer, I toss in more wire and

the post rammer. I'll give Reed that job; he needs the practice more than I do. I chuckle to myself as I pluck up two sets of heavy-duty gloves and jump back in the truck. At my whistle, Charlie bounds up and into the back of the truck. An hour later, I am at the northernmost end of the ranch.

I pull up and shift the stick before turning off the truck. Mountains stud the horizon on all sides now. Yellow wildflowers cover the sunny patches between the trees. The hilly paddock is large enough that the rest of the boundary is out of sight. The old fence is all but laying over, the cattle milling around the few clumps of old trees down one side of the hill.

Charlie jumps down and heads straight under the dilapidated fence, heading for the cattle. He trots around, sniffing the ground, as if too scared to interact with the cattle, tail between his legs. Wimp. Reed drives up along the side of the fence as I start unloading the gear. He shuts off his truck and wanders to the trailer. "Surprised Harry hasn't sent us up here before now."

He has always called the old man Harry. Beats me how he gets away with it. I sure as hell won't be trying it. "I'll dismantle the old fence. You start laying out the new posts."

"Yes, sir."

"Don't call me that, Reed."

"Why not? You're gonna be the boss around here in less than a year, aren't ya?"

I grunt. *God willing.*

He rolls his eyes, shrugging as he slides a post from the trailer onto his shoulder. "You know, Huddo, if you don't want to end up like the old man, you should probably stop acting like him."

I snip the stretched and bent wire and slide it out of the holes in the weathered, splintered posts. Reed has always liked to offer sage advice when it's not wanted. I've gotten used to ignoring him. But something in my gut twists with that particular piece of advice. Because, deep down, I know he's right.

He's not the only one, either. Jemma knew it. I'm hard to love. Don't open up easily and get invested even less easily. As much as I hate to admit it, I am a chip off the old block. Harry's right hand, and on the hard days, his fall guy. His yes-man.

Kind of a rite of passage being the oldest, I reckon. But we are more alike than I care to admit. Even through my carpentry apprenticeship, I felt different to the other guys. Not the fun-loving, partying type that the rest of my class was.

Ma calls me an old soul. But I'm about ninety-five percent sure that's her diplomatic way of saying I am a boring grump.

"Like I mean, seriously, Huddo. Look at you. Lean, mean, and all muscle. A Stetson, blue t-shirt, and Wranglers. Brown hair, blue eyes for years. And that jaw . . . Now, you got *that* from the old man, you lucky prick.

You're not bad on the eyes, big brother. Ma's got a point. The ladies are missing out. Let someone in, Hudson, anyone. I'm begging you!"

I toss the pliers at his head, and he ducks. Wouldn't want to mess up that pretty face.

"Shut up, Reed. More posts, less words."

"You know, women are always asking about you when I'm out. I know at least three that would die to climb you like a tree. You're not gonna be short of choices." He winks at me and shoulders another post. Cocky little upstart. Trust him to take Ma's side.

Mama's boy.

Chapter Two

ADDY

The machines attached to the horse's muzzle hiss and whir. The green material draped over the gelding's body rises and falls with the steady rhythm of its breathing. I clamp off the last of the small vessels and cauterize it. The dank tang of burning flesh creeps behind my mask, but I don't even care.

I did it.

The final surgery of the day. One more patient fixed up and on the road to recovery.

"Excellent work, Addy. Stitch him up. I'll meet you outside to talk to the owners," Joe says. He's my mentor of three years—during my last year of vet school and the two years I have interned under his wing in the New York Equine Veterinary Clinic. Of all the places to intern, this was a magnificent opportunity.

And I would stay here in a heartbeat, if I wanted a

narrow field of focus. But I want to learn from others and garner experience from every horse industry I can. I plant the last stitch into the gelding and hand him over to the very capable nurses.

Pushing through the swinging theater doors, I pull off my face mask and untie the cord at the back of my gown and toss them all into the linen cart. Now down to my scrubs, I wander through the next set of doors to where Joe and the owners wait in the well-lit hall.

"Here she is now. Addy, how is Bandit?"

"He's doing great. Just closed up, and his vitals are stable. The recovery should be straightforward."

The man and woman stand with polite smiles, their high-end clothes immaculate. Her blonde hair is styled and neat, his brown hair swept to the side, and they release a collective breath. "Thank goodness. That gelding is worth a fortune. Out of competition is not ideal. Thank you for your work, Doctor . . . ?"

"Dr. Howard. But you can call me Addy." A smile blooms over my face. I will never tire of being called Dr. Howard, but Addy is much better.

"Thank you, Addy," the woman says, gripping my hands with hers.

"You're most welcome."

"Right, well, I will show you to recovery. You can wait for Bandit to come to, if you like?" Joe says to the owners.

"Yes, absolutely."

They follow him as he shows them down the hallway

and through the next set of swinging double doors. I lean on the wall, blowing out a breath. It's so surreal to be done. My phone vibrates in my pocket. Pulling it out, I open my eyes. The instant I glance at the name, I smile. Dad.

I swipe the screen.

> All done! Adds, we are so stinkin' proud of you, my girl.

> Thanks, Dad.

> Your mom wants to know if you have time to come over for lunch tomorrow, to celebrate?

> Ah, sorry, Dad, have to be in Montana in four days. I'm leaving this afternoon. Only need to load the Cherokee up with my few boxes and I'm off.

> Well, you drive safe, and remember, if those cowboys don't appreciate you, you can always come home. Joe will always take you back.

Joe is my dad's best buddy from college. So, I guess you could say he is more like an uncle to me. And he rode me hard when I first started. Six of us started, and only four of us stuck it out. The pressure is intense in a prestigious clinic like this. Horses are worth thousands; their owners are not always easy to deal with. But it was worth every mistake, every heartache, every handful of days that I stayed awake for too long to make sure my patients had continuity of care.

Will do, Dad. Love you both. Kiss Mom for me, will you?

Ten four.

With a sigh, I close my eyes briefly. Everything is lighter. Almost as if the closing of one chapter and the beginning of the new one I am about to embark on is so right. Down-to-my-bones right. Something in my soul knows that in Montana, in the mountains, in that rugged wilderness, I am going to find myself. Prove my mettle. Excited is an understatement.

"Adds, you're done! You're free!" Joe's excitement almost matches mine as he strides back down the corridor toward me.

I chuckle and push off the wall. He slings an arm over my shoulders. "Fancy a drink to celebrate?"

Everyone wants to celebrate. It's nice.

"Sorry, long drive, and I leave this afternoon."

"Bummer, well"—he removes his arm and turns to face me—"you know, if things don't work out in Hicksville, we will take you back with open arms."

"Thanks Joe, but hopefully, it will be what I need."

Another thing I am hoping to get out of moving halfway across the country—distance from Adam. The one person who I am happy to be leaving behind. Ex-boyfriend, classmate, and utter douchebag. Well, at least that's what I tell myself when he tries to crawl back. Every time, I cave and let him back in. It never lasts—he always finds a new way to hurt me. Honestly, I have no idea why I let him, but a face like that is hard to say no to. And he's familiar, comfortable. Not to mention the British accent . . .

And so not happening again.

Like ever.

Thousands of miles should be enough to let me move on. Here's hoping. I make my way to the staff room and spin the dial on my locker. It opens, and photos of my parents flutter. I pull out my tote bag and pluck them from the metal door, smiling at the sweet face of my best friend, Ruby.

I will miss her. So much. But Rubes promises to visit. She is always traveling with her job, anyway, as an events coordinator working with high-end companies, new and established resorts, and travel destinations. I tap out a message to her.

> Hey Rubes, I'm heading west this afternoon. I'll call you when I get there.

My phone pings a second later.

> Yes, please do, drive safe. Promise to visit you out in cowboy country asap!

Tapping out my goodbyes, I shove the rest of my belongings into my tote and shut the locker. All that is left to do is hand in my key card and say my goodbyes.

When the last box is piled into the trunk of my Cherokee, I take one last sweep around the small apartment that has housed me for the last eight years. I never thought I would ever miss this space, but seeing it void of the things that made it my home, I feel a little sad. Not dwelling, I shut the door and head back to the car. Time to bust these city limits.

I turn the keys over and start the car. The Bluetooth connects. "Siri, play Montana playlist."

The twang of the country music playlist Joe compiled for me floods the car. I chuckle a little at the foreign sound, but after an hour, I am humming along to some of the tunes. They're actually not too bad.

Lewistown is my destination. And if these songs are worth their salt, the place should feel like home the moment I step foot on Montana dirt. But I won't hold my breath. As long as I have a job vetting horses and am miles away from Adam, everything else I can figure out as I go.

Settling in for the long drive, I swear my singing gets better with every mile.

Four days later, the welcome sign for Lewistown comes into view. I pull over at the first gas station and pull up the address for my apartment. I punch the deets into the phone and let the GPS lady guide me home. GPS Gwen. No secrets here . . .

Gwen and I are on a first-name basis after the last four days and one never-ending road trip. We're besties now. I snort a laugh at my own ridiculousness. Rolling through the quiet streets of Lewistown, I get a sense of what it's like to live a slower-paced life. And I'm pleasantly surprised by the absence of honking horns, miles of bumper-to-bumper cars, and crossings packed with people.

It's so calm. I can't help the smile that grows over my face. When Gwen finally says "You have reached your destination," I'm inclined to believe her.

"Gwen, you may be right."

She doesn't answer, of course. If I have learned anything about her over the past four days, it's that she is the strong, silent type, apparently. I pull into the drive of the quaintest little townhouse I have ever seen. Its blue paint and white trim are gorgeous. The planters that hang from the windows on either side of the red door make me smile. "Wow."

A good start to my next chapter. Made it here safely, check. Country cottage that feels like home, check. I turn off the ignition and climb out of the car. Kneading my hands into my lower back, I shut the door and slide my phone into my back pocket. Key's under the front mat, the email from Sally, the receptionist of the clinic I will be working for, had said. I step up onto the small white porch and lift the coarse-fiber welcome mat. Sure enough, a single house key sits on the white-painted wood.

I slide it into the lock and open the door. The inside is as gorgeous as the outside. I walk into the foyer. The wall to my right is lined with brass hooks. A small, dark wooden side table stands underneath. The entrance opens to a living room and kitchen. The white farmhouse-style kitchen is gorgeous. There is a glass back door and a set of stairs to the left of it. I wander through the house, exploring.

Every room that I find makes me squeal.

"I can't believe this is all mine!" I reach the top of the stairs. A queen canopy bed sits in the center of the largest bedroom I have seen in the last decade. A bathroom is joined to it on the left. With a tub! Ugh . . . Holy mama, these country bumpkins might be onto something.

I flop on the bed, arms out and eyes closed. With a laugh, I open my eyes and look to my vibrating phone.

Sally.

You have a call out first thing tomorrow morning. Harry Rawlins, mares for a checkup. Twelve mares, foaling date mid-late November. Don't be late. He is a stickler for punctuality. 8am sharp. Rosewood Ranch, 40 miles out of town. Hillview road.

P.S. Welcome to Lewistown! Looking forward to meeting you tomorrow after the Rawlins' visit. :)

Holy shit.

I squeal and kick my legs and swing my arms in the air. Time to get this city girl unpacked. I jump off the bed and take the stairs two at a time. An hour later, I am unpacked and headed to the downtown area to grab some groceries. With the last four days catching up to me, I yawn. It's around eight when I decide tomorrow's worth turning in early for.

The alarm I set blasts my eardrums. I groan and roll over, still slightly stiff from days of driving. I roll out of bed and pull on my jeans and a button-down shirt with my boots from the internship, comfortable but steel-capped and sturdy. I head to the kitchen and make a coffee before locking up and driving to the clinic.

I walk to the back, where the night shift nurses still have the door unlocked, and walk in to grab some gear. With all my supplies gathered, I double-check the address and tell Gwen. She is on it right away, and we set off, two girls heading for the hills of Montana.

Chapter Three

HUDSON

"**S**end him around again." Harry stands on the bottom rail, arms resting on the top rail, spouting orders as usual. I toss the lariat behind the colt, and he takes off around the round yard. He has learned go, stop, and come to me. Quick learner, this little guy.

"Good. Should have him running along in a few weeks." Harry slips from the rail and walks toward the homestead. "Oh, Hudson, the vet will be here in half an hour. Take him to the mares for their monthly workup, then I want that fence line sorted out. Reed can help you."

"Yes, sir."

I send the colt again before stopping in the center of the yard. Letting the rope loosen, I wait for him to come to me. He slows and, after a quarter way 'round again, he turns and walks to where I stand. "Good boy."

I rub a hand up his forehead and over his eyes before pulling a treat from my back pocket—a couple of slices of carrot I stole off the counter while Ma was chopping vegetables for tonight's supper. He gently takes them from my flattened hand.

A dusty Cherokee pulls into the drive at the homestead. Not the usual vehicle Dr. Randall brings. Must be a rental. And he's early . . . Unless my half-an-hours have shrunk?

I lead the colt back to his paddock, let him loose, and turn back, shutting the gate. A woman steps out of the car. I stop short. Definitely *not* Randall. Her curly light brown hair whips around her face in the breeze. After hauling a large bag from the trunk, she walks to the front door.

Who on earth is that? Some friend of Reed's? The only thing my brother likes better than his shiny machines is a pretty girl. Maybe she has come to move in—serves him right. I chuckle and make my way back to the house to wait for the vet.

The woman stands just inside the doorway, bag still in her hand. For one of Reed's girls, she looks a little too smart. Her curly brown hair sits around her shoulders, the morning sun turning it golden brown. She glances at me when I move further into the room. Her brown eyes find mine.

Holy fuck.

A smattering of freckles sits over her cheeks as she smiles at me.

And . . . my gut flips. My mouth gapes. I snap it shut and clear my throat. Pa's gaze alternates between her and me.

Harry shakes her hand. Something doesn't add up. Why is he shaking her hand?

"Thanks for coming out, Dr. Howard. Hudson here will show you up to the mares."

Argh. Jesus.

Hudson, you fucking idiot.

"Please, call me Addy. And that would be wonderful. I can't wait to meet them all." Her face is lit up with the brightest smile.

Goddamn, she's beautiful.

Harry grunts, dismissing her. Ma stands at the kitchen counter, glancing between Dr. Howard and me. *Oh no, Ma, don't you even think it.* I clear my throat, desperate to get out of the house before my mother starts trying to make plans neither of us want. "We can take my truck."

I walk out the back door, not waitin'. Ma says something to Addy, but she excuses herself. The back door bangs behind me a moment later. "Hudson?"

I keep walking. "Yeah."

"Ah, how far along are the mares?"

I turn back, and she almost slams into my chest but grips the bag in front of her instead and takes a step back. I tilt my head. "They are due late November."

"If you have an accurate due date, that would help."

I fold my arms. She frowns but schools it to a polite smile a heartbeat later.

"Third week of November; that's as accurate as it gets around here, Dr. Howard."

"Okay, great. And please, call me Addy."

"Whatever you say, Dr. Howard."

I turn and walk to my truck. She sighs but follows me. I'm being an ass, but that beautiful face, those brown eyes have caught me off guard. And I'm not sure I like the heady feeling I'm getting, being so close to her. *Get your shit together, Hudson. Jesus.*

I open the passenger side door and lean on it. She steps into the space, and I take the bag from her hands. My mother's ways are ingrained into my brain, even when I don't want them. I put the bag in the back of the truck. Brushing past me, she climbs in, and the scent of apples and spice tangles through the air around me. Clearing my throat, I shut the door and count to ten as I walk around the back of the pickup and take four long, steady, and deep breaths.

I jump into the truck and fire her up. Addy is looking around, her focus on the horses in their paddocks. Her gaze finds Silver and stays there. A small smile pulls up on her lips. I grip the wheel tighter and slide the stick into drive. "You're new at the clinic, I take it."

"Yeah, got in yesterday. You guys are my first visit." And there is that pretty smile. I swing my eyes back to the road. We head toward the mares.

"It's so stunning out here," she says, turned toward the window. Her hair shifts over her shoulders, her waist pulling in above her low-cut jeans. One fine, elegant hand rests on her thigh, the other over the rolled-down window of the truck.

"Yep."

She chuckles and turns back to me. "Gosh, you are so lucky to live here."

When I don't reply, she stares at the road ahead. The gateway up ahead is closed.

"I can get that," she offers.

Nodding, I slow the truck. She pushes the door open and jumps out, wandering to the gate. Her ass sways in those tight jeans, the button-down shirt only just covering a leather belt. I can't take my eyes off her. *Fantastic, Hudson, ogle the new vet.* Absolutely what she needs, I'm sure. But something about her has me unable to pry my attention from her.

Addy follows the gate around as it opens, but she's not looking back at me. Her focus is on the twelve mares that graze in the paddock. I drive the truck through, and she closes it behind me, and I shut off the engine. Adjusting the hat on my head, I suck in a breath and step out of the truck and round the back, pulling out her bag. She meets me, taking it from my hands. "Thanks." Her smile beams.

I nod, not trusting my stupid words right now.

"So, I am going to make each mama her own chart. No mix-ups that way. I don't want to miss anything."

"Okay."

No other vet has bothered with that before. Then again, no other vet has been excited to meet my horses or referred to them as mamas. I lean on the truck, and she frowns. "You don't want to be with them when I check them out?"

Is she serious? Course I do, but most vets, most *male* vets, get weirded out when owners are babying their animals. But these girls are no mere animals. They are my legacy, my life's work. My girls. I push off the truck, and she walks toward the first mare. Vanity raises her head and nickers as we approach.

"Hey there, Mama. How are you doing?" Addy says, offering out her hand. Vanity stands, chewing. She lowers her muzzle to Addy's hand and sniffs before going back to eating. The woman clearly knows her way around a horse, and—by the soft words and touch she has with Vanity— loves them as much as I do.

Addy gets around Vanity. Checking her over, she listens, prods, touches, and does an internal exam. She pulls the long plastic glove from her arm and tucks it into a rubbish bag and grabs up a manila folder and flips it open, filling out information and her findings. She drops it back into the bag and grabs the bag up, brushing a stray curl behind her ear. "Who's next?"

"Whimsy. You been doin' this long?"

I walk toward the mare, and she files in beside me. "I finished an internship at the New York Equine Veterinary

Clinic last week. But I've been around horses my whole life." She smiles, but it's forced. What's that about? The life with horses? The internship? Clearly, she loves horses, choosing the equine clinic. Maybe the last part, the part where she has been around horses her whole life. What happened to this girl to make her sad to talk about horses in her life?

"I've heard of the clinic. Must have been an experience."

"You could say that."

We stop at Whimsy, and she goes through the motions again. Talking to the mare and taking her time, like they are old friends. Making it impossible not to like her. And when those brown eyes meet mine after she finishes the last set of notes and packs up her bag, I have to shuffle to rearrange myself in my jeans.

I excuse myself and make my way to the truck. She follows, looking around, her face lit up by wonder and happiness. I think of anything other than the sway of her hips, the curves of her chest, those pretty, dark eyes, and the bounce of her curls.

Raking horse shit.

Getting tossed off a yearling and hitting the rails.

Taxes . . .

Nothing helps.

Fuck me.

She opens the door and slides onto the seat. The bag must be in the truck bed already. I look back, and it sits in the tray. "Oh, I got it in there okay." She sweeps the hair from her neck. I force my gaze onto the closed gate behind us. I start the truck and turn it around. She moves to get the gate.

"Nope, my turn," I say, my voice gravel.

Shit.

Throwing the Chevy into park, I fly out of the seat like it's on fire. Needing distance between us. Us. *You idiot, Hudson.* She is absolutely unaffected by the proximity to me. I roll my eyes at myself and unlatch the gate. I give it a shove and let it swing open and walk somewhat slower back and climb in. Holding the door half shut, I drive through and park, jumping out to shut the gate. When I climb back in, Addy is on her phone, texting.

"Everything okay?" I know it's not my business, but the words leave my mouth before I have a chance to shut them down.

"Yep. Talking to my boss. You know him?"

"Justin? Yeah, we went to high school together. He treatin' you alright?"

"Ah, I haven't actually met him in person yet. I came out here first thing."

Justin Morley makes Reed akin to a saint. Probably the reason the last female vet they had a few years ago left, if you believe rumors. Which I don't. But with Addy now on his team, I might pay closer attention. So, I simply nod, remembering she asked me a question.

"He seems nice." She locks the phone and pushes it back into her back pocket.

I pin my stare on the road ahead.

"What? He's not?"

"Never said that."

"You didn't *not* say it, either."

Clever girl. "Nope, didn't."

She frowns. Crap, now I have her thinking there's something wrong with her new boss. *Great job, Hudson.* "Justin has a reputation. A warning, is all."

"Thanks," she drawls, and it's the first time she has given me anything but sunshine. Sore topic? This girl is beginning to feel more and more akin to a detailed work of fine art that can only be understood with time and care. Go figure.

"Sorry, didn't mean to ruin your day."

She huffs a little laugh. "You would have to do much better than that to ruin my day, Hudson Rawlins."

A stone grows in my throat, thick and fast. I snap my eyes to the road. We pull up at the homestead. I hear him before I see him. Charlie. I rush from the truck, wanting to intercept him before he realizes she's in the truck and growls or snaps at her. The way he does with everyone. My family included.

I round the front of the truck. The passenger door slams. The truck is empty. I jerk to a halt. Addy is squatting on the gravel.

"Hey there, little man. Oh my goodness, look at you,"

she coos. The front half of Charlie is in her lap. She is rubbing him up, playing with his ears and belly. And that little traitor is loving every single second of it. She falls onto her butt, and a very happy Charlie laps at her face. She giggles. My gut flips for the second time this morning.

"Charlie." He ignores me.

With a whistle from me, he bolts from her lap and skulks behind me like he got scolded. I offer her my hand, and she slaps hers into it, pulling herself up. Her fingers slide from mine before she dusts off her jeans and straightens her shirt. When her gaze meets mine, it's pure fucking sunshine.

I force a smile and breathe past the stone that has turned to a boulder. "Sorry, he's not usually a people person—I mean, people dog."

"He's the sweetest thing."

I stare at her in utter disbelief.

"Oh, good, you're back. How're the mares progressing?" Harry interrupts the awkward moment that hangs between us like electricity. At least on my end.

"They are thriving. You are taking brilliant care of them," Addy says.

"Hudson's mares, Dr. Howard. His touch, not mine."

"Oh"—she turns back to me—"you're doing a fine job."

I grunt.

Charlie trots around me and sits at her side.

"Will you look at that. Lucifer has made a friend."

Harry chuckles, glancing between the two of us. "Who'da thought."

Addy bends down and pats him. He jumps up.

"Charlie," I growl.

He pops down to the ground and slinks behind her. I raise an eyebrow, shaking my head, and he whimpers.

"Hey," Reed says, appearing beside Pa. "See you made a fool of my big brother's dog here. I'm Reed." He holds out a hand, and she shakes it before returning to Charlie.

"Nice to meet you, Reed." Unlike every other woman on the planet who melts when Reed Rawlins walks in the room, she pays him no heed and rubs Charlie up some more. When he rolls over, she pats his belly before pushing back up. "Well, I better be off."

"Before you go, I wanna make sure you're on board for the winter roundup. Around seven weeks' time. We always have our vet ride along with us," Harry says.

Addy stiffens. Something like fear flashes in her eyes before she meets Harry's. "Ah, sorry, I don't ride. But I can check if another vet can go along?"

"Hudson?" Pa asks.

I raise my hands. Not up to me. "It's her call, Pa."

Harry shakes his head, giving me a pointed look. "Actually, it's mine. You will ride with us."

"I—" Addy's eyes widen a little, and she shifts on her feet.

"Obviously she doesn't want to, Harry," Reed says.

"Why not?" he snaps.

"I haven't—I mean, I don't ride."

"We got that part. Why not?" The old man folds his arms, settling in for an argument that I know she can't win.

Fuck.

I feel like I should be defending her, waving a white flag or something. I know exactly how my father is going to take this. Badly. And it won't end well for her.

"You need to get back in the saddle. Hudson can help you back onto a horse. You have seven weeks."

"Pa." I step forward, brows drawn, hands by my sides.

"I wasn't askin', Hudson. You can start Saturday. I assume they give you weekends off, Addy?"

"Yes." Her voice is light, shallow. A shell of the vibrant woman that was loving up on Charlie a moment ago.

Goddamn, Pa.

"Hudson?"

"Yes, sir."

"That's sorted, then. Reed, I need a hand with that fence line, son."

Reed winces and offers a sympathetic smile before waving and following the old man.

"You can say no, you know," I offer, but the words don't fit right. And for the first time since she got here, she squares her shoulders to me, eyes searching my face.

"Like you did?" A heartbeat later, she walks back to her car and puts the bag in the trunk.

Charlie trots after her, and I resist the urge to call him

back. Poor girl. She should transfer back to New York. But for some reason, that twists like barbed wire in my veins. I should be mad on her behalf for Harry's particular brand of tough love, but I can't get past the fact that my old man gave me a way to see her again.

Well, fuck.

Chapter Four

ADDY

"Yeah, sorry, Adeline. You will have to go with, I'm afraid."

I stare at the face of my boss. The one with the apparent reputation. Ugh.

"But I don't ride anymore. I probably won't even be able to keep up."

He leans back in his office chair and flips a pen through his fingers. His blond hair and green eyes are easy enough to look at, but that menacing smile that doesn't meet his eyes may as well be swinging a giant red flag around. And he is my boss.

Hudson's words replay in my head every time my boss gets close. Even just to help with procedures. But I can't shake the icks when he's near. This is going to be a long six months. That's the length of my contract, with the opportunity to stay on if I want to—or more like, if they want me to stay. Or not, if they don't.

He gives me the same kind of vibes Adam used to. So, I will be keeping this as professional as it gets. No friendship like I had with my fellow interns and Joe. I nod and walk from his office. Luckily, I have patients to check on. One unlucky working dog, a couple of cats with injuries from various scrapes they got themselves into. No other horse visits this week, as far as I know. And I find myself looking forward to Saturday. For the horses. It's been too long since I was around my favorite beauties.

I finish my shift and head to the grocery store for a few things. After buying a few treats and some white wine, I head home to the townhouse. I pack away the food, keeping everything organized and stored away in their categories: dairy, fruits, vegetables, meat, grains. Wine for the freezer. A habit I picked up from my mom so many years ago. Her way in the kitchen is influenced by her long and very successful career as a chef. Dad and I always ate well. I miss her cooking. I miss her. I miss Dad. I pluck my phone from my back pocket.

Hey, busy?

I send the text to Mom.

The phone vibrates in my hand a heartbeat later. Incoming call. Mom. I slide to answer.

"Hey, Mama."

"Hey, Adds. All settled in okay?"

"Yeah, I guess so. The place they set me up in is amazing. The clinic is small but busy. Had a call out first thing yesterday to a ranch."

"Wow! First day and on call out already. Go Adds."

I chuckle at her enthusiasm. My parents have always had my back, no matter what. And I hesitate with my next words. "I guess. They want me to go on this roundup. And I would have to ride. I mean, I have to ride along."

The phone is silent.

"Would that be a bad thing, hon?"

"Mom," I say, the word a pull between a plea and whisper.

"It's been over eight years, Addy. And the accident was not your fault. Riding was such a wonderful part of your life. If you have a chance to get it back with these ranch people, you should at least try."

"Maybe."

"Did they offer to help you ride again, or is it part of the job?"

"Um, both?"

"Oh?"

"The man that owns the ranch, Harry Rawlins, he must have some sway around here. He wants their vet along on the roundup. And since that's me now, he said his son can help me get back on a horse."

"His son?"

Her voice has risen an octave, and I huff a laugh.

"Yes, Hudson. Apparently, he has a way with horses," I say, using my most ridiculous voice. She bursts out laughing.

"As long as he doesn't have a way with their riders," she teases.

"Oh god, Mom, seriously, no. He is like the grumpiest guy I have ever met. Utterly icy. I wouldn't be surprised if he doesn't even show up to our first lesson."

"When is it?"

"Saturday. Ugh, should I not go?"

"Absolutely not! You want this job, and I wouldn't look a gift horse in the mouth, my girl. Pun intended, sweetheart." She laughs.

I groan and she cracks up.

Mom and her lame jokes. But she has a point—I want this job. It's part of my plan. So, I guess getting back on the horse with Hudson's help is also now part of the plan.

"Love you, Mama. Kiss Dad for me, will you?"

"You know I will. And, Adds?"

"Yeah?"

"I am so excited for you. You got this, my love."

"Thanks, Mama."

She hangs up and I slide down the kitchen cupboard and sit on the floor. I study the white-paneled drawers in the center island. So, I'm doing this. I'm getting back on the horse . . .

And if I am honest with myself . . . I'm scared shitless.

The ranch is quiet when I pull into the driveway of the homestead early Saturday morning. I kill the engine and step out. I brought riding boots and a better button-down shirt. I haven't ridden in anything but jodhpurs and top boots my entire life. It's odd to be about to ride and not dressed like an equestrian. But I am not about to wear tight-fitting pants around the grumpy cowboy.

"Hello there!" a woman calls, and I recognize her from the start of the week. Mrs. Rawlins.

"Hi," I call back with a wave. She beckons me over, and I walk through the quaint white gate flanked by hedges and into the yard. Flowers are planted under each of the ancient trees that are dotted around the yard.

"Addy, come inside. I'm Louisa. Hudson will be along in a moment; he's with one of the older mares."

"Oh, thanks. Your homestead is gorgeous."

She waves me off, but a smile splits her happy face. Her dark blonde hair is tied up. Her face is like her youngest son's. A diamond face with prominent cheekbones and green eyes.

"Would you like a cup of coffee or tea while you wait? Just made a fresh batch of cookies for the boys."

The boys. Adorable.

"Sure, that would be lovely." I follow her inside. Reed

sits at the table, mug in one hand, papers in the other. He looks up when he realizes someone is following his mother. "Hey, Addy."

"Hi," I offer, and Louisa ushers me to a seat at the table and slides the plate of cookies toward me.

"She's feeding you. She likes you," Reed says and winks, but goes back to his papers.

I stifle an awkward laugh and take a cookie, shoving it into my mouth. The kitchen is huge. My mom would die for a setup like this, and I can imagine her in this space, whizzing around, magnificent aromas drifting through the place. Louisa returns with a pot of coffee. "Sorry, I only have drip coffee at the moment."

"That's wonderful, thank you."

I take the mug from her, and she fills it. "You take cream and sugar, lovely?"

"Ah, just cream. Sweet enough, thanks."

Reed smiles behind his papers, schooling it back to a thin line the second he sees me look at him. Okay . . . He seems around my age, but I can never be sure. The papers appear to be tax papers of some sort. I sip the coffee. It's hot and bitter. I love it.

"Ma, have you seen—" Hudson stops in the doorway.

"Oh hey, sorry, I was early." I wave and offer him a tiny smile. Reed puts the papers down, his eyes trained on his big brother. Hudson clears his throat and steps inside.

"We should get started."

Hello to you, too. I resist the urge to roll my eyes at him.

"Hudson Andrew Rawlins, manners," Louisa snaps.

"Sorry, can we please get a start, Dr. Howard?"

Reed raises an eyebrow as I stand, leaving the coffee on the table. "Thanks for the coffee, Louisa."

"You're most welcome, hon." She smiles at me and turns back to her work.

I follow Hudson out the door. He is halfway to the barn before I catch up to him. "What are we doing today?"

"Chores."

"Chores? So, not riding."

He stops and turns back. He does that a lot. "Nope, you're not ready."

What the hell? He doesn't know a thing about me, let alone my riding abilities. "Can you call me Addy?"

"No." He turns and walks toward the closest barn. Reluctantly, I follow. *Like father, like son.*

"If I am not going near a horse today, what's the point?"

He doesn't answer me. Instead, he turns back and hands me a scooping rake. For horse shit.

"With all due respect, Monty Roberts, how are you supposed to get me back on a horse without an actual horse?"

I mean, I had to psych myself up for the past three days to have the nerve to do this, and now he is telling me I can't. What the hell is his problem?

"When you're done there, the water troughs need

draining and scrubbing. All six of them. We break at lunch."

My mouth gapes as he turns to walk away. "Hey!"

He stops and looks back. "What?"

"How the hell do you know what I'm not ready for without even assessing me around or on a horse?"

He closes the space between us in a heartbeat. He is a solid four inches taller than me. With him this close to me, my breath disappears, and I grapple a swallow. I meet his gaze. But it's not angry, only searching.

He tilts his head. "I saw the way you reacted when Harry brought it up the other day. That's all I need to know. You're not ready." He pushes the rake toward me, still in my grip. "Chores."

I grunt in annoyance and turn back to the barn, assuming the shit shoveling happens in here. Making short work of the first stall, I'm starting on the next when I hear the rumble of a big engine. I stand and stretch my back, sinking my hands into my lower back to ease the ache. A silver semi loaded with hay bales pulls up outside.

The other side of the barn is empty, but the remnants of old hay litter the ground. That's a lot of hay. Hudson appears a moment later, talking to the driver. The older man shuts off the engine and gets down, heading to the house. Reed jogs over to the semi and helps his brother remove the tie-down straps.

I move to the next stall and start raking the piles into the rubber tub outside the door. Hudson climbs onto the top of the load of hay and starts tossing the bales down. They hit the ground with a hiss and Reed carries them into the barn, stacking them neatly against the wall. After an hour of the same, both men are sweaty, and Hudson pulls his shirt over his head.

I finish the last stall and move to the first water trough. It has a float. Crap, how do these things work, again? I forget how to shut it off. Which sweaty, muscle-bound guy shall I ask for help? I snort out loud at my stupid thoughts. Guessing Reed is a safer bet, I wander into the barn hoping to find him stacking the bales.

Hudson is busy stacking bale upon bale as I stop in the center of the barn. His arms flex, his back works as he tosses the bales on top of each other and straightens them. His light brown hair that I haven't even seen in full until now is messy, with bits of hay sticking out of it. I chuckle and he spins back.

He stands, chest heaving, arms at his side, his hard stomach tight. The jeans and boots he is wearing are also covered in bits of hay. My heart rate quickens as butterflies take flight, filling my stomach. Holy shit.

His blue eyes narrow. "Done already?"

"I—" I clear my throat and huff a strangled laugh. "Ah no, how do I disable the float? I couldn't remember."

He walks to where I stand. He smells hot and sweaty and goddamn amazing. A mix of hay and sandalwood. And that face. His jaw. He runs a hand through his hair, pulling out a few short lengths of hay, flicking them to the ground. "Flip the small metal clasp at the joint where it meets the rest of the mechanism. Then pull the stopper at the end of the tub."

"Thanks," I say, but the word is weak.

"Anytime, Dr. Howard." He doesn't move, staring at me as I stare at him. At his very well-toned chest. Fuck.

I force a small, weak smile and turn back, heading back to the trough and said float, internally berating myself the entire way. How can someone so frustrating be so goddamn hot?

Life is utterly unfair.

Utterly.

I do as he directed and drain the trough. I have no idea why I am cleaning it; it's one of the cleanest I have seen. I shift my focus up from scrubbing when Hudson walks past, leading a colt. The chestnut yearling is high-stepping, most likely anticipating what is coming. They enter the round yard, and Hudson adjusts his hat before removing the lead from the halter.

I stand and wander to the rail to watch. He clicks his tongue, and the horse trots around the pen. The communication between man and horse is invisible and mesmerizing. He flicks the rope behind him, and the colt breaks into a lope.

He is stunning. The horse, that is.

Watching the two of them makes me miss the bond between horse and rider.

"Woah boy, woah." Hudson holds a hand up, and the

yearling slows. This time, the man waits in the center until the colt comes to him. He rubs a hand over his forehead and eyes before clipping the lead back on. They walk past the rail I lean on, heading for the gate. I pop through and open it for them. Hudson tips his hat as he walks past, but after a few steps, he stops and the horse halts behind him. He finds my gaze and I straighten, waiting for his next annoyance-laced words.

"Now, that look right there on your face, *that* is the reaction you should have around a horse, Dr. Howard."

My eyes widen as I realize my mouth is gaping and my heart rate has peaked. And he's right. This is the feeling that I once had with horses. I thought I had lost it forever. But somehow, this grump of a man knew where to find it.

There's no turning back now . . .

Maybe I *can* do this.

Chapter Five

HUDSON

A week has gone by since Addy was here, and it may as well have been a month. Not sure why I'm fucking counting. And when her Cherokee pulls into the driveway, Charlie flies from the barn to her door. Apparently, I'm not the only one who is glad she's back. Before she gets out of the car, I remind myself that she is here because of her job. And my father. Things have to stay professional between us. It's better for her that way.

Her door opens and she jumps out, dropping to her knees to fuss over Charlie. He's going to get used to that, and it's going to break his little heart when she eventually leaves. They always do. For now, she rubs his belly and laughs at his overzealous enthusiasm for her affection. She is wearing a light blue t-shirt and dark jeans with riding boots, and her hair is up, but wisps of curly hair have already escaped.

She looks to where I stand, now leaning on the rake. And she stands, brushing herself off. Charlie prances at her feet expectantly. She walks to the barn and my little buddy follows. The moment she is inside, her eyes find mine. "Chores again, I suppose?"

I try to flatten the smile that plays over my mouth and shift on my feet, breaking eye contact. Anything to stop the heat that grows with every second she looks at me. "That all depends, Dr. Howard."

"On what, the look on my face? And can you *please* call me Addy?"

With a grunt, I shift my focus back to her face. Her features are so soft in the muted light, her lips pink, the angles of her cheeks blush. Her brown eyes burn into mine, and I realize she is waiting for an answer. "Let's go for a drive."

Her eyes narrow a little. "Where are we going?"

I lean the rake against the wall and make for the truck parked at the side. When neither she nor Charlie follows, I poke my head back inside. "Come on."

She gives me a quizzical stare but starts walking for the truck. I hold the door open, and she climbs in. Charlie whimpers on the ground by her door. "Sorry, bud, not this time."

I climb into the driver's seat and start the truck. As I

reverse away from the barn, Reed comes trotting around the corner on Magnet, his steel grey gelding. But he claims to have called him Magnet because the ladies can't resist a man on a horse. Still remember shaking my head at him when he came up with that name. He tips his hat at Addy, and she waves back. "Hi, Reed."

Her eyes light up watching my brother ride past, on his way to the heifers in the southern paddock, if he knows what's good for him. Pa gives out a list of work for us each morning; that one was on his list. The last thing we need right now is to lose cattle to the wolves. Addy glances back at me. "Are you going to tell me where we're going, Hudson?"

My name on her lips never gets old.

"Nowhere particular. I have chores to finish before we start your lesson."

But I am hoping that taking her into the mountains will help her open up and tell me what happened, why she doesn't ride anymore. If I am going to help her into the saddle, it would be real helpful if I knew what got her out to start with.

"Oh, okay. Can I help?"

Absofuckinglutely.

"If you feel up to it, sure."

"Okay . . ."

I shove the truck in drive, and we head to the northern fence line that Reed and I were working on last week. It's started, and by no means finished. She looks out the window as we drive out. The higher we ascend, the more excited she becomes. "Oh wow, this is magnificent."

When we finally reach the hilltop with the old fence line, I park and turn off the engine. Addy climbs out before I do, wandering to the front of the truck, turning in circles to take in the epic mountain view. I thought she'd like it. But the wonder on her face takes my fucking breath away. And like that, I'm hard.

Jesus.

In all honesty, we could have done her lesson first up. But selfishly, I wanted more time than an hour with her. Even if this can never amount to anything, I made her smile. It was worth it. Something hits the door, and I startle and turn. Addy is standing at the door, hands gripping the frame where the window is rolled down, smile permanently etched on her lit-up face. "You getting out of the truck?"

"Yup."

She backs off the door and spins back to wonder at the mountains. I rearrange myself in my pants and push past the door, shutting it behind me. I come to stand beside her. She turns and looks up at me, those dark lashes fluttering upward. "You really are so lucky to live here. It's so peaceful. Just stunning."

I watch her mouth as she speaks. And every last ounce of blood rushes from my brain south. I run a hand over my face and think about taxes. When I don't respond, she frowns. "So, did you need me to help you with something?"

I shake my head, as if clearing my thoughts. "Right, how are your fencing skills?"

"Nonexistent?"

I make my way to the truck and grab my tools—strainers and pliers. I turn back, and she is inches from me. "Sorry, I thought you might need me to carry something."

She's too close. Something like the scent of apples catches my attention. Her shampoo. The vanilla and spice of her skin. I force my focus to stay on her face and not drop to where her shirt hugs the swells of her perfect fucking chest. That is now rising and falling faster than it was a moment ago.

Putting space between us, I hand her the pliers. She takes them and turns back to the fence. I drag in a lungful of air, willing my body to calm the fuck down, and walk to the fence line to apply the strainers. Reed and I built the fence, but it has been a week, and it needs one last tightening before we leave it to the gods and the wandering cattle. Addy appears, pliers in hand. "Tell me what you want me to do."

She studies the strainers, glancing to the mountains every so often. I snap the wire into the feeder and pull back the lever. "Here, crank this as tight as you can make it."

Sliding the pliers into her back pocket, she takes over

the lever, her hand brushing mine. She tugs at it, and her face twists with annoyance.

"Harder," I offer.

She puts more effort into it, getting through a few cranks.

"Sorry, that's as tight as I can go."

I take the lever from her hand and pump it over a few more times with one hand. Her gaze drops to my cranking arm, traveling to my bicep. And she stills. As if something occurred to her. Something shocking. She turns and wanders toward the path of trees a little further down the fence line.

"Four more wires to go yet, Howard. Don't slack on me now."

She glances over her shoulder, giving me a small, meek smile. What's that all about?

I fix the wire and release the strainers. Dropping them to the ground, I follow her to the trees. She leans against one, her eyes closed, arms folded. Her t-shirt has risen up, a sliver of her tummy exposed. When I am close enough that my shadow covers her, she opens her eyes. I hold out a hand, and she frowns, tilting her head.

"Pliers," I grunt.

She holds my stare for a moment and pushes off the tree, closing the space between us. And once again I am enveloped by her vanilla and spice. I stifle the groan that wants to rattle up my throat at being this close to her. And she unfolds her arms, passing the pliers. "You don't really need my help, Hudson. I can barely operate that contraption."

I can't help the smile that blooms over my face when she says my name. "You helped. A little."

"You don't have to be nice to me. It doesn't suit you." She pushes past me and walks back to the truck.

What the hell?

To be fair, I haven't exactly rolled out the welcome mat. I guess the way I feel really is one-sided. That should make me happy. But my gut sinks like a stone. *It's better this way.* I repeat the phrase all the way back to the truck. After straining the last four wires like a man on a mission, I toss the tools into the back of the tray and jump into the truck.

Addy stares out the window, lost in thought. I want to ask her if she's okay. How the hell I managed to dampen her sunshine. But when she doesn't take her attention from the mountains as I start the truck, I shift it into gear and head home.

Reed is unsaddling Magnet when we make it back to the barn. Addy chats away to him, bright and bubbly as usual. That gets under my skin more than it should. I find Charlie and head for the gelding paddock. Addy will meet Sergeant today, my first horse after Silver. He is old, experienced, and the calmest with unsure riders. He will take good care of her. And once again I am brought back to wondering what happened to her to make her stop riding altogether.

The way her eyes lit up when I was working the colt

tells me everything. Horses are part of her. It must have been something terrible to keep her away from them all this time.

When I have Sergeant saddled, I walk him to where Reed is entertaining Addy with his dramatic retelling of something he has done. She laughs and asks questions. They get along well. I grind my teeth to stop myself from telling Reed off, to go find another chore and leave her be. But she turns when she hears us coming and her mouth gapes.

"Have fun, Addy," Reed offers and walks to the homestead. She glances at his retreating back for a moment before turning to face Sergeant and me. The bay gelding rubs his face on my back, pushing me forward. She huffs a small laugh, but her face falls.

She's scared.

Fuck.

"Dr. Howard, meet Sergeant. The oldest gentleman on the ranch."

She takes a tentative step forward. She wasn't like this with any of the other horses. Maybe it's because she thinks I expect her to ride this one that's making the difference. Making her nervous.

"It's alright, he knows how to take care of his riders. You will be more than safe."

"Uh-huh."

She holds out a hand for Sergeant to sniff. He nudges

her hand, and I lead him to the round yard, Addy following at my side. Her hands shift from her pockets to across her neck to her pockets again. When we reach the gate to the round yard, she darts forward and opens it.

I walk Sergeant through and come to a stop in the center of the yard. The sun has reached its apex by the time I double-check the girth and walk the gelding in a few circles. Addy stands by the gate, stiff. Her usual sunshine is clouded by a storm, visible in her eyes.

I hang the reins over Sergeant's neck and walk back to the gate where she stands. Her cheeks are pink in the heat of midday. I take off my hat and plop it on her head. "Can't have you getting burnt," I say, my voice gravel.

"I don't know if I can." Her eyes are glued to Sergeant.

"I'm right here; take your time. Even if you only mount and dismount. That's okay. Sergeant isn't going anywhere. He has all day."

She nods, but her pulse thunders in her neck. Her breaths have turned shallow.

Dammit.

All I want to do right now is fold her into me. To take away the fear and that desperate look on her face that is tearing at my heart. Instead, I clear my throat and walk back to Sergeant and gesture for her to follow.

She takes tentative steps to where we stand, eyes studying the gelding as if hunting for any sign of danger. I extend an arm, ushering her closer. She steps into my space by my side, as if I am all of a sudden safer than the horse in front of her. I'm not too sure about that.

She drags her gaze from Sergeant and finds mine. "You will be right here? You won't step away?"

"Right here, Howard. Not going anywhere."

She blows out a low, shaky breath. And nods.

I resist the urge to tell her how to mount. She knows what to do. Sergeant nickers, and she pauses. Her hand waves to the side, hunting. I grab her hand, and she forces a wobbly smile. A stone lodges in my throat. I push air in and out of my lungs. Sergeant shifts on his feet, resting a back leg. Bored already. Good man.

She releases my hand and takes the reins and a handful of his mane.

So far, so good.

"You're okay. Nice work."

She hovers from foot to foot and her eyes close. As if she is hyping herself up to mount the gelding. As if being on a horse is akin to the worst experience on the planet. *Fuck, Addy. What the hell happened to you?*

The breeze rustles through my hair, and she turns back, studying my face. Maybe gauging whether she really trusts me to do this.

But when she lifts her foot and slides it into the stirrup, I move forward, ready to catch her if she bails. She grabs the back of the saddle with her other hand and goes to push up into the saddle. But her body trembles, and she shakes her head violently. "No," she chokes.

She is out of the stirrup and backing away before Sergeant even knows she's gone.

"I'm sorry, Hudson. I can't do this."

Her face breaks as she turns and shoves through the gate with a breathy moan.

Fuck.

Chapter Six

ADDY

I can't do it. And I'm going to lose my job.

Sliding down the wall of the barn beside Hudson's truck, I shove my head in my hands. Knees up. Body shaking. I can't even mount. Why did I think I could do this? A strangled groan spills into my hands. Harry is going to be disappointed. And then it hits me—is he going to be angry at Hudson, too? He did assign this job to his son. And from what I gather, he is not used to being let down.

A wet snout hits my arm. I lift my head to find Charlie. I put my legs down and he makes himself at home on my lap. He nuzzles into my lap, and I rub his head and face. "I bet you're not scared of anything, little man."

"Oh, he is. His food bowl being empty."

I look up to find Hudson's worried face. His blue eyes are narrowed, his hair is messed up, and I remember I still have his hat on. I pull it off and hold it up to him. But he shakes his head. "You still need it, Howard."

I lift Charlie from my lap and stand. "Hudson," I say with breathy disagreement.

"This is how I see it. You need to ride. Something happened that makes you scared to. But Sergeant isn't going to let you down, nor am I."

"I—"

He holds up a hand. "Tell you what. You hop on that old man and take one turn around the yard, and I will take you camping on that mountain top you loved so much under the stars. Deal?"

I open my mouth to object but close it. Sleeping under the stars in the middle of the mountains. That would be breathtaking.

"But I couldn't even get on."

"It's alright; it takes as long as it takes. I'll honor my half of the deal if it's today or next month. That okay with you, Howard?"

"Fine, deal. But I wish you would call me Addy."

He huffs a laugh. "Maybe, one day."

What is that supposed to mean?

He holds out a hand and I shake it. His hand is warm, his grip firm. And butterflies explode in my belly. *Just a physical reaction.* I ignore it.

"Good. Let's head back to Sergeant before he thinks you stood him up."

He winks at me, and I feel heat flood my neck and

face. Shit. He walks in front of me all the way to the round yard. His Wranglers are tight in all the right places. His broad shoulders flex, the t-shirt he wears moving over his back muscles as he strides for the gate.

He holds it open for me, and all the humor that was there a moment ago is gone. Sergeant waits exactly where we left him, one leg still up, resting. Hudson takes the rein by his muzzle and tilts his head, gesturing for me to try again.

I suck in a breath and take purposeful steps toward them. Blood thunders through my veins and my heart flings in my chest, but I take the reins again and put my foot in the stirrup.

"Good job. You're okay." Hudson's words are soft and sweet, and I glance at him. His face is calm, his stance solid. He really does have my back. I trust this man. I pull on the saddle and push up off the ground. The second I swing my leg over Sergeant, I know this isn't going to end well.

Fear prickles up my spine and tears burn behind my eyes. Sweat pops over my brow as I grip the pommel of the saddle. Every breath is too shallow. Hudson's hands rest over mine, those blue eyes looking up at me.

"You're okay. Steady."

Sergeant shifts on his feet. Visions of Jewls flood my mind. Her still body, trapping mine on the sandy arena. The fear in her eye when she shook her head and blood streamed from her nose. The moment my parents told me she was gone.

Bile rises in my throat, and I shake my head violently.

"No, no, please. Get me down, Hudson."

His hands are around my waist a heartbeat later, and I fall into his hold and off the horse. His hat hits the ground. I cling to his t-shirt, and he stiffens. I choke through ragged breath, trying to hold back the sobs clawing up my throat. His arms fold around me and hug me tight.

"You did good, Howard. It's the first time; I promise it gets easier."

My chin wobbles. But I refuse to let him see me cry. I push out of his hold and swoop down to grab his hat. I hold it out to him, tears welling in my eyes. But I set my shoulders back, raising my chin, and he takes his hat. Sergeant stands, unbothered. "I'm sorry."

Hudson shakes his head and pushes his hat onto his head. "Do you *want* to do this, Howard?" His words are kind, not harsh like I expected.

"I don't know, I—" I swallow and stare at his hand that now runs behind his neck, his arm flexing. "Yes," I finally say, almost a whisper.

"What happened when you sat in the saddle, what went through your mind?"

My hands tremble by my sides. And I shove them in my back pockets and stare toward the homestead. *I saw Jewls, that's what.* I don't want to make another bad decision and cost another beautiful horse their life. I trust Hudson. It's *me* I don't trust. Hell, I even trust Sergeant. And that's the biggest problem. I'm the problem. "I—"

But the air chokes from my lungs as I try to force out the words. Hudson lifts his hat and runs a hand through his hair before setting it back down. "You know, just because something happened once, doesn't mean it's gonna happen again, okay?"

I nod.

"I'll give you two choices. You can either tell me the story that has you this way around the animals you clearly adore, or you can get back on and I will count to twenty before you get off."

I open my mouth to protest.

"I ain't askin', Howard."

After a moment, I groan and walk back to Sergeant.

He raises a brow. Obviously, he thought telling my story would be easier. I disagree. I'll take my chances with Sergeant. I grab the reins and slide my foot into the stirrup for the third time. Third time's the charm, right?

This time, I don't wait for him to be beside me. I swing up and into the saddle like I have done thousands of times before. And when fear starts clawing at my insides, I force air in and out of my lungs like my life depends on it.

Hudson's face lights up with the most gorgeous smile. "There you go."

"Are you counting?"

"Oh yeah. One . . ." he drawls.

"Not funny," I growl.

He chuckles. "Two . . ."

Oh god, this is going to take forever.

"Relax. And how 'bout some love for Sergeant here? He has been nothin' but patient."

Running a hand over his mane, my hand shakes a little. I slap it back to the pommel. Hudson counts, ever so slowly, as he walks around the back of the horse, adjusting my feet in the stirrups like I don't already know where they go. "You want to send him 'round the yard?"

"No, absolutely not."

"Okay, guess that camping trip will have to wait."

I go to take my foot from the stirrup and dismount and Sergeant moves. Hudson has his hand on the reins by the bit. He clucks his tongue and Sergeant walks on.

Fuck.

I grip the saddle. "Please, stop." The words are so breathy, stars appear in my vision.

He halts the horse and turns back. "You sure?"

I nod.

"Alright, probably too much for you, anyhow."

He moves to the other side of the horse and holds his hands up, as if he is going to help me down again.

"I can do it."

"Yeah? Okay. I'll get the gate then."

He walks away.

"No wait, where are you going?"

"Gate."

Shit. I grip the pommel and remove my foot from the stirrup and swing my leg back over, dismounting with a wobble. The ground under my feet feels like a luxury. I take the reins and move them over Sergeant's head to lead him. Before I have the chance to walk him away, his muzzle nudges my arm. He chews on the bit, and I rub his face and loose a shaky breath.

"You two comin'?"

I lead Sergeant toward the gate. He walks behind me, close. When we reach Hudson, he reaches for the reins, but I don't hand them over. "It's okay, I got it."

He steps back and tips his hat. We walk through the gate, and he shuts it behind us. I make it back to the barn before I realize I have no idea where he unsaddles his horses or where the tack even goes.

"Behind the barn; you wash him down and I'll pack away."

I lead Sergeant around the back of the barn. There's a concrete pad with a tie rail and three hoses connected to faucets. Hudson is by my side in the next heartbeat. He unbuckles the girth and slips the saddle and blanket off Sergeant before handing me a halter. Unbuckling the bridle, I move the browband down before waiting for him to give me the bit.

I slide the bridle over my arm, and Sergeant lowers his head for me to slide the halter on. I have missed this. So much. I rub his face and ear and lean my forehead on his for a moment. Tears well in my eyes. It has been so long. I breathe him in. That distinct horse smell. The grounding earthiness of him.

"You two need a room?"

I huff out a laugh, my eyes still closed, and rub my thumbs over the gelding's jaw before leaning back and opening my eyes. Hudson is staring at me. His face is lit up with happiness and something else I can't quite place. "I'm glad you guys are getting along. You should probably take it slow, though."

I scrunch my face up and poke my tongue out at him. He hollers a laugh, low and hearty. It's fucking gorgeous. My gut flips and my heart slams into my ribs. Oh no.

That is not, absolutely never, happening.

This is professional.

But deep in my gut, it's like something else entirely. I'm sure Hudson Rawlins has no interest in some passing-through vet with horse baggage.

"Is that it for today?" I ask.

His face falls a little and he clears his throat. "Yup. Once you turn him out, you're free to go."

"Thanks." I turn my back to Hudson and turn on the tap. The water spills from the mouth of the hose and I turn back to say something, anything. But he is walking toward the homestead. I shake my head and hose Sergeant off.

When he is clean of sweat, I wipe him down with the scraper that hangs by the tie rail. I lead him away and toward the paddocks that hold the horses. Their names are written on plates on each gate. We walk to the first one. Silver.

The old mare lifts her head from her grazing, and I smile. She appears healthy for an old horse. He really does love his horses, this man. The care and attention he takes with each one is impressive. I turn back and glance at the homestead. Hudson is talking to his mother. They both turn my way, noticing I've stopped at Silver's gate.

"Come on, mister, which one is yours?"

He follows as we make our way further down the small lane between paddocks. Fifth one along, I find his name. I open the gate, walk him in, and remove his halter. He doesn't walk away, though, and I give him one last rub before walking back out and securing him inside.

I lean over the rail and take in the place around me. I have seen a lot of establishments. Many horse farms and equestrian setups. This one is like home mixed with horse husbandry. It feels good. It's not harsh or money-focused. It's horse-focused. Like Hudson. Like I used to be.

As I wander back down the lane toward the barn, Charlie flies toward me. I drop to my knees and wait for him to jump into my arms. I chuckle as he licks my face like it's a lollipop. "Hey, little man."

This time, I stand and give him a little whistle. He trots behind me as I make my way back to the barn to hang up the halter. I walk into the barn and head toward the back where the tack room is. Stepping through the doorway, I find saddles on racks on one wall, bridles and halters on the other. I find an empty spot and hang it up. The doorway darkens, and I turn back. Hudson stands in the doorway, arms crossed over his chest, a frown twisting his face.

"What? It doesn't go there?'

"No, it goes there."

"Okay?"

"Ma wants to see you."

"Oh, she does?"

He nods and walks from the doorway. I follow, jogging to catch up and fixing my hair. He glances at me before getting the small white gate that leads into the homestead yard. Louisa is sitting at a small outdoor café set. Something cold is in a jug with three glasses. She gestures to the seat opposite her, and I sit. "Hi, Mrs. Rawlins."

She smiles and pours three glasses of what looks like cold juice. "Call me Louisa. How was your lesson?"

"It was good, actually."

Hudson's face flickers between surprise and confusion. It was. I know it probably didn't seem like it, but I was glad to make progress. I can't lose my job. And part of me is desperate to be part of the horse-and-rider dynamic again. Hudson drains his glass, and Louisa takes it back.

"Hudson, Reed wanted a hand with something. He's inside."

He nods and walks through the front door and inside.

"How was your lesson, Addy?"

I stare at her. She sent him away. Does she think I'm

not telling her the truth because he was standing there? "It was good. I was on Sergeant for, like, twenty seconds?"

She takes a sip from her glass, studying my face. "I know my husband can be a hard man, but he knows what his family needs. What people need. Have you tried riding before now?"

"No."

I sip the juice. It's cold and refreshing, and I hope it takes away the heat that has flooded to my cheeks with this conversation.

"That's fine. If anyone can help you back on a horse, it's our Huddy. He has a way with horses."

"He seems to."

She smiles at me, then sits up in her chair abruptly, delight lighting up her face. "Tomorrow, Sunday lunch, you have to come."

"Ah, I don't want to intrude on your family time."

"Nonsense. It's no intrusion. And we all know Charlie will be happier if you're here."

I laugh at that, and she winks at me. I finish my glass and place it on the table. "Tomorrow, then, for Charlie. Can I bring something?"

"Just yourself. Or if you have a chance, something you would like to eat for lunch, a side dish?"

"I can do that."

She stands and grabs the jug and glasses.

"Thanks, Louisa."

"See you tomorrow, Addy."

I wave and wander back to my car. Charlie is waiting for me. "I'll see you tomorrow, buddy."

He gives me some love and I climb into the car. I start the engine and wait for Charlie to move away before driving off. Reed stands by the barn, Magnet's reins in hand. He salutes me with a hand at his brow, and I chuckle at the silly notion and wave. The only thing I can think of for the next forty minutes on the way back to town is the fact that I got on a horse today.

And the part of me that lived for horse riding swells as the biggest smile claims my face and happy tears blur my vision.

Chapter Seven

HUDSON

Happy Birthday, sweetheart.

Happy birthday, Adds!! 

Addy's phone sits on the kitchen counter as she helps Mom and putters around, chatting about New York as if they are old friends from way back. Wearing an elegant yellow sundress with flowers that ends above her knees, and topped with a heart-shaped bodice and half-moon straps, she's fucking stunning. I track her as she moves around the kitchen, chatting. They talk about her work at the clinic. And when Ma brings up her accident, Addy masterfully redirects. To her credit, Ma leaves it. Addy's phone is buzzing.

It's her birthday?

Shit.

Happy birthday, babe.

From Adam.

The air stalls in my lungs. *Who the fuck is Adam?*

Reed is plonked on the sofa, watching sports. Probably riding out his hangover from town last night. I can't remember the last time I went out on the town. But then again, my life has been strictly horses and ranching since Jemma.

You can't have your heart broken if no one has a chance to sink their claws into it.

"Earth to Hudson," Ma calls.

"Hey, what? Sorry."

"I was telling Addy you went to New York a few times." Ma raises her eyebrows. Yeah, because I really want to talk about my ex in front of the woman I can't get out of my head right now.

"Twice was enough for me." I take the tray of meat for the grill and walk outside to get started. Ma chats away, trying to make up for my abrupt comment and departure.

"It's okay, Louisa. I'm used to getting the minimum-word treatment from Hudson."

My hand stills over the knob of the grill. It's her fucking birthday, and I can't even be civilized. *Prick.* Then it hits me. Did Ma know it was her birthday? It's not unlike her to invite folks over, but this is far too coincidental for my liking. She likes her, I can tell. Harry's probably in on it, too.

Never figured my parents would resort to playing matchmaker for their thirty-four-year-old son, but then I guess I haven't exactly had a life since Jemma. I press and turn the knob and the grill clicks, flame bursting through the iron plate. I toss the steaks and sausages on and they hiss, sending up smoke.

"Need a hand with anything?"

Addy stands in the doorway. Her hands grip the frame as she leans onto it, one foot kicked back. Her brown curls fall around her shoulders, the pink in her cheeks flushing out her freckles, her brown eyes on me. "Your mom said you might need a hand?"

Of course she did.

"Nope."

She forces a smile and nods slightly before pushing off the frame and walking back inside. God, I am a world-class dick. I drag a hand down my face and resist the urge to groan. Her looking like that and me in close quarters is not a good idea. Charlie appears at my feet, sitting patiently, nose sniffing the steak-aroma-filled air around us. "Not a chance, buddy."

He lies on the patio and closes his eyes. Laughter comes from the living room. I move to the window. Reed is sitting on the sofa with Addy, facing her with his leg bent over the side of the chair, re-enacting something she's finding hilarious. He makes an exploding noise, throwing his hands up.

She tosses her head back and loses it. Her laughter is

the prettiest thing I have ever heard. And it's all for my brother and his stupid antics right now. Heat grows in my core, and not in the way it usually does around her. I throw the tongs on the side of the grill and stalk inside.

"Howard, you got a job." My words are growly, like some kind of Neanderthal. Ma raises an eyebrow and tames a rueful smile before going back to her cooking. Addy pushes off the sofa and excuses herself from Reed's storytelling. He rolls his eyes at me behind her back.

"Sure, where do you want me?" Addy says.

Reed's eyes widen as a shit-eating grin splits his face. I give him the look he knows all too well, the one that says *don't*. Brows lowered, head tilted. He raises his hands like he's in an old-fashioned stickup and turns back to the TV. The second we get to the doorway, I panic.

Shit, I don't actually have a job for her. Maybe a healthy dislike for her around any other guy. Even if it is my youngest brother. *Especially* if it's my youngest brother. She turns back once we're outside. "What is it?"

She is looking around as if it should be obvious.

"Charlie actually needed you, sore paw or something," I grunt.

Lame, Hudson.

Fucking lame.

But to my surprise, her eyes light up and she drops to the ground and cuddles him into her lap. This fucking woman, I tell you. The sound of hooves tells me Harry is back from the northern fields. Lunchtime will be as soon as he is washed up and ready. Ma's rules. He may be the boss, but she captains this ship. The only person on Earth that outranks our father.

The gate swings. Harry wanders toward us down the path. His gaze snags on Addy on the ground with Charlie. "Addy." He dips his hat, and she ushers Charlie from her lap and brushes off, standing to greet my old man. He asks her polite questions, and she answers. *Smooth, Howard.*

If he hasn't taken her down a peg by now, he must like her. Or at least want her around for one reason or another. Pa walks inside. Ma's calling for him to wash up the second he crosses the threshold. Always predictable, my parents. Reed appears through the doorway and hooks an arm around Addy's shoulders. "Come on, I'll show you to the table."

"Reed?" I call out.

He turns back. The scowl on my face must have said it all, because he removes his arm from Addy. "Oh yeah, that should probably be Huddo's job."

"I don't mind, really," Addy says.

Great, now she's indifferent to me. I think I liked it better when she gave me attitude. Fuck, I am all over the place. What the hell is going on? My mouth moves before my brain does. 'Bout time I got my shit together.

I drop the tongs on the grill and Reed files in to take over. "Don't screw this up, Huddo."

"Mind your own business."

I walk to where Addy stands waiting and run my hand

across the back of my neck. The t-shirt and jeans I'm wearing feel underdressed next to her flowery yellow dress. But she smiles at me. Lightning flings through my veins a heartbeat later.

"Ah, this way." I walk to the white gate and hold it open for her.

"Thanks," she utters.

I head for the table under Ma's favorite ancient weeping willow, and she's right beside me.

"Happy birthday, Howard."

Her mouth gapes a little and then she chews her bottom lip. The last of the blood circulating in my misfiring brain sinks south. Jesus.

"Thanks."

"Sorry about my family. They think everyone should belong here, whether they want to or not."

"It's sweet. You're lucky to have them."

Charlie trots between us and ahead toward the tree, leading the way.

"You have lunch out here a lot?" Addy asks.

"Every Sunday. Kind of a tradition now."

"Wow, that's amazing."

She looks around. The breeze plays with her hair, and I resist the urge to sweep it from her cheek and behind her ear. We reach the table. Shit, I should have brought the cutlery and cloth.

"Oh, we could have brought some things out with us. I

didn't even think of it," Addy says, but she wanders under the weeping willow tree and peers up into it.

Her face is pure wonder as she takes in the gnarled and twisted branches and the many, many veils of weeping green. She runs a hand through one and huffs a soft laugh. I sit on the end of the table and cross my arms over my chest.

"Howard. How old are you?"

She turns back, surprise lighting up her eyes, her lips tipped in an incredulous smile. But she walks to where I sit and tilts her head. "Why?"

I wasn't expecting that. Although by now, I really should, since she constantly surprises me.

"I don't know, was just thinkin'."

"Did it hurt, Hudson?"

My mouth gapes, and chuckling, I shoot up from the table. "Hey!"

She spins away and prances away from me, giggling. Heat tingles through my core. For all the hard edges of me she gets, she takes everything in stride, evening out my roughness with her sweetness. I sink back onto the table as she goes back to wandering around the tree, running her hand through the green veil of willow that she gets close enough to. I could watch her all damn day long.

The white gate squeaks. Ma is heading our way, arms full. I push off the table and jog over to take the load from her arms. "Thank you, Huddy."

Her focus lands on Addy, still wandering, looking. Ma

smiles and walks back to the house. Reed meets her half-way, his arms loaded with dishes. I make my way back and set down the cloth and cutlery. Addy appears by my side and takes the cloth. I pick up the things from the top as she throws it up and lets it settle over the old, weathered boards. I move around the table, setting five places. Two either side, and one at the head for Pa.

Reed dumps the food down.

"Wow, it all smells wonderful," Addy says.

Reed puffs out his chest and nods. "Yep, was up all night making this lot."

She laughs and smacks his arm. He grins at her, and she shakes her head. They get on like a house on fire. Reed walks back to the house, slapping me on the shoulder as he goes. Wish he would stop acting like a fucking idiot.

"Hungry, Howard?" I ask.

"Starving," she says, leaning down to smell a baked dish. The neckline of her dress swells. Suddenly, I'm goddamn parched. She tucks a strand of hair behind her ear and smiles up at me. What I would do to that mouth, those breasts. Fucking hell. My cock stretches my jeans, and I run a hand through my hair.

As she stands back up, her eyes darken and hold mine. Blood thunders in my veins, my heart flinging against my ribs. Sweet Jesus. Her gaze drops lower, and her breathing turns ragged, before her gaze lifts. "Are *you* hungry, Hud—"

"Take a seat, y'all," Ma says from behind me.

Addy's attention snaps from me, and she rolls her bottom lip through her teeth. "Um, where am I?"

Ma points to the seat by where I stand. Addy walks around the table as I pull out her chair, and she glances up at me. "Thanks." But the word is soft, choked.

Oh good, it's not just me, then.

As she sits, I take the seat beside her. Reed sinks into the chair opposite us, and Ma sits next to him. Pa appears with the meat, cooked and steaming on an oversized plate. He sets it down before taking his seat at the head of the table. Everyone bows their heads and I wait for Addy to do the same before bowing my own.

"For these and all His mercies, may His holy name be praised," Pa mutters. The second the last syllable leaves his lips, Reed is into the food. Ma slaps his hand like a naughty child, and Addy stifles a light giggle. And just like that, my blood drains south again. I focus on the food, hoping my body will calm the fuck down. But sitting this close to her, breathing her in with every breath I take, makes it harder and harder. Literally and figuratively.

"Thank you for the salad, Addy," Ma says, taking a huge portion with huge serving spoons that I don't think I have seen her use more than once before.

"You're welcome. It's my favorite."

Pa grunts. Ma gives him a warning look. Reed ignores them both, shoveling food into his mouth like he's shoveling shit onto a burning barn. Not a lot of leafy greens get eaten around these parts. Cowboys and the like mostly live on meat and potatoes. That, and whiskey.

Reed passes the bowl to Addy after taking a large serving, and she smiles at him. She dishes out some for herself and then turns to me. "Salad?"

I eye the leafy greens and then catch a glimpse of her hopeful face. "Sure, load it on."

She snatches up a pile of leaves and places them onto my plate. Great. I force a smile as she huffs a quiet laugh before returning the bowl to the center of the table.

"So, Addy. How is the riding coming along?" Pa asks.

She stiffens beside me, and I grip my fork with white knuckles. When she doesn't answer, I alternate my gaze between her and Harry. He waits patiently, chewing his food as if he'd asked her about the weather.

"Um, okay, I guess." Her words are weak.

Shit.

He's going to jump on this. I know it.

"Will you be ready in time for the roundup?" Harry continues.

"Hope so," Addy offers, pushing her salad around her plate.

"Yes or no?"

"Yes, sir."

God, she sounds like me, placating the old man. It grates. I shift in my seat.

"Why did you wait?" he continues again.

Addy shifts in her seat, placing her fork by her plate. "What do you mean?"

"Riding, after your accident. Why didn't you get straight back to it?"

"I ah—"

Fuck.

Pink flushes her cheeks, and she swallows. Even Reed notices it from across the table, by the pity on his face aimed at her.

"Well?" Harry prompts.

Her shoulders rise, rapid and shallow, and her hands have dropped to her lap, clutching the skirt of her dress. Ma shoots a warning look at Pa, but it's too late. Addy chokes on a tumble of words before pushing up and out of the chair. "Excuse me."

She rushes across the lawn like she's being hunted.

Sweet Jesus.

"Good one, Harry," Reed drawls. Ma pushes up from her chair, I assume to go after Addy, but I hold up a hand and she sinks back onto her chair.

Dropping my cutlery, I stand. "Jesus, Pa."

I stalk to the house.

Chapter Eight

ADDY

I am well aware it's my birthday, and I don't want to cry. But here I am, trying to stifle the tears that burn behind my eyes as I wander around the homestead, trying to locate a bathroom, a box of Kleenex. Anything. What's worse, I let Harry get to me. I have been so good at deflecting that question and making excuses about why I never rode again. I walk down the hall from the kitchen, hunting for a bathroom.

I find an open bedroom door. Inside is a dresser with a box of tissues. I go in and pluck a few tissues from the box. Sitting on the edge of the bed, I dab my eyes, sniffing back a fresh torrent of salt water. When I catch my breath, I take in the space. It's a man's room. One of the guys', I suspect. A queen bed and a flat screen TV mounted on the opposite wall.

Horse trophies and photos of various mounts sit on

the top of the drawers and adorn the walls. It's like a shrine to horses.

Hudson.

All of a sudden, I feel something entirely different. Curiosity. I stand and walk to the dresser. A photo sits in the center. I pick it up. A younger version of old Silver in the paddock closest to the house. A boy, maybe around ten, sits on her back, the widest smile plastered over his cute face.

"You alright, Howard?"

I startle and drop the picture. It falls forward and I catch it before the glass hits the wood. Setting it straight again, I back away from the furniture like it's on fire.

"I'll live."

Accurate.

I lived. Jewls did not.

I scrunch the tissue up in my hand and head for the door where he stands, arms crossed over his chest. "Sorry, I was looking for a bathroom or tissues. Found these first. I'll get out of your space."

But he blocks the doorway with a wide stance. "Don't let the old man get to you."

I huff a strangled laugh. Easy for him to say.

"I'm serious. He will rail on you until you stand up to him."

His face is soft, his mouth pulled up but in a way that completes his concern. I meet his gaze. "Why don't you?"

He drops his arms to his side. "It's complicated."

"Uh-huh. Reed doesn't seem to think so."

"Reed is a brat. The youngest of the four of us."

"There are four of you? God forbid."

He chuckles and runs a hand through that gorgeous hair. His bicep flexes, and I suck in a breath.

"Luckily for you, you only have to tolerate me and Reed. For a little while, at least."

I drop my focus to the floor. My contract is only six months. Then it's on to another job, another location. Or back to the city. I have no idea yet. I was focused on getting through the next few months.

"You want to talk about it?" he says, his voice deep and soft. And something inside me warms at the sound.

"Which part? The part where I can't ride when it used to be my entire life? Or the part where I'm only here for six months?"

His eyes widen, and his lips part. "Whichever one."

"I—"

He walks to the bed and sits down, patting the spot beside him. I hesitate, but eventually come to sit by him. He hands me another tissue, as if I'm going to need it, and I huff a laugh.

"After the accident, I couldn't—"

His blue eyes find mine. He is so still, as if on tenter-hooks with every syllable.

I take in a lungful of air and start again. "After the accident, my hips were smashed up bad. It took months to walk again. All the doctors told me I wouldn't have a career with horses anymore, at least not riding, anyway. So, I kind of shut that part off. That huge, enormous part of me that was my everything . . . until it wasn't."

Tears stream down my cheeks. Hudson shifts on the bed. When I meet his stare, his eyes are lined with silver and his jaw feathers. He swallows like he's eaten hot coals. "Shit, Addy. I'm so sorry."

Addy.

He called me Addy. I smile a wobbly smile and choke out a laugh.

"You called me Addy."

His face crumples slightly, but he doesn't move.

I have the overwhelming urge to nestle into his chest and let him fold his arms around me. But instead, I scrunch up my nose and dry my face before standing. He sits on the bed as I walk out of the bedroom and head down the hall to find a bathroom.

When I finally come to a half bath, I splash water over my face and pull myself together. As hard as that was to say out loud, I'm glad I told him. I'm glad I'm here, with the chance to get back the part of my life I have desperately wanted but not dared to hope for.

"Come with me, Howard," Hudson says from the hall.

I dry my face and meet him in the hall. His face is pulled up with a smile and he offers me a hand. "Wanna show you something."

I place my hand in his. It's warm and folds around mine so well. "What is it?"

"You'll see. Come on."

He drags me through the house, out the white gate, and to his truck. When he opens the passenger door, I glance to the table where the other three Rawlins are still eating. "Um, I don't want to be rude to your folks."

"Jesus, Howard, after what Harry just put you through, feel free to ditch lunch. It's your fucking birthday."

How did he know? He tousles my hair with one hand, the other guiding me into the truck.

When he starts up the engine, Reed and his mom take pause, watching us. I feel like a naughty kid but resist the urge to slink down in the seat to avoid them, just barely.

We drive toward the horse paddocks. When we reach the gates, Hudson gets them, insisting it's only fair, since it's my birthday. I should have brought my phone to check for messages from Mom and Ruby. I could have taken some pictures of this stunning place. After another couple of gates and almost forty minutes of driving, we ascend a large hill. When we crest it, the view takes my breath away.

A vista of lake, mountains, and pine firs lines the span from the foot of the hill to the horizon. It's like nothing I have seen before. But that is not what steals my breath. Sitting on the rise is a half-built, sprawling, ranch-type timber home. It's massive. And gorgeous. The enormous window spaces. The multi-gabled roof with *four* chimneys.

My door opens and Hudson offers his hand again. I take it, and this time he leads me to the tip of the rise. He drops my hand before skipping up the stairs to the impressive porch that skirts the home. With no side rails, he plops on to the edge and swings his legs over. "Come here, Howard."

I walk up the stairs. The wind billows under my dress, and I hold it down. I sit beside him, fixing my skirt around my legs before scanning the magnificent view from the spot. "What is this place, Hudson?"

He grips the edge of the veranda on either side of him. "My house."

"This is yours?" I spin back, trying to see more of the inside.

"Yup."

"When will the builders finish it? I was wondering why you still live with your parents." I nudge his shoulder with mine. His gaze drops to my lips before sinking further. Heat flushes my neck and face. And I want nothing more than his hands on my face, my neck. As my breaths shallow out, I clear my throat and return to admiring the vista. "It's an amazing spot here. You must be keen for them to finish."

"There is no them, Howard. I'm the carpenter."

Now, *that* I was not expecting. I spin back again, and this time I rise to my feet and walk to the space where I imagine huge double doors will hang one day. I run a hand over the wood. "You built this?"

"Yup."

"Hudson, that's—"

"I did a carpentry apprenticeship before I was ranching full time. Ma's idea. Paid off. But after—"

The words die in his throat. Hurt and pain flood his eyes. *After what?* I return to the edge of the veranda, but this time I sit with my legs tucked under and to one side, closer to him than before. "After what?"

"After a rough breakup, I needed something to occupy my head and my hands. I'd designed this house years ago, so when I had no reason to be anywhere else, I got started on this place. That was over five years ago now."

"You have been working on this for five years?"

"Ah, yeah. It's kind of slow with only one person."

"Yeah, I bet." I lose my train of thought and stare out at the vista. Such a stunning place, still heartache lives here, as it does anywhere. Hudson glances at me but returns his gaze to the pristine mountains in front of us. After a while, he jumps up and wanders inside the house.

I take in the crisp, cool mountain air and close my eyes and lay my head back. Gosh, it is magnificent here. And I let my mind start to wander, imagining what it would be like to wake up here. To watch the sunset on this porch. To sit in front of the fireplace and huddle up next to—

"Howard."

I snap my eyes open and straighten, turning back. Hudson stands with his hands gripping the top of the doorframe. His shirt is pulled up a little, exposing his hard stomach and the V of his muscles, his biceps bulging. His eyebrow raises, and I shake my head and school my face and my thoughts. I scramble to my feet. "Yep, coming."

The breeze tugs at the skirt of my dress as I walk across the porch to where he stands. He drops his hands to his sides. "Grand tour?"

"Sure," I say, smiling.

He swings an arm through the door in a dramatic, grand gesture, and I chuckle, walking over the threshold. The inside is even more impressive than the outside. "Oh wow."

"So, living room." He opens both arms and spins back, walking through the bare space. "Kitchen will be here. Something like Ma's, possibly; not sure on the design of that yet." He turns back and walks to where I am. "Do you want to see the rest?"

"Yes," I say, the word all but a whisper.

His eyes burn into mine for a moment, and my heart stammers. I chew my bottom lip before pulling it through my teeth. He shifts on his feet, his jaw feathering. But he crooks his arm, and a smile kicks up on one side of his mouth. "Milady?"

I giggle and slide my arm through his. We wander down the hall in the center and he points out the study, a few spare bedrooms. Then we get to the last door.

"What's this one?"

He turns but hesitates. "Master."

The word is gravel. My pulse kicks up, sending thunder through my head. Of course it is. Heat pools in my belly, and I stutter through a shallow breath. I slide my arm out of his and wrap my arms around myself. "It's nice."

This close, it's too easy to feel something that may or may not be there. Too easy to let myself want something I can never have. I force a smile and walk back toward the front of the house. An enormous fireplace claims the external front wall. I missed it before, too busy looking in to notice it.

Everything about this house is gorgeous, including the man who is building it. Choking on my next breath, I smooth my skirt before fixing my hair. And I remind myself why I am here in the first place. The deal is, I ride along on the roundup, I get to keep my job. Hudson is my coach, that's all.

Shit.

An incredibly sweet, albeit grumpy most of the time, but patient coach. Like that's not a contradiction, but he's different when he's in his element. *Ugh, Adeline Howard, you are in big trouble, girl.* I lean against the post of the porch and run a hand through my hair and wait for my heart to slow.

"What's going through your head, Howard?" Hudson comes to lean on the next post along.

"Just thinking how lucky you are, Rawlins."

"Ha, Rawlins. Guess I deserve that. As for lucky, more like trying not to fail at this and let Harry down. That's how I see it."

I push off the post. "You think you'll let him down? How?"

"I don't know. Screw it up. Lose the ranch or run it into debt. It happens to a lot of others, especially these days. It's not like it used be."

"What does your mom think?"

"Ma? She thinks all her boys can do anything." He chuckles. But he runs a hand behind his neck. "Maybe she's right. But she's most likely just being a good mom."

I close the distance between us. From what I've seen, there isn't anything Hudson Rawlins can't do. He is the most grounded, forward-thinking guy I have met in a long, long while. "Do you want my two cents, Rawlins?"

He dips his head and meets my gaze. "Give it to me, Howard." Then he smiles, lighting up those blue eyes of his. I adore this side of him. He's not like this when he's around his family. He's all-business Hudson. Get-the-job-done Hudson.

I rest a hand on his shirt, just under his collar. He swallows. "*I* think you have an incredible gift with horses and people. And it doesn't matter so much what your parents want you to do. It only matters what you want to do."

My hand slides from his chest.

He nods, slightly.

I offer him a small smile. It's the least I can do for him.

As for me, Harry is right.

"Your father, tactless as he may be, is right about me."

I turn and search the vista. "I should have tried to ride the minute I was able. That's what I regret most of all."

"If I can give that back to you, Addy, I will."

My chin wobbles and tears prickle behind my eyes. "I know you will, Hudson."

"You busy tomorrow?"

"Nope, you?"

"I have this rider that needs some extra attention. Sergeant and me, we're gonna be busy." He scrunches up his face and his blue eyes are lit with mirth. He's talking about me. Of course he is.

"It's a date, Rawlins."

"Absofuckinglutely, Howard."

I chuckle and wander down the steps. And like that, Howard and Rawlins are a team. And it's so goddamn right. And every which way I look at it, it looks a lot like the start of something that could very well be once in a lifetime.

Only it can't.

Chapter Nine
HUDSON

I lie in bed, trying to push away the image of Addy on my porch in that fucking sundress. All she wanted to do was talk about Harry and horses. All I wanted to do was flip that pretty yellow skirt up, pull her onto my lap, and let her sink onto me. Over and over, until every last one of those horrible memories from her accident were a distant memory.

But since I'm a fucking gentleman, I did no such thing. But the second her hand touched my chest, I was hard as hell. How can she do that to me with only the lightest touch? A smile and a look from those deep brown eyes. The curve of her lips. What I wouldn't do to taste those.

And now I am painfully hard. Fuck. A grown man, thirty-fucking-four for god's sake, hard just looking at this woman. Jesus. It's for the best she is leaving at the end of her six months. Because this is starting to feel very much like it could wreck me if we went there and it went sideways. Memories of tough days and impossible nights after Jemma flood in.

Like that, the blood rushes back to my brain. Nope, rider and coach, client and vet will have to be as good as it gets for Addy and me. I will have to make sure that it stays that way. It's better for her that way.

The smell of pancakes finds its way to my room, and I roll out of bed and head to the kitchen. Ma stands behind the skillet, flipping methodically. The coffee already dripping away, I grab a mug from the top cabinet behind her.

"Addy coming today?" she asks.

"Yup. Needs to make better progress if she's going to make the roundup."

"Hudson, you're not pushing her too hard, are you?"

"Of course not."

"I know what your father expects, and what her reality is may not exactly line up. I have been doing some research on her fall—"

"You what?"

She tilts her head and gives me the *don't shoot me* expression. "I was worried about her; I thought it would help if we knew what she went through, that it would help you—"

I slam the mug on the counter. "Howard will tell us when she is good and ready, not a second before."

"Huddy. She—"

"Nope." I hold a hand up.

All of a sudden, I ain't hungry. I walk out and back to my room to change. I pull on jeans and a t-shirt before socks. I make my way to the porch and slide on my boots, grabbing my Stetson and shoving it on my head, fire still coursing through my veins with Ma's good intentions. What the hell was she thinking? After Harry's lack of tact yesterday, I thought they would realize it's best to let things play out in their own time. But no, she decided to snoop instead.

Fuck me.

I whistle, and Charlie is at my side a heartbeat later. "Hey, boy. Least you make her happy. Come on. We have work to do."

He trots alongside me. Low clouds threaten overhead, the air thick with moisture. Addy's car pulls up as we clear the white gate, and she gets out of her car, making a beeline for Charlie. Lucky bastard.

Great start Hudson, be jealous of the fucking dog.

Addy's jeans hug her frame and her cream half-sleeve top is done up with a bunch of metal clasps, like a V-neck, resting over the swell of her chest. Her silky brown curls are loose and around her shoulders today. I remind myself why she is here, for the thousandth time this morning.

"Hello, little man. You with us today?" She is on the ground with him. Charlie licks her face, and she roughs him up.

"Morning, Howard. Ready to take a turn around the yard today?"

Her fussing stops and she meets my gaze, looking up from the ground. "Hopefully."

"Let's go." I march to the barn, and she walks behind me, talking to Charlie. Making my way into the barn, I grab a halter before her shadow fills the doorway to the tack room. Charlie waltzes in, sniffing the floor around the room.

"I will meet you in the wash area. I'll help you saddle him up." I hand her the halter.

"Okay," she says, scanning my face, as if trying to find what's different since yesterday.

"Go on."

Something like hurt flashes in her eyes before she schools it back and nods, turning and heading to the paddocks. Fuck, I am the world's biggest ass. But it's better this way. She doesn't need this. She needs to keep her job. To ride again. Whatever else this is, it's not why we're here.

I grab up Sergeant's bridle, blanket, and saddle and walk to the pastures and out to Silver. Charlie is stuck to Addy's side. Traitor. I rest the saddle and bridle on the top rail and climb through a lower one and walk to where Silver stands under her tree. She is thinner than a few weeks ago. Old age, maybe.

When Addy halters Sergeant and walks past, I slip through the rail again, pulling the gear into my arms. I pass her the bridle as she slips the halter off. She talks softly to the gelding while she slides the bit into his mouth and the headband over his ears.

I saddle him, taking in the words she uses. The tone of her voice. There's no fear. A little sadness, but no fear. When the girth is done up, I step back and give her a nod. She leads Sergeant toward the round yard. And now I see it, her stiff shoulders. The awkward sway of her gait. Her ribs flaring under that tight-fitting cream shirt with every quick breath.

Once inside the round yard, I tighten the girth and turn back to Addy. Her eyes are slightly wider, her hands wringing together, that bottom lip pulled into her teeth. I drop the reins to the ground and close the space between her and me.

I take her arms in my hands and tilt my head down a little. "You are okay. Sergeant will take good care of you. We both will. Once around the yard, and that's it. No more."

She nods, fast.

I turn to face the horse and move in beside her. "What are you thinking, Howard?"

"You should go first." She is shaking now, her breath ragged.

"Will that make it easier, if you see me go around first?"

"Uh-huh."

"Righto."

I move to the gelding, pluck up the reins, and grip the

pommel before swinging into the saddle. Her gaze lifts to mine. Her lips part, and she drops her hands to her sides. With a cluck from me, Sergeant walks on. She tracks us as we make our way around the yard, turning on the spot, her focus not wavering. When I complete the revolution of the round yard, I pull the horse to a halt.

"Your turn, Howard." I dismount and lead Sergeant to where she stands. She rubs his forehead with a shaking hand.

"I will walk beside you, okay?"

"Okay," she whispers.

"You need help getting on?"

She shakes her head no and moves to the side, raising her foot into the stirrup. She glances at me before gripping the reins and some mane. I move beside her and hold Sergeant steady, and she pulls up and mounts. She rearranges her hands and adjusts her feet in the stirrups. Her seat is perfect, her posture impeccable. She would have been one hell of a rider.

Something flips deep in my gut. "Right, you want to rein him around, or me to lead him?"

Her gaze, that has been frozen on the two ears flickering back and forth in front of her, snaps to mine. "You lead." She's almost out of breath.

Jesus.

"Hey, Addy?"

Her wide eyes find me.

"You're alright."

She nods, but I can see she doesn't believe me. What will it take to get this girl back to being at home on a horse? We have six weeks to find out.

I lead the gelding at a slow walk around the yard. When we come full circle, I steady him to a halt and look up. She's frozen. Her breathing is rough and raspy. Oh shit.

"Addy."

She doesn't move. Her eyes, not seeing, are fixed somewhere ahead of us. I pull her foot from the stirrup and slide mine in and push up, leaning on Sergeant to move in front of her. "Addy?"

She sucks in a staggered lungful on a soft whimper.

"Howard?"

"Hudson?" she rasps.

"I'm right here. I'm gonna get you down now, alright?"

But she doesn't respond right away. "No, please." Her stare snaps and her face crumples. But she takes the reins up. "Let me try again."

"No, Howard."

"Let me try again." She is so close to me, her breath lands on my face. "Please."

The way she begs shouldn't affect me the way it does. But with my heartstrings thoroughly plucked, I slide back to the ground and remove my foot from the stirrup and replace it with hers. Her hands shake around the reins, but she gives me a stiff nod.

I step back from Sergeant, and she gives him a squeeze

with her legs. Shoulders back, jaw tight, she moves with him in the saddle as he walks on. Addy is the bravest soul I have ever met, and I don't even know her story. Hell, I don't even know what Addy is short for. I make a promise to myself to do better from now on. For the ranch. For her.

When they are halfway around, she sucks in a breath and holds it. I track her body movements. Her legs squeeze the gelding, and he breaks into a trot.

Shit.

But to my surprise, she rises and falls with the gait like a pro with every outside front hoof step. And a small, wobbly smile flickers over her face before she reins Sergeant in and pulls him to a halt.

Well damn, she did it. Surprising me again. I walk to the gelding and rest a hand on the rein near the bit, rubbing his face with my free hand.

"That was . . . " Her words peter out.

"Epic, Howard, that's what that was. Guess who's going camping next weekend?"

"Yes!" She pumps both fists into the air before bending down and hugging Sergeant's neck. The storm clouds rumble overhead.

"We should get this old man squared away in his paddock before the sky bursts." I offer my hand, but Addy swings her leg behind her and dismounts, removing her foot from the stirrup. When she turns back, she's inches from me. And for a heartbeat I don't move, taking this incredible woman in as she stands, still shaking. The smile that beams over her gorgeous face is addictive. And I tip my hat to her, a well done for a hard-won task. "Well done, Howard."

"Thanks, Hudson. We should go before we get soaked."

I'd pay good money to see that cream shirt soaked through. So, I take my time leading the gelding back to the barn. Addy walks beside me. She's quiet, and I know she is processing what just happened. I pray that it is all good progress from this point onward, but I know from experience that sometimes it's one step forward and two steps back. Especially when it comes to rider psychology.

It's a huge undertaking to trust an animal with your life again, especially after a traumatic accident. A tiny part of me wishes I knew what happened to Addy. What could possibly have someone like her, with such a love for horses and obvious riding prowess, out of the saddle? If I am lucky, maybe one day she will let me in and share her story. If Ma doesn't find it by hunting it down first . . .

As we release Sergeant to his paddock, thunder cracks overhead and rain pours from the dark clouds. In seconds, we are both drenched through, and I force my focus back to the barn when Addy takes off running for its shelter. I follow, flying into the barn after her as she scrambles to a halt, chuckling.

Her hair is dangling over her face, neck, and shoulders. The cream top that she has on is almost translucent. The dark bra underneath snags my attention before I train it elsewhere. Addy walks in a circle, ringing out her hair and then her shirt. It lifts as she wrings it between her hands, her belly exposed up to her ribs.

I track my focus to outside, but it's too late. My cock is rock hard. Heat swells in my belly and my heart thunders.

"You're all wet, Rawlins."

I stifle the groan that wants out of my throat. The blood from my brain well and truly migrated south, I don't dare turn around. And she appears by my side a heartbeat later. Her shirt is back down, but the navy bra shows through the wet material that now clings to her skin, over the swell of her breasts, the curve of her ribs, narrowing at her waist.

I shove both hands through my hair and think of anything but the woman beside me. And then she moves. Closing the distance between us, she stands right in front of me.

Fuck me.

"What are you thinking?" she breathes.

Her chest rises and falls erratically. As if she read my mind, her gaze drops to my mouth.

"Addy," I rasp.

Her hand rises as if she wants to touch me. "Thank you for today, Hudson."

I clear my throat. "You're welcome. Just doing my job."

Her hand falls, and she takes a step back. "I guess I'll see you next Saturday, then."

"Yep. Don't forget your camping gear."

"Sure thing," she says, but the words are flat, and she turns back and walks into the rain before getting into her car and driving away. Her taillights disappear in the misty downfall, and I swallow hard.

Sweet Jesus, why did that feel like the worst moment of my entire life?

ALEXANDRA DAVIS

Chapter Ten

ADDY

So, I now know two things. One, I have officially been back on a horse and nothing horrific happened. Kudos to Hudson. Two, he is *definitely* not interested. Which in hindsight, is good. Right?

At any rate, we are camping after my lesson next week-end, and I am stoked. I can only imagine how magnificent the stars will be from the top of that hill.

But first, I have to make it through this week. I have been assigned to small animals this week, with Justin taking over the equine work. Something about rotations being fair for all veterinary staff. But I'm not convinced. Did Harry have a hand in it, not happy with my riding progress? Or is Justin punishing me for not responding to his borderline inappropriate flirting over the last three weeks?

Whatever the case is, I am on dog and cat duty for the

next five days. I can only hope something more interesting than routine vaccines comes in. Here's hoping.

Is that bad? Ugh, who would know.

"You have a procedure booked for this afternoon," Sally the receptionist chimes in, breaking apart my musing daydream.

"Great, which theater am I allocated?"

"None. Justin wants your work done in the treatment rooms. Something about priority cases only for the theaters?"

"You can't be serious. That's not even best practice."

"It is when you're in rural Montana, love."

Fine. Just fine.

Whatever you say, Justin. Lord, how far we have sunk in three short weeks. I am sure there is cause for reporting the practice to the veterinary board, but that would most likely cost me my job. Which I desperately need.

And there is no way I am missing the roundup with the Rawlinses because some small-town, unrequited Romeo got a bee in his bonnet. It's almost as bad as Adam and his spam texts. Every night since my birthday, he has been texting multiple times. I moved across the country to get away from him—you'd think the man would take a hint.

With only one more appointment before lunch, I start prepping the treatment room for a routine procedure, taking stock of the cart and the medicines. I am busy cleaning down the treatment table in the center of the room with disinfectant when Sally pops her head back in.

"Your twelve o'clock canceled, hon. And there is someone here to see you. You should take your lunch break while you can."

"Oh, thanks, I'll be out in five."

"Okay, I'll tell him."

Him.

I stiffen a little at the thought that Adam could've tracked me down. Finishing up the cleaning job, I pull off my white coat and hang it over the back of the office chair. I straighten my scrubs before walking out to the waiting area. Hudson sits reading a magazine about cats and dogs, one ankle resting on his knee. His Stetson is sitting on the chair beside him.

I stop right in front of him. "To what do I owe the pleasure of this visit, Rawlins?"

He startles and tosses the magazine on the table and grabs up his hat, standing. He studies me up and down. "Nice scrubs, Howard."

"Well, they wouldn't let me wear my swimsuit, so this is the next best thing." The joke is lame. Heat flushes my cheeks, but Hudson doesn't seem to notice. "Did you need an appointment?"

"Don't think you'll ever geld that one, Addy," Sally pipes up from behind the reception desk, muffled giggles following the comment. I raise an eyebrow at her, and she holds up both hands in a *please don't shoot me* plea.

"Um, okay?" I say to Sally before turning back to Hudson. "So, what do you need?"

"Actually, I'm here for you."

"You are?"

"Ma's idea, since we kind of ruined your birthday the other day."

"Oh, I see."

"It's your lunch break, right?" His gaze flicks to Sally briefly.

I huff a laugh. "Yes, it is. I'll get my bag."

"No need, our treat. Since Harry spoiled your day."

Pointing behind me, I turn back a little. "In that case, I'll grab my phone."

"Sure, meet you outside."

Walking back to my treatment room, I snatch my phone from the desk. Another text from Adam. Two from Ruby. I slide it into the side pocket of my pants and walk outside. Hudson is sitting on the tailgate of his truck. When he sees me coming, he jumps up, folding up the tailgate. "Right, the place is two blocks away. You like Italian?"

"Lead the way."

He walks quietly beside me as we travel past quaint shops and handfuls of locals. Some say hello to Hudson.

"I wanted to apologize for the other day in the barn," he starts.

"Forget it, Rawlins, I got my wires crossed. I know exactly where you and I stand. Coach and rider, at a stretch . . . sometimes friends. It's all good." He opens his mouth to object, but I interrupt. "I'm starving, you?"

He adjusts his hat. "Yup."

We cross the street, and he leads me through the door to the only Italian joint in town, Mama's Place. The divine aroma of garlic and pasta sauce hits me. We walk to a table and Hudson waits until I am seated before sliding into a seat opposite me. "Busy day at the clinic?"

"Not really. One procedure this afternoon, then routine check-ups for the rest of the week. Without the equine visits, it's kind of slow."

"You're not working horses?"

"Nope, Justin thought it was best to share the cool jobs around. So, I'm not back on the roster for ranch visits for another couple weeks. Good news is my days are much shorter. Like nine 'til three."

"Oh, damn." His face is unreadable. But he picks up the menu and studies it intently. I do the same, but with a little less vigor.

"If you're finishing earlier now, did you want to add more lessons to your schedule?"

"Won't that put you out? Surely you have other things to do apart from me." When a cheeky grin splits his face, I realize my mistake. "I mean, apart from *helping* me."

He chuckles and drops his menu. "Howard, I will always have time for you. You can come out every after-noon, if you want."

I feel heat rise in my neck and flush my cheeks. "It's a

fair bit of drive time. Maybe Tuesday and Thursdays, on top of our Saturday session?"

"Sergeant will be thrilled. You realize Tuesday is tomorrow?"

"Yes, Rawlins," I drawl.

"Good. We'll see you then. For now, what do you wanna eat?"

"Nothing beats spaghetti Bolognese, please."

He raises a hand, and the waitress scoots over. "Two spaghetti Bolognese, please. And some water and bruschetta for the table."

Glancing between us, she scribbles down our order before rushing away.

"You know, something has been bothering me these last few weeks. And you can tell me if it's none of my business, but . . ."

I lean back in my chair. It's either about a man or a horse. And by the sympathetic look that claims his gorgeous face, it's not about a man. He wants to know about Jewls. And I want to tell him, so badly. I have, ever since that first lesson. But across the table feels so far away from him when I am about to pour my heart through my sleeve. So, I pick up the chair and come to sit by his side and he turns in his seat.

I open my mouth but air lodges in my throat as memories replay of the day. That course, the decisions I made.

"It's, alright, Howard. Whenever you're ready." I

glance up and his jaw feathers as he leans forward. "Maybe—"

"No, it's fine. I want you to know . . . It was my fault."

He doesn't say anything. Doesn't dismiss the way I feel or the way I remember that day. Not like my parents did.

"Her name was Jewel. Jewel of the Nile. She was a half-Arabian, half-warmblood show jumper. We were at the qualifiers. I was last to ride. Our round determined who went through to the Olympics."

Hudson swallows, his face still soft.

"We had cleared the first lot of jumps and just gone over the hedge when I felt something wasn't right." My chin wobbles as I pull in a breath. His hand appears on my lap, upturned, like a lifeline if I need one. I inch my fingers closer, letting the tips find his. His hands are warm, so warm. Tears burn behind my eyes.

"She was off, and I pushed her. I had no idea what had happened at that stage. But we went for the next jump. And she seemed okay . . . but when we took on the triple, she crashed headfirst into it. I remember the way she looked at me. As if—" Tears stream down my face and Hudson shifts in his seat until his knees are on either side of mine. He takes my hands in his, and I have to keep going. If I stop, I don't think I could say it all again. "She was scared, confused. She was dying, and I had no idea."

"Addy." His voice is raw. His thumbs rub over the backs of my hands.

"There was a taipan in the hedge that we'd jumped

over. And after twenty other horses and riders, it was very much riled up. It bit her on the flank, and she was gone minutes later."

I choke through a sob.

Hudson pulls me into his lap and cradles my head, and I sob into his chest, hard. "It was all my fault. She tried to tell me, and I was so caught up in making a good time, I didn't listen. I didn't listen, Hudson, and she died. Afraid and helpless."

"Addy, I'm so sorry."

My lungs impossibly tight, I sob in his hold. When I have finally recovered from my grief and removed myself from his lap, I clear my throat and reinstate myself in my place on the opposite side of the table.

"You said you had to learn to walk again?"

"My foot got hung up when she went down, and I was crushed underneath her. Both of my hips were shattered. The surgeon did a great job, but it took so long and multiple procedures that the muscles in my hips, abdomen, and legs had atrophied too much. So off to physical therapy I went, to walk between the bars. That part, at least, wasn't too bad. I mean, it was painful and frustrating. But nothing like losing Jewls. We were together for five years. The day we met . . . She changed my life." Tears burn again, but I dab my face with a napkin, taking in the cozy little restaurant. And for the first time since the accident, I feel as if the weight I have carried since that day is almost gone. I don't think

Hudson will ever know how much of an impact he has had on me.

The waitress appears with two oversized bowls of steaming spaghetti Bolognese, bruschetta and water.

"This smells amazing," I say. But when I look up, Hudson's face is slack, his eyes narrowed, his breath short.

"It's okay, Rawlins; I'll live." I force a smile, and he swallows before breaking eye contact.

I twirl my fork in my spaghetti and shove the steaming pasta into my mouth. It's epic. God, this is divine. After a while, Hudson picks up his fork, but instead of diving right into his food, he shunts it around on his plate.

"Eat, Hudson, I can't have you hangry on top of grumpy." I scrunch my nose up at him, and he huffs a laugh and twirls his fork.

We finish the meal, and Hudson grabs the check. We wander back to the clinic on the opposite side of the street so I can check out some more shops. We pass a florist, and Hudson ducks inside. I hang around outside the next shop, a little gift shop, and peek at the handmade gifts. Mom would love some of these neat little spice jars and bundles of dried herbs. I make a mental note for later.

Bright yellow daisies are shoved under my nose, and I step back and chuckle. "I think you giving me flowers might breach the rider-coach agreement we have, Rawlins."

"Since this was Ma's idea, I'll send her the bill. Then

they're from her, not me. Problem solved." He hands me the flowers again. I grab them, covering his hand. And he closes the space between us.

"I'm glad you're okay, Howard. And for the record, taipans are always fatal. There wasn't anything you could have done. It *wasn't* your fault, Addy."

I close my eyes and let his words sink in. It will take a while for me to believe that. I know he is right, logically. I'm a vet, for goodness's sake. But I will always carry the loss of Jewls with me. Especially when I'm on a horse. Something brushes my cheek and I open my eyes to find Hudson sweeping a stray curl of hair behind my ear. My heart thunders against its cage.

"Come on, I better get you back before Justin has a conniption," he mutters.

I nod and he releases the flowers, taking his hand out from under mine. It takes me a moment to follow him down the street, spice jars and bundles of whatever long forgotten.

Hudson holds the clinic door open for me and tips his hat in a goodbye. Justin calls out as he goes to close the door, "Here to check up on your empire, Rawlins?"

"Justin," Hudson grunts and waves to me, letting the door close behind him. I turn back, daisies in hand. Justin grunts and grabs a pile of charts from the reception desk before slinking back to his treatment room. Ugh. That guy is starting to give me the creeps. Sally gives me a knowing smile. "There was a call for you when you were out. Someone called Ruby?"

"Oh shit. Yeah, I'll text her back. Thanks, Sally."

I walk to my treatment room and plop onto the office chair. Phone in hand, I slide it open and tap the messages icon. Ruby's messages are top of the list.

> Hey, Adds. Checking in to see how things are going. Awesome news, I have a job at an inn not far from you. Will let you know when I hit Montana.

> Adds, answer me, girl! Or I'm coming to hunt you down . . .

> Adeline Howard, I am on my way.

I huff a laugh and text her back.

> Hey, Rubes. I'm good. But I can't wait to see you if you're serious about Montana, that is.

The three dots appear on my screen.

> Already left NYC. See you in a few days.

> Like four days, Rubes, don't drive like a crazy woman, please!

> Fine, old lady. Four days, tops.

Yay!! Can. Not. Wait!

Me too, babes. Me too.

Chapter Eleven

HUDSON

I send the colt around the yard again. Harry hangs over the rail, barking orders. But all I can think about is Addy. The pain in her voice, in her eyes when she told me about Jewls. And how she blames herself for it. It was like someone had sucked the oxygen from the room and replaced it with electrified concrete. I had expected some kind of trauma related to horses, but not that. Not losing her champion partner to something like a snake in a hedge jump. That's beyond belief.

"Hudson!" Harry snaps.

I shake my head and realize I have let go of the lariat. The colt is standing near the rail, facing me. Fuck. The last thing I need is the old man getting it in his head that I can't do my job. Sweet Jesus. I snatch up the lariat and send the colt around.

"I want him under saddle in the next month," Harry says.

"Yep."

"Also, how is Addy coming along with her lessons? She needs to be on that roundup."

"Good. Back on the horse, just need to get her moving out." A slight exaggeration. But we have extra lessons now, so she won't be far off from riding out in the fields.

"Nice work, son. I'll see you at dinner."

"Yup."

He stands there for a moment, studying me, as if what I'm not saying is written on my face and in my body language. The same way I look at a horse. Reading body language. But he shakes his head and wanders back to the homestead, and I cluck my tongue to send the horse into a lope.

When he handles the basic commands at all gaits, I bring him to a halt and throw a blanket over his back. He shuffles on his feet, nickering, but doesn't shy away. Good start. I rub his face and talk softly to him before sliding the blanket off and back on again. After a few rounds of blanket treatment, when he is calm with the new weight, I call it a day and walk him back to his pasture.

I saddle up my own dark gelding, Rocket, and lope down the laneway. Charlie trots beside me. Time to check on my mares in foal. I will have to schedule another visit for them with Addy. It's been almost a month since their last checkup. I make good time to the mares' paddock and ride between them.

Everything appears fine. Their bellies grow bigger with every week that passes. I make a mental note to bring Addy down on Saturday after her lesson. Twelve foals will make for a fine little herd to sell, either broken or green. And it will be a boost for the ranch's finances nonetheless.

I ride home and put the horse and tack away, making a beeline for the homestead. There is one last section of fence line to be done. Reed can help me. I walk through the front door. "Reed?"

"Kitchen." His voice is flat. Probably trying to think of a way to weasel out of the fencing. *I have news for you, little brother.* I file through the foyer and into the kitchen. He is reading a sheet of paper at the kitchen table.

"We have that last section of fence left. You're *it*, lover boy, let's go."

He folds the page in half and places it on the table.

"What ya readin'?"

"Nothing, some instructions for the post-factory gadget for my truck." But his gaze is stuck on the sheet of paper, not meeting mine. Liar. I lunge for the paper. He dives for it, but he's too slow. I leap over the sofa, and he groans, stopping before the chair, his face screwed up with something like regret, arms limp by his side.

With a frown, I open the paper. It's a printout of a news article. The title in bold print is like a slap to the face. **Talented Almost Olympian, Adeline Howard, Survives Freak Accident at Qualifiers.**

Reed's face turns pleading. "Huddo, sorry man, Ma found it. We only wanted to know what happened."

I stare at the article. The image of a younger version of Addy. Her horse, Jewls, stands beside her. They make a stunning pair. And my gut sinks like a rock. Because I know exactly how this story went. And how much that mare meant to her. Absentmindedly, I hand the paper back to Reed over the sofa. He takes it tentatively. "She didn't tell you?"

"She told me yesterday."

"Fuck bro, sorry. I know what she means to you."

With that, I snap my head up. "What's that supposed to mean?"

"You know, like she's your captain."

As if some imaginary force slapped me hard on the back, the air in my lungs disappears. "Don't be fucking stupid," I finally rasp.

My little brother tilts his head. "Seriously, Huddo, you must be the only one who can't see it. Even the dog can see it."

"Howard is my client. She is our vet. That's it."

"Yup." His eyebrows are raised and pinched.

"Fence line, Reed, now!"

I turn on my heel and stalk out the door and to the truck. I have no idea why I am angry at my family. If anyone deserves wrath, it's me. For being so goddamn stupid. For letting my heart get involved when I am in no position to give it away. Not after last time.

Reed makes quick work of the fencing while I haphazardly help, lost in thought. How did things change so much in a month? I crank the lever on the strainers and make one last adjustment to the bottom wire.

"How's the house coming along?" Reed interrupts my tortured thoughts.

"Fine."

"You know, when you take over this place, you're gonna regret building so far away from the homestead. All that drive time, Huddo."

"I'll live."

I'll live. The same thing Addy said to me after she told me about her accident. I push the thought out of my mind. The most we can be is friends. Captain or no captain, Addy isn't interested in commandeering this ship. For fuck's sake, she's leaving after her six months is up. It's a wasted effort thinking about it.

I huff a laugh at myself.

Reed raises an eyebrow at my muttering self-talk.

Don't think about Adeline Howard. Tell that to my gut, my aching chest. To every hardened inch in my pants when she's around. You may as well tell me *don't breathe.*

The tantalizing scent of pot roast wafts from the kitchen to the dining table. Harry and Reed are already sitting down when I wander in. Ma rushes down the hall toward me, muttering something about burning veggies. I take a seat at the table. "What's with Ma?"

"She's been like this all day. In and out of the study, like a woman possessed."

"Still digging up things she should leave well enough alone?" I ask.

"What's she digging up?" Harry chimes in, putting his paper on the table.

"Ma found an article about Addy this morning," Reed says.

I flick the knife on the table around on its weighted handle. It spins easily on the polished wood.

"That so? What did it say?"

"A write-up about her losing her horse in the accident."

"Oh, how did that happen?" Harry asks.

I flick the knife harder.

"Snake bite on a show jumping course." Reed's answer is short but accurate. As if he can sense my growing annoyance at the both of them talking about Addy.

"Show jumper, hey," Harry says, as if imagining Addy sailing over a jump.

"At the Olympic qualifiers, too. She must have been really something, Harry," Reed adds.

I slam the knife on the table. Both men snap their

gazes to where I sit, knife still under my hand. "Stop talking about her like she's some topic of gossip!"

Reed throws both hands up over his shoulders. "Take it easy, Huddo. I'm only telling Harry her story."

"If she wanted you all to know, she would have told you." I push up out of the chair and storm to the study. The laptop is still on. I don't dare look at the tabs Ma has open. I don't want to see or hear or imagine anything else about Addy hurt or scared or in pain.

Fucking sweet Jesus.

I run both hands through my hair and my shortened breaths steel my steady footing. I slump on the reading chair in the corner before I sink to the ground. I close my eyes and breathe through my nose. Thinking of taxes, shoveling horseshit, and anything that will get that picture of young Addy and her beloved horse out of my head. And when her broken face from yesterday stops flipping through my mind on replay, I sigh and open my eyes.

Ma stands in the doorway.

"She told you?"

I don't trust my words. Anger, frustration, and something like helplessness are still coursing through my veins. So, I simply nod.

"We wanted to understand, Huddy. It wasn't meant to be intrusive."

"Great job, Ma."

She swallows, and I know I hurt her feelings. And when I am sure I won't say something even stupider, I stand and walk to where she leans on the doorframe. "Sorry, Ma. I don't know why this is riling me up so much."

She pulls an incredulous face and tilts her head before patting my chest. "My love, I am one hundred percent certain you'll figure it out."

Dinner is quiet. Only the sounds of cutlery clinking make it past the guilt-ridden murmurs of my family.

"Oh, I forgot to say, Mackinlay is coming home this weekend. He got off tour early." Ma's face lights up.

"Awesome, I could use some better company than king grumpy over here." Reed points his fork at me.

I throw him a scowl, and he huffs a laugh.

"How long does he have off?" Harry asks.

"A few months, possibly three if the other team can fill in for his unit. He won't be here for Thanksgiving." Ma's expression deflates. She misses him and worries like nothing else for Mack. Having a son in the army wasn't part of her plan for us boys. But Mack has always done what Mack wants. And when he enlisted, she supported him the only way she knew how—with unconditional love and a shit ton of baked goods.

"Speaking of family business," Harry starts. Reed puts his fork down and steeples his fingers. I slump back in my chair. "We should go over the last quarter for the ranch and the company holdings."

"Fire away," I say, waving my hand in the air.

Harry sits up in his chair and picks up a small manilla

folder from the table by his plate. "This will be the last roundup I'm on. You will take point this roundup, Hudson. And when we get back, the money from these cattle will go towards our off-ranch investments, namely the clinic. Justin wants out. So, we will be buying him out. Along with the clinic, we have half shares over in Great Falls. And with the equity that brings, we will start looking at other ranches. Adding another two into the business is smart. However, all this is to say that the outcome of the roundup will be your testing point. It's high time you called the shots. If you are to take over the ranch at the end of the year, I want to see some leadership. The ranch doesn't need a yes-man, son."

Reed's gaze is firmly fixed to the plate in front of him. Harry's burns into mine.

So, this is it. This is how my old man makes me step up and take the reins. I knew it was coming. In all honesty, I thought he would have had this conversation with me four years ago. And I have spent the last four years trying to give him whatever he wants, thinking that was what it would take. And I couldn't have been more fucking wrong. Yes-man, Pa's version of a pushover. No wonder he waited. Goddamn.

"Yes—" I shift on my seat. "Alright, I'll make it happen."

"Good. You will need to have Addy ready. I won't lose any animals because of a lack of a willing ride-along vet. And the foals, half of those will need to be sold after the roundup. It will take every last penny to buy out that hack, Justin. God knows he has had long enough to run the clinic into the ground. And besides, we will need that equity for further growth."

"On it."

"Good. Now, onto more pleasant business. Where you planning on takin' Addy for her camping trip? It would be good for her to see how the ranch operates and the pure scale of this all."

My eyes widen, how the hell does he know about that?

"Um, she loved the hill under the new fence line on the north end. Probably there."

Reed clears his throat.

"What's wrong with that?"

"I dunno, Huddo, why don't you take her to the vista? It's much nicer. Unless you're worried she'll notice that half-built house of yours . . ."

"I've already taken her up to the house," I grunt and slouch in my chair, folding my arms. Why is everyone in this house so damn invested in a simple camping trip? Reed drops his fork, his eyes widening.

"You have?" Ma pipes up. Her face is lit up with excitement. Now I get it. They all think Addy and I are a thing. *Sorry to disappoint.* "Yup, I had to get her out of here when Harry couldn't mind his own business during Sunday lunch. Was a quick visit, don't read into it, Ma."

"Oh, I definitely won't."

Reed sniggers and runs a hand through his hair. I glare at him until the stupid expression on his face slips.

But it's Harry's face of stone that sees us all quiet. "Don't want to get involved with her, son. In a few months, you will practically be her boss. One of them, at least. She's off-limits." His brows are pulled down, eyes studying me deep. And then it dawns on me: if things don't go well with the clinic, or if it's a mess when Harry takes over completely, Addy's job might not be safe. And I will be part of the decisions around what happens to the clinic *and* the employees.

No pressure, Hudson. You only need to ensure twelve healthy, salable purebred foals, pull off the biggest roundup of the year with a vet who can't get out of the round yard on a horse, bring in every last head of cattle to make sure the business side of our—what did Justin call it . . . dynasty, or was it empire—can thrive and not sink like the fucking Titanic.

Not be romantically involved with the most incredible woman I have ever met. And finally, prove to my old man that I have what it takes to run a ranch and not follow orders like some idiot. *Nah, no pressure at all.*

Oh, and all before Thanksgiving.

Fuck my life.

Chapter Twelve

ADDY

Sergeant moves under seat a little as I readjust my stirrups, and I ignore the panic that creeps up my insides. Hudson is right beside me. I am safe. Sergeant is safe. Everything is going to be A-OK . . .

My knuckles whiten around the reins. If I can make it through all three gaits today in the round yard, Hudson wants me to try the small paddock attached to the barn. And the thought of that much freedom on a horse ties my stomach into a thousand knots.

But we have three weeks left until the big roundup. Despite extra lessons and Hudson's endless patience, I'm terrified. Not for me. I've fallen off horses more times than I care to count. What I can't handle is that I might do something or make a decision that endangers Sergeant. And the thought of this wonderful boy getting hurt or me letting Hudson down gives me hives.

Hudson is distracted today. The usually light banter that took weeks to establish between us is strained. He's tense. Is he worried about the camping trip? Maybe he thinks I expect things to heat up between us. I'm not gonna lie, that thought has crossed my mind a few times. Who am I trying to kid—it's more like a lot. When I can't sleep late at night . . . in the shower. Heat pools low in my belly thinking about it.

"Walk on, Howard," Hudson says.

All business today. Righto . . .

I push the horse into a walk and shorten the reins. *Two can play that game, Rawlins.* I squeeze Sergeant into a trot and rise and fall with his footfalls. But Hudson's brows lower and he puts his hands on his hips. Ugh. I squeeze the gelding into a canter and lope around the yard for a few revolutions.

Hudson doesn't even look at us. He isn't watching my body language, or Sergeant's. His attention is somewhere else entirely. I pull Sergeant around and canter to where Hudson stands, sliding to a halt only inches from him.

Wow, that felt amazing. Sergeant takes two steps back automatically. I pat his neck. I *am* ready for the paddock. "Earth to Rawlins."

He snaps back from wherever he was in that mind of his and jerks when he realizes we are standing right in front of him. "Shit, I'm sorry. Did you want me to lead you around?"

"Ah, no. Didn't you see what we did?"

"I, ah—"

"What is going on with you today?"

"Nothing. Did you want to try the paddock?"

I frown at him and gather the reins again before dismounting. He watches me, jaw clenched, as I lead Sergeant past him and to the gate. Opening the gate, I make my way to Sergeant's paddock. I glance back to find Hudson and Charlie are trailing behind. I walk into the field and double-check the girth and my stirrups, waiting for Hudson to catch up. He closes the gate behind him and climbs up onto the rail. Charlie lies on the grass below him. "Show us what you've got, Howard."

I huff a nervous laugh as the knots in my gut turn into a pit of writhing snakes. But I am not quitting now. I slide my foot into the stirrup and swing into the saddle. Charlie watches, his little head popping up from his paws for a moment. As if he can sense the snake pit in my gut, too.

Pushing the gelding into a walk, I track along the fence line, away from Hudson. The paddock is a perfect rectangle of grass, one horse shelter for bad weather, and a handful of trees. It's secure, controlled, and in no way intimidating.

We break into a trot along the fence, and I shorten the reins, rising with his outside footfall, the way it was drummed into me in my early equestrian coaching days. Gosh, that was almost twenty years ago.

If only eight-year-old me could see what's become of me.

She would be so mad. Going for years without riding. I can only imagine the pout I would get from her. With a soft laugh at my ridiculous inner monologue, I push Sergeant into a canter. We lope around the short end of the paddock, past the shelter and the first clump of trees. Happiness bubbles in my chest.

Hudson has a hand over his face, as if sheltering his eyes, as he watches us lope toward him. I pull back on the reins and slow to a walk as we close in on the fence-sitting duo.

"That was fantastic, Howard. Well done!"

"Thanks," I say, almost out of breath. I shift in the saddle, and my hip twinges a little on the right.

Charlie bolts to his feet, hackles up. Hudson swings around to see what he's doing. And then I see it. A snake in the grass, less than ten feet from Charlie. Ringing starts in my ears. Sergeant shuffles on his feet—he must have seen it, too.

"Fucking hell," Hudson growls. "Charlie, away!"

Charlie barks at the snake. It pays him no heed. Winding its way through the short grass toward us. My heart beats so fast, my breath shallows out. A whimper leaves my lips. Hudson moves so he is between the snake and Sergeant.

"No," I choke.

Charlie moves closer. His barking intensifies to shrill yapping. Stars encroach on my vision as bile claws up my throat. Hudson pulls off his hat and tosses it at the snake. But it rears up at him, hissing.

Hudson stands his ground, thumping his feet, yelling at it to get out of here. Then I shift my gaze to Charlie. Everything moves like molasses, so slow. He leans back on his haunches, growling. Then pounces.

My heart flies into my throat. "Charlie!"

Sergeant whinnies and backs away from the chaos. I hold the reins tight.

Charlie snaps his teeth around the snake's neck an inch before its head and shakes it until it goes limp. Growling the whole time. He only lets it go when Hudson tells him to drop it. The mangled snake lies limp at his feet. I take a shaking foot from the stirrup and clamber from the horse. Hudson turns back as I duck under Sergeant's neck and fall to the ground and crawl to where Charlie sits.

"Shit, Charlie." I run my hands over his face, neck, and torso. Making sure the snake didn't have a chance to sink its fangs into him while it was getting tossed about. Hudson comes to stand behind me, close. I hug the pup tight. The snake twitches on the ground beside me. Hudson slams a boot onto its head, grinding into the ground.

"Are—" Hudson starts, his voice cracking. "You alright, Howard?"

I nod, letting tears fall onto Charlie's head.

A moment later, Hudson and Sergeant walk past and

out the gate. I pick up Charlie and prop him over my shoulder. I walk to the barn and sit on the hay bales and love him up, scratching his belly.

"Aren't you the bravest boy I know?"

He pants, rolling around under my hand.

Hudson appears, saddle in one hand, bridle in the other. "You shouldn't fuss over him so much. He's supposed to be a ranch dog."

"Well, this is a well-earned reward, Rawlins. What's got your goat today?"

He doesn't answer; instead, he heads to the tack room. I dot a kiss to Charlie's head and wander to the tack room. When I don't hear any movement inside, I wander over. Hudson is standing at the back of the room, hands pressed against the back wall, head hanging. His back muscles ripple with every heaving breath he takes. What is going on with him?

I close the distance between us and stare at his back, trying to find something to say.

"Hudson?"

He doesn't respond. Charlie trots around us but finds a scent and tracks it back out of the tack room. Like he didn't just kill a snake. I make my way over to the feed bins, a row of rectangular sectioned feed storage with multiple hinged lids. I sit on the middle one and wait for him.

When I think he isn't going to talk to me, I push off the bin and head for the door.

"I'm sorry, Addy."

I stop in my tracks. Slowly, I turn back. He has spun around. His hands hang by his sides. His face is wrecked. My gut flips, breath caught in my lungs, not moving.

"It's fine. Not your fault," I choke out, shoving my hands into my back pockets, not sure what to do with them. I bite my bottom lip and suck in a breath.

He steps forward but hesitates. So, I close the space between us. He dips his head and meets my gaze.

"Charlie will be okay, he didn't get bitten," I offer.

He closes his eyes and shakes his head. "I'm not worried about the dog."

I raise an eyebrow. Since when is Hudson Rawlins not concerned about his horses, and his faithful little buddy Charlie? "Is Sergeant okay?"

"Yeah," he chokes.

"Good."

When he doesn't open his eyes, I make my way to the door. I should get my gear ready for the camping trip. I hope what happened before doesn't wreck the whole trip.

"Adeline." His voice is gravel.

I stop, hands gripping the doorframe.

Holy shit.

That's the first time he has *ever* used my full name.

He walks up behind me. "Turn around, Addy."

I close my eyes; the rawness of his voice shallows everything out. I swallow past the rock wedged in my throat and drop my hands. My breath rises and falls in deep cycles. Fire floods my veins with every heartbeat as I open my eyes.

"Addy," he whispers, desperation lining my name.

I turn back. His hat hangs in his fingertips by his side. His chest heaves. His disheveled hair is swept from his face. His blue eyes burn into mine when I reach them. A moment later, I drop my gaze to his lips, throat, and back to his eyes. Those blue pools swallow me whole. God, what I wouldn't do to have Hudson Rawlins's mouth on mine right—

His hat slips from his fingers, and he takes my face in his hands, sinking his mouth over mine. I wrap my fingers around his collar. He deepens the kiss, and I open for him. Desperate for more. Heat floods my center. I run my hands inside his shirt, sweeping up his neck and into his hair.

He groans against my mouth. I press my body into his, and hardness rubs against my stomach. Suddenly, I don't feel close enough to him. This is not enough. It never was. I am desperate for every part of this man. All of Hudson Rawlins.

Nothing less.

I break the kiss, and he rests his forehead on mine, breathing heavy.

"Want to go camping, Huddy?"

He chuckles. "You know, my mom calls me that."

"Yeah, I know. But it's sweet. It suits you."

"You think I'm sweet, Howard?"

"I think you are many things, Rawlins."

His hand cups my jaw as he dots a kiss to my nose. "And I you, Addy."

He releases me and walks out the door, sliding his Stetson onto his head. Charlie darts from somewhere behind the hay bales and follows his master. I chuckle and fix my hair and straighten my clothes before making my way to my Cherokee to grab my camping stuff.

When Hudson pulls up alongside me in his truck, Charlie barks from the passenger's seat, head out the window. I toss my bag and sleeping bag into the back and shut my trunk. I open the door, and Charlie moves to the center of the bench seat. I hop into the truck and close the door. "So, where are you taking me?"

A grin splits Hudson's face, so bright, I can't help but smile back. It may have been the kiss, the all-encompassing way he held me, or the way the light fills his eyes when he looks at me. But after all those weeks of grumpy Hudson, I'm irrevocably addicted to this side of him. And I know this is gonna hurt when it eventually goes sideways.

He shifts the stick into gear, and we roll down the gravel road toward the paddocks. We are going the same way we did to get to his house, but when we come to the foot of the hill, instead of going up, he tracks to the left, on a rough road that heads in the opposite direction.

We bounce along for around twenty minutes before the

road starts to ascend. Trees have closed in around us, and I can't see anything except the road ahead of us. Charlie curls up on the seat and closes his eyes.

When we start the climb, the trees thin out a little. A little while later, we reach the peak of the hill. And I am like a kid hanging out the window, gushing over the most magnificent view I have ever seen. And when Hudson turns the truck and backs it up a little, I swing my gaze to his smiling face. The truck jerks to a stop.

"Hop out, Howard."

He turns off the truck. I push out of the door and wander to the back of the vehicle.

Oh. My. God.

Now I understand why they call this God's country. Its stunning. We are on a hill that connects to others. Below, a crystal blue lake fills the space between us and the opposite hill. Hudson puts the tailgate down. I turn back to scan the horizon. And is that . . . ?

"That's your house, Rawlins!" I gape at the sight of it. I mean, I saw the lake last time, but from this side of the vista, it's like some kind of oil painting.

He laughs and lays an arm over my shoulders. "Yep, that's my half a house."

I laugh and he takes his arm back. He sweeps me off my feet, an arm under my legs, one under my shoulders and sits me on the tailgate. With the next breath, he is sitting beside me. I breathe him in and rest my head on his shoulder. "It's so magnificent up here."

"Yeah, the view's pretty damn fine." I look up at him, but he's not looking at the mountains. His eyes are locked onto me.

"Hudson," I protest.

"Adeline."

I huff a laugh. God, why does Hudson saying my name make me crazy in the best way possible?

He holds out a palm and I rest my hand in it. His warm fingers curl around mine for a moment before they unfurl. He traces a rectangle on my palm with his finger. "This is what you can see of the house from here. What you can't see are the parts I haven't built yet. The stables go here." He draws a long rectangle behind the house square. "The homestead vegetable garden goes here." He draws another rectangle to one side of the house. "And the trees and the swing seat for two," he says, his voice thickening, "that goes right here."

"Who you gonna sit next to, Huddy?"

"I guess I'll know her when she turns up." His voice is raw, and he tries to force a smile. But his chest sinks deep with every breath.

"Like the way I turned up?"

His face splits into a happy smile. "Yeah. Something like that, Howard."

I groan at him and swing my legs to one side before pushing up to my knees. When I move closer, he shuffles back a little. I step over his lap and sink, straddling him.

His blue eyes darken. His hands find my face, and I claim his mouth.

Mine.

For a little while . . .

Chapter Thirteen

HUDSON

Never before in my life has following Harry's orders been so goddamn hard. *Don't get involved with Addy.* Simple enough order. The concept is solid. But the reality of that is so much harder. As is my cock. It's aching, it's so fucking hard.

Some things are worth Harry's wrath. If I wasn't sure about Addy's feelings for me before, now they are crystal clear and driving me to the brink. Not one woman has ever had this effect on me before. Not a single one. Not even Jemma.

Her hands trail down my neck. It's taking every ounce of willpower I have to stick to kissing this gorgeous woman. It's like torture, beautiful fucking torture, *only* kissing her. But over hell's warmed-up body am I going any faster than she wants to. I drop my hands to her waist, and she moans. If she keeps making those sweet-as-fuck little noises, I'm likely to explode in my pants.

When I hear the first call of a night bird, I push her away a little. Her eyes are warm, all browns and golds. Stunning. Her lips are swollen from kissing me. And I can't even stop it when my mind goes to those elegant lips wrapped around my cock. Fuck.

"We should start a fire before it's dark, Addy."

"I thought that's what we were doing."

I laugh. She's not wrong.

"One with actual fire to keep us warm."

She raises an eyebrow. I kiss her lips briefly, and she pushes off my lap and jumps down from the tailgate. I follow her, and Charlie trots beside us. "Grab anything dry enough to burn."

"Sure."

I bundle up wood in my arms as I go, and Addy does the same. When we both have a load, we head back to the truck, dumping it by the back wheel. I start building a fire a few feet from the tailgate. We will need it close to keep warm overnight.

"What's for dinner?" she asks.

"Ah, you will have to wait and see."

"Please don't tell me we have to catch our own?"

I holler a laugh and her cheeks turn pink. "No, sweet girl, no having to catch your own dinner tonight."

Her blush deepens. Sweet girl is a nice color on her. I

could watch those pretty eyes and make her blush all night, if she'd let me.

I light the fire and stay stoking it for a while before jumping up into the back of the truck. I brought a picnic basket with dinner and some breakfast, a double swag tent, and some clothes. Addy wanders around, Charlie by her side. He's got it worse than me, poor little guy. She chatters away to him as I set up the bedding and organize the picnic dinner.

The cooler bag I have has wine, beers, and whiskey in an ice slurry. Picking out a beer for me and the bottle of wine for Addy, I double-check I have everything before hopping down to find her. I follow the sound of her voice.

And when I finally find her under a low-hanging tree branch, I stop, not wanting to disturb her. Eyes closed and head resting against the trunk of the tree, she is sitting on the grass, Charlie in her lap. Her curls flick around her shoulders in the breeze.

Something snaps in my chest. This woman is beautiful, inside and out. Brave as fuck and more determined than my stubborn, hard-headed father. She's incredible. Charlie pops up from her lap and she opens her eyes. A gorgeous smile blooms over her face. I walk to where she sits and she tilts her face up at me, her smile deepening. "Hey."

"Hi." I study her face with an ache in my chest as I take in her freckle-dusted cheeks, soft pink lips, and stunning brown eyes that are now searching mine. "Hungry?"

She holds a hand up and I take it in mine. It feels right.

Like the answer to an ageless question that only she and I know. A perfect fit. She pushes to her feet, and I pull her into me, sinking my face into her hair. "God, Addy."

She chuckles. Her hands slide between us and to the opening of my shirt before her soft fingers grip my jaw. I push back a little and claim her mouth. One way or another, this is going to be a long night. She opens her mouth and I plunge in, tasting everything she is willing to offer me.

How the hell did I ever live without this? Without her. Charlie barks, and we pull apart. He is barking at the fire. Running circles around it. Yapping like an excited little kid.

"Come on, we have some dinner to eat," I rasp.

She nods and follows when I lead her by the hand back to the truck. Charlie sits, watching the flames flicker and crackle, head tilting when an ember hisses and flies into the sky from the fire.

"After you, Howard." I extend a hand to the blankets on the truck bed, and she climbs up and makes herself comfortable on one side of the spread of food Ma sent with us.

"This is wonderful, Hudson. Thank you."

"Anytime, Howard. And if I remember, you earned this. I didn't do much."

She shakes her head and pops the cork on the wine bottle. "You want some?"

"Nah, I'm a whiskey man."

"But there are beers here."

"Yeah, nice for a change."

Plus, I don't want to end up wasted and miss a second of Adeline Howard in the great outdoors.

"I'm starving," she says. I climb onto the blanket and pull off my boots and drop them onto the tailgate. She does the same and tucks her legs underneath her. She takes a sip of the cold wine in the plastic tumbler I brought along for her and sighs.

"What ya thinking about, Addy?"

"Everything"—she takes another sip—"and nothing."

I chuckle and crack the top off my beer. It's cold and refreshing, and I take a long mouthful. The work of my very enthusiastic mother lays between us. Entrées, meat on sticks, cheese, and two covered dishes with her famous Irish stew and mashed potatoes and veggies. I grab a meatball on a stick and pluck it from its stick with my teeth. Addy nibbles on the cheese and chopped-up carrot, celery, and cucumber.

"When do you find time to work on your house?" Addy's gaze is homed in on the house across the vista.

"Weekends and some afternoons."

"But that's when I'm here. Hudson, am I taking up your free time?"

Free time, on a ranch? *Yeah right.* "Nope."

She tilts her head, as if she doesn't believe me.

"I swear, I still work on it."

"Can I help you?"

"You want to help me build a house?"

"If you'll let me."

"You got any carpentry experience, Howard?"

She laughs and takes a sip. "Not really. But what I lack in skill, I can make up for with enthusiasm and work ethic."

"I bet you would." I stare at her. This woman who has buried her way into my heart. As much as I hate to admit it, Reed may be right. But how do I keep Addy and carry out Harry's orders? Right now, it feels like it has to be one or the other. Maybe for tonight, we can just be Addy and Hudson.

Not vet and client. Not coach and rider. Not boss and employee—well, almost, at any rate. And what happens when her six months are up? She goes back to the city and drags my heart along behind her like some banged-up tin can.

It's too much. I take another pull of beer and shove a meatball into my mouth before my mind can make me say something stupid. Or my heart cracks all over my face.

"You okay, Rawlins? You went quiet there."

"Yeah, I'm okay." But my voice betrays me, raspy and shot through. I clear my throat. "What are your plans *after* your time is up in Montana?"

"I don't know yet." Her focus drops to the food between us. "I was hoping Justin would extend my contract. But I'm not exactly his favorite employee."

"What do you mean?"

"I'm off equine for another month."

"What the hell? That's what you moved here for."

"Yeah, I was kind of annoyed when he told me, but I don't know, maybe I should be doing other things."

"Is he—Did he, I mean. Hit on you?"

She huffs a strained laugh.

That fucking asshole.

"Not directly, I guess."

My grip around the beer tightens. "Addy, you tell me if that little shit bothers you."

"I don't need you to ride in and save the day, Rawlins."

"No?"

"No, but you could send Harry?" She loses her shit, doubling over laughing, and I pluck a piece of cheese and toss it at her. She squeals and grabs a carrot stick and pegs it at my head. It bounces off my forehead and she is crippled by laughter.

It's the most amazing thing I have ever heard.

When Addy has finally recovered from her own joke, she clears her throat and sips her wine. "On a more serious note, tell me more about this roundup. About you. About everything I missed the past thirty-four years."

"Which part do you want first?"

"You, definitely you."

"Alright . . ."

She holds a hand up. "Actually, start when you graduated high school."

"This is gonna take a while, Howard. We should make ourselves comfortable."

"Agreed." She shifts the food, and I pack up the drinks. Supper can wait. When we have space on the blanket, I lay back, folding my hands under my head, and she lies beside me. Her hair fans out around her head and shoulders as she scans the sky. The first stars pop through the hazy grey of the sky.

"After high school, Ma insisted I do a trade. I'm not really one for career paths, but I had always loved building things with my hands, so I signed up for a carpentry apprenticeship. That took four years. Then I worked for a company building houses for around eight years. I enjoyed it but living out here and traveling every day got old, so I eventually quit and worked the ranch full time. Started breeding quarter horses about a year later, when I was desperate for something a little less Harry-intensive, you know. Horses, as much as he works with them and likes the extra income they make, were never his thing. So, I sunk my spare time into getting my herd started." I hesitate on the next part. "Then, I started building the house."

"Why?"

I guess there is no getting around it. "I needed something to occupy my mind. I told you that part."

"You did, but why, Hudson?" She pops up onto one elbow, her face resting on her palm.

"Jemma and I met when I was with the building company. She was one of the clients' daughters. Was my first real girlfriend. We were together for almost three years when she left for the city."

Addy's gaze drops to my chest, and she swallows.

"I was pretty broke up after that, after her."

Even now, the sentiment still hurts even though I got over the girl. And now, with my heart bleeding all over my sleeve, I roll on my side and prop my head on my palm, imitating Addy. "What about you, Addy?"

Her finger traces the pattern on the blanket between us.

"Adam."

"The guy who still texts you?" My brows lower, and my gut flips, like it has fucking permission.

"Yeah, that Adam. We were together during the last half of our internship. But he was always doing stuff like going out with other girls, telling me they were friends hanging out and stuff, but Ruby, she saw them. They were definitely not his friends. I tried to break up with him a few times. A few times, he convinced me I was being paranoid. And then when my time was up at the internship, I decided to move. That would be the best way to make my decision about everything. And I was hoping that he would take the hint, you know. Like moving hundreds of miles away from someone would be the breaking-off point. But he still texts. I don't want any part of whatever it was that we had. Being strung along while he did whatever . . ."

"Shit. I'm sorry, Howard."

It takes her a while to look at me. "I'm not, Hudson. It led me here."

Her hand brushes my jaw. *Fuck.* I let my eyes fall shut. Her lips press to my forehead. "Sorry to bring down the mood, Huddy."

Opening my eyes, I grab her wrist and press it to my lips. "Nope. Don't ever be sorry for explaining yourself, sweet girl."

"God, Hudson, when you—"

A blush covers her face. I smile against her wrist. "When I do what, sweet girl?"

Her breathing shallows out. Those gorgeous breasts heave with every breath.

"Addy," I rasp.

"Uh-huh?"

"I really, really want to kiss you."

"What on earth are you waiting for?"

I sit up and pull her over my lap. My cock digs into her center. Her very wet center.

Sweet Jesus.

I smash my mouth to hers and she palms my shoulders before her hands grip the hem of my t-shirt. "Can I?"

"I am all yours," I breathe.

Her face breaks a little. "Good."

She lifts my shirt off and tosses it onto the blanket. She stills a little, running a finger over my chest, from my collarbone to my breastbone and down the center of my stomach until she hits my jeans. My cock twitches with the movement. Then I still, leaning my head back, and groan.

"What? What is it?"

"I didn't bring a condom, Howard. This was supposed to be a friends-celebrating-a-milestone kind of camping trip."

"Oh."

"I have a better idea. Hold tight." She squeals as I grab her ass and pull her into me. I may not be able to bring her to climax with my cock, but there are other ways to worship this gorgeous woman.

And I am going to take my fucking time.

Chapter Fourteen

ADDY

Hudson flips me over so I am laying underneath him. Those blue eyes pinning me to the blanket take my breath away. And I'm still nowhere close enough. His gorgeous, toned body, propped up over me with those huge arms, tenses with every move he makes. The fire in my center is aching for him.

But I have way too many clothes on and no condom. It has been a long time since I have been with anyone. Adam wasn't exactly the generous type when it came to getting me off. And with all of his other extracurriculars, I wasn't exactly first priority.

Hudson waits until I am settled before he tucks a stray strand of hair behind my ear. My heart flutters like a caged bird.

"I want to touch you, Addy."

"I want you to."

"If you want me to stop, just say."

Like that is going to happen. How long have I waited for his hands on me? His warmth and hardness against my skin.

"Sit up," he rasps.

I do as he says, and when I'm sitting, he nudges between my legs and kneels before resting on his heels. He takes my shirt and lifts it up. I lift my arms, and he slides it up and off. The dark lacy bra and panty set I chose for today are paying off now, as his gaze darkens. But he doesn't touch me.

"Please, Hudson."

His eyes flicker downward and back up. "You sure, Addy?"

His pants are stretched by a hardened ridge. His breathing is erratic and choppy.

"About you, Hudson Rawlins? Always."

A smile flickers on his lips before his face turns feral. He grabs my hips and tugs my jeans down. They give way, and he tosses them onto the blanket with my shirt.

"Jesus, Addy."

"You're still not touching me," I whisper.

"Give me a moment to look at you."

Heat rises to my face. But I lay back and stare up at the bursts of stars above us. I'm pretty sure this is heaven. I have found it. Naked and adored by Hudson Rawlins in the bed of his truck, under the magnificent sky full of stars. With the fire crackling. His hands, strong and warm . . . His breathing, heavy.

He leans down and kisses my mouth before tracking down my neck. His lips are warm, soft, and hungry. Tracking over my collarbone, he presses kisses to the swell of my left breast, then the right. *Oh god.* His hands cup each one as he nips each hardened peak. I whimper and arch off the blanket. A deep, soft laugh rumbles through his throat.

"Hudson, take it off."

His hands slide underneath me as he unclasps the bra and I wriggle out of it. He swallows hard, jaw feathering, as my breasts bounce with the movement. A heartbeat later, his mouth finds my nipple. I release a breathy moan. He grips my hips, his weight pressing into me a little more.

I can't help but move my hips to push my aching center against his throbbing hard-on as I grip the blanket. He moves to the other nipple. His teeth scrape over it, and he sucks it, releasing it with a pop.

"You are divine, Adeline."

A sob cracks in my chest. No one has ever had me this way. Discovered my body like this. Taken their time to make me feel everything. Let alone think I'm *divine*. How the hell am I ever going to come back from this?

I stifle another sob. Hudson stills, his eyes tracking back to mine.

"Please don't stop," I beg.

"Addy, what's—"

"Please don't stop, Huddy."

His eyes widen slightly, studying mine for a moment before he returns to my chest. I push my hands into his hair. He groans around my nipple, and I moan. This time, I arch off the blanket involuntarily. He gives each peak a last pluck with his teeth before kissing down my stomach. My hips swivel with anticipation. I want his hands on my apex. His fingers inside me. When his mouth finds my aching center, I gasp.

Oh. My. God.

Another thing I've never done.

He growls and pushes against the inside of my thighs, opening me wider for him. "Jesus, sweet girl, you are so fucking wet."

I can't respond. He rubs a thumb over my apex, and I whimper. Then his tongue sweeps over it, and my hand fists his hair, and he chuckles. The sound sends electricity through my core. He suckles and licks my throbbing clit. Every stroke of his tongue sends me higher and higher.

"Hudson," I moan.

"Not yet, Addy. We're taking our time, remember."

Too breathless for anything else, I nod.

He slides a finger into my core.

"Oh god, Hudson."

He sucks my apex, sweeping his tongue over my folds, and I can't help the cries that spill from my lips. His hand slides up my belly, and he tweaks my nipple between two fingers. I arch again, and he slides another finger inside me. Heat floods my center. My tipping point is so close.

"Come for me, sweet girl."

He slides his fingers in and out roughly. My mouth waters. Fire builds in my core. He sucks my apex. I grip his hair and the blanket as I explode around his fingers.

"Hudson, Huddy . . . Hud—"

His name is a plea, a chant. And it sinks into my soul, like it was waiting to come home.

When I settle from having Hudson send me higher than anyone ever has before, I push up on my elbows. The sweetest smile is on his face and the evidence of my release is all over his chin.

"Come here," I breathe.

He crawls up to me on his hands and knees, and I wipe his chin before kissing his mouth. He sinks into the kiss like a man starved. And I bet he is. I can imagine how hard he must be right now. I tug at his jeans and release the button before sliding the zipper down.

"Addy," he rasps. "You don't—"

Pressing a finger to his lips, I whisper, "I absolutely do."

He groans and lets me remove his jeans and boxers. His hard length springs from its confines as I slide his clothes down. Holy shit. He's big and perfect. The bell end on this man makes my mouth water. He stays on his knees, and I shuffle backward. "Hold the headboard, Huddy."

He raises a brow but does as he's told. I take him with one hand, and he sinks down to kiss me, hands fondling my aching breasts. But he breaks from the kiss and takes my chin in his free hand. He groans and rests his forehead on mine. "Fuck, Addy."

"All in good time, Huddy. Now, hands on the headboard, mister."

He straightens and takes the headboard. I lower my mouth onto his cock and his grip turns white. Taking in the head, I lick and swirl my tongue over him. He melts and tenses all at once. I let his velvety soft head pop from my mouth. He shudders and groans.

"I thought we were taking our time, Rawlins?"

He huffs a growly laugh. "With those pretty lips around my cock, Addy, I don't think I'm going to last as long as you did."

I smile and sink onto his head again. His stomach muscles tense as he tries to stay still, and I slide down a little further. Taking up a smooth rhythm and sucking and teasing the tip of him, I pump him with my hand.

"Addy, fuck," he groans.

"Mhmmm?" I feel the sound of my hum sink into him.

He starts to shake. I pick up the pace.

His hands snap from the headboard and around my face. "Addy, stop."

I pause for a minute to catch his meaning. His face is wrecked. He is so close. I slide him deep into my mouth.

"Addy, are you sure?" he growls, low and gravelly.

I nod.

Come for me, Hudson.

Let me taste you.

I swirl my tongue over his tip and take him deep, pulling up and plunging deep. His hands are in my hair. His gaze is on mine. He chokes for breath. Those gorgeous blue eyes are lost to release as he spills into my mouth. I keep up the pace and swallow every drop he gives me.

When he offers up no more, I slide him from my lips and clean the corner of my mouth with my thumb. He drops onto his heels, breathing heavily. I crawl into his lap, and he folds his arms around me. We stay locked together until the cold finds us.

Cold, I snuggle closer to Hudson in the bedroll. My own sleeping bag is somewhere on the ground, still rolled up. We didn't even bother getting dressed last night. After we lay talking until the moon had reached her apex, I fell asleep on his arm. Now, he is wrapped around me. I lift the canvas. Dawn's light splinters over the eastern mountains. I stifle a groan, drifting back to sleep.

Something tugs at my nipple. Warmth is splayed over my ribs, sliding up to cup each breast. I force my eyes open in the bright morning light. Hudson hovers over me on his hands and knees. His scruffy brown hair is messy from sleep. His arms flex as he moves around my breasts, dotting kisses. I can feel his morning hardness against the inside of my thigh, so close. We could move an inch and he would be inside me. And I would be in heaven. I know it. I run my hands through his hair.

"Morning, sweet girl."

I chuckle. "Good morning, Hudson."

"Will be in a moment for you."

He kisses his way downward. I gasp as his mouth finds my apex and it thunders to life, throbbing under his tongue. I arch again. He slides two fingers into me, and I cry out. His hand reaches for my nipple, but I grab it and slide two fingers into my mouth. He groans when I suck them and release them.

"Jesus, Addy."

"Jesus ain't here, Rawlins, only you and me."

He laughs, his head hitting my stomach. He loses it, rolling off me and slapping his chest. I can't help but laugh, too, and when he closes his eyes to push through the last little bit of laughter, I roll on top of him. His breath shallows out when my wet center meets his hard cock.

"God, you have no idea how bad I want to sink into you right now," he rasps.

"Maybe this will help." I slide down and duck under the blanket. My mouth finds his tip a heartbeat later, and his hands grip the blanket underneath us. This time, I suck and pull with one hand, teasing him with my tongue on every upstroke. I can taste myself on him from a moment ago. I moan and he growls.

I love that sound. The way he falls apart when he hits his release. I fold the blanket back so I don't miss his gorgeous face. He looks down at me with hooded eyes. His hand finds my hair, and I pull up with more suction and release him with a pop. He groans, deep and heady. He liked that.

I do it again.

His breathing shatters. I graze the tip with my teeth, swirling my tongue around the base of his head. I plunge him deep into my mouth and suck upward, letting him go again.

"Adeline," he rasps.

I pick up the pace until his entire body trembles and his grip turns to a fist in my hair.

"Stop, Addy. Please, stop."

I shoot up and out of the blanket. "Huddy?"

His face is torn between agony and bliss.

He finally opens his eyes. "You don't—" He sucks in a breath. "You don't have to."

I raise an eyebrow and slide a hand up between the valley of his chest, over his throat, and cup his jaw. "I *want* to."

"I can't stop when you—"

I press a finger to his lips. "Shhhh. Let me make you feel good, okay?"

He swallows and nods lightly, and I slide back under the blanket. The head leaks with precum. I take him into my mouth, gripping him with a hand. And I pull up with suction, and my mouth pops from his tip. He is fisting the blanket. I pause, taking his hand and shoving it into my hair. I want his hands on me for this.

"Come for me, Huddy."

I tangle my tongue around his tip and slide down, pulling up with hard suction. His hand grips my hair. *Good man.*

I pick up the pace and deepen with each pass until he is trembling under me. "Now, Hudson."

I take him as deep as I can and suck my way back up. He explodes in my mouth with a groan. I pump him with my hand, taking everything as I swallow.

When I have cleaned him up, I kiss my way up his hard abdomen. Halfway up, rough hands pull me up until I'm face-to-face with a very happy Hudson.

"Your turn to hold the headboard, sweet girl."

"What?"

"Hold the headboard and spread your legs, Adeline."

My face must give away my shock, because he chuckles and lifts me above his head. I settle with my knees on either side of his head. And, as instructed, I hold on to the headboard. His tongue finds my very wet center a second later, and I try not to collapse on his face.

"You are so fucking wet, Addy. You should be on my cock right now."

I huff a laugh, but he sweeps his tongue through my wet center and I almost crumple. One hand slides up my stomach, finding my hard nipple. He tweaks it while sliding two fingers inside me. He sucks my apex, flicking his tongue over it, all the while pumping his hand in and out. Heat builds in my center, and every breath is a soft cry. He works my breasts, pushing and pulling, rolling my nipples through his fingers. When he sucks hard on my apex, I whimper, so close. My grip on the headboard turns white.

"Hu—Oh god!"

His movements intensify, and I explode. I cry out, bucking on my knees. Breathless, I clamp around his fingers, beautiful agony coursing through me.

"Good girl."

I melt against the headboard.

When both of us are cleaned up and dressed, we sit by the embers and have some breakfast. I stare over the vista at the house that Hudson built. A tiny part of me wants to be the one on that swing with him. I swallow past the rock lodged in my throat. We're more than friends. But we're not serious by any means. And I'm leaving before the end of the year.

Suddenly, I'm not that hungry. "We should get going."

"We can stay a little longer, if you want. Personally, I never want to leave this spot."

I wish I could stay here. Replay the last twelve hours, actually. When it was only Hudson and me. Suspended in time, wrapped in each other's arms. No reality needed. No asshat boss. No contract that will come to an end all too soon. No pressure to succeed.

No reason to leave.

I smile, but it doesn't reach my eyes. "Yeah, we could stay here forever."

Chapter Fifteen

HUDSON

After last night and this morning, I can barely concentrate on anything but the replaying vision of Addy. Her soft little moans, her body against mine. Her lips wrapped around my cock. After a quiet ride home in the truck and a change of clothes, we are up at the house.

Addy is on all fours on the floor, marking out the dimensions for kitchen cabinets and the like. Her ass is the perfect fucking view. And I am hard as a rock. If it wasn't for her being so quiet all day, I would spin her around and kiss her senseless. But something shifted between us. And I don't know what it was.

"Do you want a wide refrigerator, Hudson, or single?"

"Wide, Addy."

She chuckles. "Okey-dokey." But her smile fades as she turns back to her markings on the floor.

She wiggles backward, marking the floor with a fat piece of chalk. My cock twitches in my jeans. When she said she wanted to help, I didn't realize that would mean I would be in close proximity, watching her on her hands and knees. And it kind of has me undone. For a quick second I imagine she is here building because this is her house, too.

I shut down that dangerous fucking thought pronto. Measure the timber for the thousandth time, drop it on the saw platform.

At this rate, I'm going to be so distracted I'll end up losing half my fingers. I shake my head and hone my focus. I line up the timber I am about to use to make the horizontal porch railing and press a finger onto the ignition. The blade roars to life and I lower it. The jagged teeth make a clean cut left of my line. Perfect.

I let the saw back up and tug the timber from the platform. I rub the end and take it outside to screw between the posts. I intend on making a top rail with smaller X-configuration inserts. A design somewhere between farmhouse and the rustic log-cabin rancher homestead look my parents have.

Addy appears at the front door, leaning on one side of the frame. Her hair is tied up in a loose ponytail, her cheeks flushed with a touch of pink. It's warm today. Fall's last wave of heat before the cold rolls in. Her shorts are cutoffs, and her toned legs are not helping my constant hard-on.

"You need a hand with that?" she asks, flipping the tape measure over in her hands. The singlet top she is wearing is also not helping my cause.

"Sure," I grunt.

She frowns but walks over, placing the tape on the porch, and takes one end of the railing.

"That mark on the post, line it up flush with the top of your end of the railing. I'll fix mine and then yours."

"Okay." But her gaze doesn't leave mine, and when I screw my end secure and move to hers, there is almost sadness in her eyes.

I screw the railing to the post and put the drill down. "Okay, Howard. What's eating you?"

She startles as if I jerked her from deep thoughts. "Nothing, what d'you mean?"

"You have been too quiet all day. Is it last night? This morning?"

She drops her eyes. Her phone buzzes in her back pocket. Not looking at me, she studies the vista.

"You gonna answer that?"

"No," she whispers.

"Addy, what's going on? If it's about this morning, we can forget it, okay? Put it down to both of us needing to blow off some steam."

Her head snaps back. "Is that what it was to you?"

"I—"

Her phone rings. She ignores it. I open my mouth to tell her that of course it wasn't. It never has been with her.

But I take too long and hurt fills her eyes. She plucks the phone from her back pocket and walks down the steps and away from the house.

Fuck.

"Hey, I thought I asked you not to call anymore." She's talking quietly, but I can hear the tension in her voice. "No, do *not* do that. Please."

I lean on the post and fold my arms over my chest, well aware that I shouldn't be eavesdropping. But this feels important, and I don't want her to be alone.

"Goodbye, Adam." She hangs up and stands with her hand over her face for a moment. Her ex. The fucking asshole knows why she moved hundreds of miles away. Not letting her move on is a dick move.

The overwhelming urge to pummel this guy into the ground turns the blood in my veins to lava. If he shows his face here, his breaths will be numbered.

When Addy turns back to the house, I don't move from the post. She walks up the stairs and stops at the top step. "You know, it's rude to listen to other people's conversations, Rawlins."

"I'm aware," I say, but my voice is raw, and I can't shake the unease. When she walks past me and into the house, I know I should apologize. I walk in after her but come to an abrupt halt. She has designed an enormous open-plan kitchen for me with a simple piece of chalk.

The back wall is lined with cupboards, a massive stove-oven combo, and the wide fridge exactly where I had envisioned it. To the left is a pantry, and in front of it all is a massive island counter with an impressive double sink. She has even drawn the arched tap ware and barstools.

"Howard, this is brilliant."

"Thanks. It's what I would want if I was living here."

The air leaves my lungs.

She offers a shy smile and starts explaining the storage and types of appliances. All I can do is listen and nod, the stone that has grown in my throat turning me incoherent.

"Do you like it? I can change anything you think is not okay."

"It's—" I swallow and run a hand behind my neck. "Awesome, Howard. It suits the house."

"Yeah?"

"How did you learn so much about kitchens?"

"My mom is a professional chef. So, kitchen talk has been in my life for as long as I can remember."

"She works in one of those fancy New York City restaurants, doesn't she?"

"Yup."

We arrive at an awkward silence, and I try again. "Addy, about last night—"

Her hand shoots up between us, and her eyes snap shut. "It's fine, Rawlins; it is what it is." Her eyes open and those deep brown eyes hold mine. "I have no expectations of you. I mean, come on, I'm leaving at the end of the year. It wouldn't be fair to you . . ."

"Sure."

Of course. What else was I expecting? She will finish her contract and move back to the city. I'll take over the ranch, god willing. We go our separate ways. Hundreds of miles apart. An ache grows in my core, and I turn and walk back onto the porch. This is the way it has to be. Harry was right—don't get involved. Harry is usually right. Why would this time be any different?

When the light starts to fade, my phone rings. Ma.

Mack is home.

Excitement builds in my gut, and I start packing up the tools.

"We're done?" Addy asks. She has sawdust all over her face and neck. Her clothes are coated, too. Fucking adorable. *No, Hudson, not adorable.* She's just dirty.

God, that's worse. I clear my throat, as if I need to excuse myself from my own thoughts. "Mack's home. You ready?"

"Oh, wow! I'm so excited for you!" Her face splits into the prettiest smile.

"Let's head back."

"I can't wait to meet him. Your mom will be relieved he's home." Having mostly dusted herself off, except for the smudges on her face, she slides into the truck. I hop in and start the truck. But I hesitate. She would be embarrassed if I didn't tell her about the dirt on her face.

"Check the mirror, Howard. You don't want to scare him all the way back to the front line."

"Oh shit." Tugging the visor down, she scoffs, taking in the streaks of dirt and sawdust covering her face. She wipes her face with both hands. I hand her a rag from behind my seat, and she gives it another once-over. "Did I get it all?"

She turns to me, and I study her face. All except one little bit. "Mostly. May I?"

"Hudson, you had your head between my legs this morning, I think you have permission to touch my face."

I choke out a laugh, and she leans forward. Those perfect breasts push up, and I force my focus to her face and rub my thumb over her jaw, removing the last streak of dirt. "There. Perfect."

She sucks in a ragged breath and turns to face the front. "Ah, thanks."

I push the truck into gear. Forty minutes and three boners later, we pull up beside the homestead. The weeping willow is lit up with fairy lights. And my family is seated around the outdoor table. Double-checking I'm not smuggling a raging hard-on, I jump out of the truck and scoot around to Addy, opening her door. She jumps out, rubbing her arms.

"You cold, Howard?"

Her eyes narrow. "How could you tell?"

"Goosebumps. Don't flatter yourself."

She chuckles and I pull her sweater from the truck. It is practically a permanent feature these days. She slips it on, and we make our way to where Reed is regaling Mack with a tale of some great feat, judging by his wildly swinging arms. Ma's attention shifts to where we close in, and Mack spins around. He looks good.

I stride to where he is, and he jumps up and grabs me in a tight hug.

"How's it going, Huddo?"

"Good to have you back, Mack." The words are strained.

He slaps me on the back. I try to ignore the burn behind my eyes that follows the swell in my chest. Every time he leaves is harder than the last. And every time he comes back to us is a blessing.

Addy steps up beside me and holds out her hand. "Addy Howard. It's so wonderful to meet you, Mackinlay."

"Ah, so you're the vet who has my big brother all moon-eyed."

Addy blushes but doesn't back down. What the hell have they all been talking about in the forty minutes it took us to drive here? I snap my gaze to Reed. A shit-eating grin splits his face. He is a literal dead man.

But Mack wraps an arm around her and steers her to a seat by his. "It is so good to meet you, Addy. Finally."

She sits by Mack and peppers him with a bunch of questions. He answers, handing her a beer. She takes a sip, and her focus is on Mack. She is fascinated. Who could blame her? Mack is one of the bravest, kindest men I have ever known.

I grind my teeth, wanting nothing more than to pummel both of my little brothers into the ground. I love them to pieces, but they will take something and run with it, no matter how much it isn't true. Especially when it comes to my love life.

Reed looks at me and nods to Addy before saluting her with two fingers. *Captain.* That's what they think she is.

Luckily, Addy doesn't notice. I won't have to try to explain that one. And despite what Reed thinks, it isn't that simple. Not everyone gets a happy ending.

Charlie appears and jumps into Addy's lap. He growls at Mack before curling up on her lap.

"Jesus, Huddo. This one's a keeper. Even devil-dog is in love."

And with that, I excuse myself and find my way to the shower. Reed and Mack will have everyone entertained for the next couple of hours, so I take my time in the shower. Sawdust and dirt swirl around the shower floor and down the drain. Addy would be wanting a shower, too. The feel of sawdust and dirt stuck to sweat only gets worse as you cool off. I towel dry and wrap it around my waist, heading for my room.

"Hudson?"

I pause before turning to face her. Her bottom lip is between her teeth. Her sweater is in her hands. "I might go. I have to be at the clinic in the morning at seven."

"Shit, of course. Hold on, I'll walk you out."

"It's fine. Not like it's the middle of New York or something. I'll see you Tuesday."

She doesn't want my attention. She doesn't want me to walk her to her car. Doesn't want to talk about last night. My gut sinks.

"Sure, Howard. Tuesday."

She forces a smile and walks out of the house, leaving me staring at the spot she stood in. Watching her walk away has me rattled. Well and truly.

I walk into my room and pull on a polo and some fresh jeans before making my way back to the table. Reed hands me a beer, and Ma gives me a small smile, as if she can sense something has shifted between Addy and me, and not for the better.

"Tell me about this last tour, Mack," I ask.

Reed leans back in his chair, and Pa cracks another beer. Ma, who never wants to know, like if she knew what went on over there she could never cope, pushes from her chair and kisses her boys on the head before saying her goodnights.

When she reaches me, she bends down and cups my jaw. "Oh, Huddy, things will work themselves out. I know they will."

Maybe she could sense the tension between Addy and

me. Or she expected something to happen on that camping trip. Whatever it is, she looks as disappointed as I feel. Addy isn't just any girl to me, she's *the* girl. And I have no fucking clue how to make this work.

Not one.

No means no. Like, it literally should. And to every single other person on this planet, it most likely does. Only not to Adam Hervey. Respect has never been something he is big on with women. I should know, after three years of whatever it was I had with him. It definitely wasn't as a girlfriend or partner.

I have had more respect and felt more wanted in the few weeks I have spent with Hudson than the entire three years I spent with Adam. And it crushes me to think I wasted three good years on that asshole. And yet here I am, telling him for the umpteenth time that under no circumstances is he to come visit. Ugh, like we are friends or whatever. I stare at yet another text. Different words, same questions. All crafted by the manipulator extraordinaire.

I tap his name and scroll down, hitting the block button before tossing the phone back into my bag under my desk. There once was a time that I would feel bad for doing that to Adam. I'd tell myself he needed me or some other bullshit that I used to justify not seeing him for what he really was. A womanizing, cheating prick.

Now, I no longer suffer from such compunctions. I'm sure Hudson has had some sway with that. Not because he's a fine-ass cowboy who gets my panties wet in a heartbeat, but because his grounded and quiet ways let me know where I stand and how much he cares. The epitome of a gentleman. Albeit a grumpy one . . .

I flip the chart in front of me over and glance up at the tabby who is currently hissing at me. Horses and dogs, I have a kindred spirit with. Cats, not so much . . .

"So, how many Rawlins boys did you have to sleep with to weasel your way back onto the equine roster, Howard?"

Turning back, pulled between shock and disgust, I find Justin's scowl-lined face. *What the hell?* "I beg your pardon?"

I drop the clipboard to my side and tilt my head as my anger flares, sending fire through my veins.

"You heard me. You're back on the equine roster, permanently. Must have been a hell of a favor you did him or them. Who knows with you city girls."

I ignore my heart flinging against my ribs and step

toward him. He sinks on the desk, one leg bent over the edge as he leans back on the wall.

"Who the hell do you think you're talking to? This may be a small town, Justin, but you don't go around shooting your mouth off to employees about your business partners."

His brows furrow for a second before he pulls a red apple from his pocket and bites into it. He chews for a while before swallowing. "It was Hudson, wasn't it?"

I have never wanted to smash someone's face with my knuckles as much as I do now. I stalk to where he still sits with a ridiculous smirk plastered over his face. "Watch your mouth. Or next time I'll either let Sally hear your little rant or I will shut it for you."

"I'd like to see you try, Howard." He drops his gaze to my chest. He must be bitter about co-owning the practice. Does he want one hundred percent ownership?

Who knows, but he picked the wrong employee to take out his frustrations on.

"Maybe I will," I say lightly.

"Oh yeah, what you gonna do for me?" He stands up and stands over me, so close his breath hits my face.

"Oh, I don't know, perhaps I'll stab you with propofol and then wire your jaw shut. Creep."

I shove past him and make my way back out to Sally and the full waiting room. Right now, that's the only place I feel safe. From now on, whenever he is around, I am going to have Sally with me and press record on my phone. When I slide into the empty chair behind the front reception desk beside Sally, my hands are shaking.

"Oh, honey, are you okay?"

I shake my head no.

"I heard what he said, love. Did you want me to call someone? The police?"

"It's fine. Do I have any other appointments for today?"

"No, nothing until tomorrow. Then you have three equine visits. You'll be out all day. You want me to blank out the rest of today so you can leave?"

"No, it's fine. I'll grab the mace from my bag."

She gives me a sympathetic frown before forcing a smile. I push up from the desk and make my way back to my treatment room. Not actually having any mace in my bag, I bypass the staff room and grab up some charts. I have three more patients to check up on before I can leave.

And I don't want him to think he's won. If he lays a hand on me, I will break his fucking nose. *Miss Congeniality* was my all-time favorite movie growing up. Justin might get a singing lesson yet . . .

I chuckle to myself and walk to the back where the little overnight and short-stay ward is.

I am greeted by soft barks and meows. I do a set of vitals on Oscar, a German shepherd, before moving onto Squiggles, a ginger cat. He growls at me. "Calm down, buddy. Only here to make sure you're okay." When he relaxes a little, I pull him from his cage and pop him on the small metal table in the center of the ward. I need to check his stitches.

I run a hand under his belly, and he hunches up, growling low and steady at me. "Alright, almost done." I lean down and lift his closest leg. His stitches are fine, the surrounding skin only a little pink. No slough or infection present. Excellent. I take him back to his cage and head to my last patient.

Rosie, a dalmatian who by anyone's count should be long gone. She's old. Almost eighteen years old, and for a big dog, that's a long life. But her owners adore her, and she passed the kidney stone last night. I check her temperature and other vitals before checking her chart for urine count and records. As good as we can hope for this spotted geriatric. No more blood or ketones. So I give her a pat, and she wobbles on her feet to lick my hand. Such a sweet girl.

I return the charts to their home and grab my handbag. My phone lights up with a text. Ruby.

> Okay, so don't kill me, but I'm kind of at your house. xx

> OMG! Your timing is perfect, I really need someone to talk to today. Be home in an hour.

> Yay!! See you then.

I clean my treatment room as fast as my routine allows

and head out. I don't bother saying goodbye to Justin. He can go and screw himself as far as I'm concerned. I have no idea how Sally has worked here for so long with that twat. I close the door and head to the waiting room. "I'll see you tomorrow, Sally." I wave and make my way to the front door.

"Oh honey, is everything alright?"

"Yeah, thanks."

"Did you want to take your kits for tomorrow with you?" She waves to the storeroom behind her.

Excellent idea, then I don't need to deal with Justin first thing tomorrow. I walk back and collect two kits—one with supplies, the other with equipment.

Sally leans on the doorframe. "I'll forward your appointments and their addresses?"

"You're a lifesaver, Sally. Yes, please."

"Done and done, my love. You have a good night, hon."

She gives me a mischievous smile as I back into the glass doors to open them with my ass. She laughs and shakes her head. Outside, the warm breeze tangles in the stray strands of my hair as I load the kits and my bag into the car. I head home, desperate to see Rubes. It has been far too long.

The first thing I find when I round the street corner toward my house is the long, lean legs of Ruby Robbins. Her tan pantsuit is finished with red heels, and her perfect straight blonde hair sits over one shoulder as she taps furiously on her phone. She may be out of the city, but her work never stops. Nor does her wardrobe.

Fully engrossed in whatever is going down on her phone, she doesn't notice the car pull up, or the door slam. She looks up when my feet appear beneath her phone, almost between hers. With a gasp, she leaps up, wrapping me in a hug. I drop my bag and squeeze her back. As my best friend for the last ten years, she is practically my sister.

"Damn, have I missed you girl," she groans.

"You have no idea. Please tell me you're staying the weekend?"

"Of course, as long as you need me. My office is right here." She waves her phone in my face, and I step around her and unlock the door. We file inside, and I give her the tour. She spins around in the huge living room and holds her arms out. "Wow, Adds, all this for one girl. Geez, I should have been a vet." She laughs.

"Ha! You would be fine until there was blood or poop, Rubes."

"Ugh, you can keep it. I'll visit lots and soak up the country living and wide-open spaces."

"Speaking of wide-open spaces, I have visits tomorrow for some of my equine clients and then I'm off to Rosewood Ranch for another riding lesson."

"Oh, yes, how is that going? Come here and tell me." She flops on the couch and pats the seat beside her. I roll my eyes at her, but it's playful. I can't wait to hash this out with her. Hudson, the ride along with the roundup, Adam, and now the shithead boss I can't stand. So, I curl up on the sofa beside her and lean back before turning to face her.

"Wow, that bad, hey?" She studies my face, her body mirroring mine.

"Hudson and the coaching are going well. Better than I expected. Work is okay, but my boss is a douche. Absolute asshat. But what has me the most stressed is Adam. He keeps calling and texting, even though I told him to stop. We are not happening anymore. We're done."

"Fuck."

"Have you seen him around? He needs to move on. What's going on with him?"

She chews her bottom lip, much the same as I do. "Yeah, I saw him last week. He was freaking out that you up and left. I told him you can go wherever you want. And then . . . "

"What? And then what?"

"He kind of got weird. Saying things like you belong together and if you don't come back after the end of your contract, he's coming to take you back to the city. I tried to tell him that's not okay, and not happening. But he stormed off. I'm sorry, Adds, I think I kind of made it worse."

"How?"

"Told him you and the cowboy were a thing . . ." Her

face is pure cringe, as if that was the biggest lie on the planet.

"I don't know what Hudson and I are, honestly. If I let my heart decide, I would stay here and have his babies. But I know myself better than that. I need to be busy, and have goals and work, you know. Hudson, he's like—"

Her mouth gapes and her eyes widen with delight. "Hold on, this calls for wine!"

Ruby jumps up and runs to the fridge, pulling a bottle of white from the freezer at the top. She knows everything about me, even where I keep the wine I don't share with anyone else but her. Glasses clink and the wine glugs. She drops onto the sofa a moment later with two glasses, handing me one. She kicks off her heels and sweeps her blonde hair to one side of her neck.

"Thanks, Rubes."

"Okay, don't leave out a *single* thing."

And I tell her everything, from that first moment in Louisa's kitchen when I met Hudson and his family, to our camping trip. Her eyes widen and her jaw drops further and further with every detail. When I finally finish, she stares at me for a heartbeat.

The look on her face is pure cheek. Her hand rests over her heart like a shocked Beverly Hills housewife. "Oh my god, Adds. I can't believe you got back on a horse!"

I smack her arm. "Yeah, that's the most important part, Rubes."

She loses it. After a bout of stomach-clutching laughter, she recovers and grabs my shoulders, leaning in. "I cannot wait to meet him, Adds."

The love and excitement in her eyes send a prickle to the bridge of my nose and my heart into a frenzy, promptly flipping my stomach.

Ruby's head swings from side to side like a kid in a toy store who has never seen one before. The Montana countryside is breathtaking. And I was just as captivated on my first drive out to Rosewood Ranch. Her brown eyes are saucers, taking in the mountains, the fields, the horses, and homestead as we pass.

"You're going to hurt your neck, babe."

"I can't believe how amazing this place is."

"You have no idea. Wait 'til you see the ranch. Some of the places Hudson has taken me. So stunning."

"How have you been living here and not sent me pics? Rude, Adds. Just rude."

I turn off the road and we roll underneath the Rosewood Ranch sign. Ruby is like a kid in a candy shop. It's adorable. When we finally pull up beside the white homestead gate, I hop out and open her door. Hanging around Huddy for weeks has his thoughtful ways rubbing off on me. Ruby steps out. Her capri-length jeans and boat-necked, ribbed white-and-navy striped shirt are vastly out of place. But she is beaming. And she grabs my arm with a gasp when Hudson trots over to the car on Rocket, bringing with him a saddled-up Sergeant.

"Oh wow, you must be Hudson!" Ruby grins, waving a hand.

He tips his hat, giving me a happy but somewhat confused glance.

"Hudson Rawlins, this is Ruby Robbins, my best friend."

"Hey, Ruby, it's a pleasure to meet you. This is Rocket, and this here is Addy's current loaner, Sergeant."

"Hello boys," Ruby gushes.

"Why is he all saddled up and looking like he is about to head some place wide and open?"

"'Cause he is, Howard. Sorry, Ruby, I didn't realize you were coming, otherwise I would ha—"

"Addy! How's it going?" Reed swings an arm over my shoulder and tips his hat to Ruby. When his brows shoot up and his mouth gapes, he removes his arm from me and shoves his hands into his back pockets. Okay . . . Her face slackens and she raises an eyebrow. Reed clears his throat and holds out a hand to Rubes.

"Ah, Reed Rawlins. You must be Addy's friend from the Big Apple?"

"Ruby. Nice to meet you."

He takes her in, with a breathy huff, as if not believing what he's seeing. "If these two are off into the sunset, I can give you a tour of the Montana mountains. If you'd like."

"Um, is that okay with you guys?" Ruby asks, eyes widening in my direction, a cheeky smile on her pretty lips.

"Sure; apparently, I have plans."

Hudson chuckles and adjusts his hold on the reins.

"Huddo, I'll be taking your truck," Reed says, ushering Rubes toward the barn.

"Smooth, Rawlins. You two are hilarious, really." I laugh.

Hudson's gorgeous mouth splits with the happiest grin. God, who could deny that face. I walk to Rocket's shoulder and look up at him. "Well, then, hand over my boy."

He drops the reins into my waiting hands, and I swing into the saddle. "So you know, I'm still not confident with big spaces."

"I'll be right next to you. Soon you'll be begging to lope off into the sunset by yourself."

I screw up my face and poke out my tongue. But my gut is a tangle of knots. And not because I'm on a horse. Every time we're this close, I feel overwhelmed, but in the best way possible. Like when I step into Hudson's space, I can finally breathe. And for the first time in my life, I feel valued by a man. Worthy, and something like treasured.

"Let's go, Huddy, before I lose my nerve."

He pulls the reins to the side and Rocket walks on

toward the northern laneway. I follow and move to the sway of Sergeant's sure and steady gait beneath me. I push him forward with my seat until I'm beside Hudson. "Where are you taking me, Rawlins?"

"Somewhere fun. It's the last week of the warmer weather before the cold starts to descend on us. Gotta make the most of it."

"Oh okay, I guess I'll have to trust you, then."

"Yup." He pops the *p* and stares ahead, all cheek. The light green t-shirt he's wearing moves over his arms that jostle with Rocket's movements. His Stetson firmly planted on his head, Wranglers, and boots, he makes for one ridiculously smoking-hot cowboy. "Enjoying the view, Howard?"

I chuckle, but heat flushes my neck and face. "Always."

"Ready to pick up the pace?"

"Sure, but not too much. Maybe a slow lope?"

"Sure." He squeezes Rocket forward, and they lope down the lane. *It's now or never, Addy.* I do the same, and after the initial usual butterflies and heady feeling that have been with me in past lessons, I relax. Focusing on Hudson, I catch up, and I can't help the smile that grows on my face.

God, I missed this.

After a twenty-minute ride, we come to a river. Tree-lined banks flank the half-full bending waterway, its waterline just over the halfway mark. It's clear and steady. And so gorgeous. What a spot.

Hudson dismounts and hangs the reins over a low-lying branch. Before I can move from the saddle, he's beside Sergeant, holding his hands up to me.

"I can get down myself, you know."

"Any excuse to feel you up, Howard."

I scoff and swing my leg over the pommel, shaking my other foot free of the stirrup. My hips give a subtle twang with the movement. Hudson's hands rest on my hips, and he dips his head. "Addy—"

"Uh-huh?"

"I—"

Hudson's truck roars toward us. Ruby is hanging on to the top of the window frame. Reed has the biggest shit-eating grin on his face, like he's busted something.

Hudson sighs. "Just great."

Reed parks the truck a few trees down and rounds the vehicle to open Ruby's door. Her face lights up as she watches him, his biceps flexing to shut the door before he crooks an arm, and she slides hers through. They wander to where I am still sitting on the horse.

"You okay, Addy?" Reed says, the grin slipping from his face.

"Yeah, a little achy."

Hudson looks up, brows dropping, head tilting. I force a smile, something like a *sorry I didn't say anything*, and he mutters something I don't hear.

"Get her down, Huddo. She should stretch or something." Reed stops at Sergeant's head, and Ruby rubs the gelding's face.

"You ready?" Hudson asks.

I nod and he lifts me from the saddle. I slide down his chest until my feet hit the ground. Heat pools in my belly, fire scattering through my veins at the contact.

"Better?" Hudson whispers.

"Thank you."

He looks like he wants to fold me into his arms, but he hesitates and lets me go.

"Nothing a good skinny dip won't fix, Addy," Reed quips.

Ruby tracks her gaze between Hudson and me. "We should leave them be. Come on, show me your mountains. I'm dying to see them, since Adds hasn't shut up about them the whole time I've been here."

"Really?" Reed's eyes widen.

I roll mine at him and he escorts Rubes back to the truck. Those two are getting on like a house on fire.

When they pull away and drive back the way they came, Hudson closes in on me.

"Why didn't you tell me about your hips?" His face is pinched with worry.

"It's no big deal. And I can handle it, Huddy."

He shakes his head, and now he folds me into his chest. "Please tell me these things, Addy."

I nod against the muscles of his toned shoulder, and he dots a kiss to my hair. When I think he isn't going to let me go, I wriggle, and he unfolds with a sly smile. "Last one in's a rotten egg, Howard!"

He flies toward the river, ripping off his shirt and hat. His boots go next, then his pants, until only his boxers remain. God, the sight of him has my core liquid. I peel off my top and jump around, pulling off my boots. My jeans hit the grass before I leap into the water after him. And when he comes up for air and sweeps his hair back out of his face, I swear my heart craps out.

Chapter Seventeen

HUDSON

I could do this all damn day. The red lacy bra and panties Addy has on have me hard and throbbing. Fuck me. So goddamn beautiful. She bobs up and down a foot away from me, the water lapping against those perfect tits. When she leans back and ducks under the water, they crest the water, hover, and then sink as she dunks herself.

When she comes back up, her hair wet and plastered to her face, she sweeps it away and around one shoulder. The tips of her curls dangle over her soft breasts. And when I finally lift my gaze to those pretty brown eyes, they are laced with fire. The kind that means I'm not the only one about to combust here.

"Come here, Huddy," she breathes.

I'm through the water, hands on her face, mouth over hers a heartbeat later. She presses her body into mine. Her lips are velvet, her mouth opens, and I sweep my tongue inside her mouth, needing to taste every part of her. She's moaning, her hands in my hair. My cock throbs against her stomach. The cool water does nothing to quell it. When Addy breaks from the kiss, I drag in a ragged breath.

"Adeline Howard, the things you do to me."

She smiles that crooked smile that tells me she is going to do something crazy. The next thing, my boxers are off my hips, her hand gripping my cock hard. Groaning, I let my forehead fall onto hers. "I want those gorgeous tits in my mouth, Addy."

"They're all yours."

I make quick work of her bra and toss it to the bank. Her eyes are stuck on me as I take each breast in my hands and suck each peak. And when I swirl a tongue over one, she whimpers, falling into me. Jesus, what I wouldn't do to have her come undone wrapped around me.

If I had been smart, I would have brought a blanket. But I'm not smart, so we will have to improvise. There is a fallen log a little way downstream. I pick her up and plant her around my hips. She giggles and kisses my jaw, then down my neck. Her hands grip my shoulders. The water is a little deeper at the log that has fallen into the river. Water rushes around it.

I deposit her onto the log and slide her panties down. She wriggles as I tug them over her hips and ass and toss them into the nearest tree for later retrieval. I push my palms into the inside of her thighs, spreading her wider.

"Addy, you could bring a man to the brink of starvation looking like this, sweet girl."

I run my hands up to her breasts, cupping and fondling them before rolling the nipples between my fingers. Addy steadies herself with her hands on the log on either side and spreads her legs a little further. I swipe a thumb over her swollen apex, and she whimpers. She glistens with wet heat.

That's for me.

I do that to her.

My cock swells at the thought.

I press kisses to the inside of her thighs, and she squirms when I purposefully avoid the place where she is desperate for me. For my tongue, my mouth.

"Huddy, please."

"Tell me what you want, Addy."

"I want your mouth on me, your fingers inside me. I want you."

I lower my head and run my tongue through her wet seam. The taste of her goes straight to my balls, and they tighten and lift. I groan, the sound vibrating through her clit, now caught gently in my teeth. Her hand finds my hair, her fingers running through it before turning to a grip.

I flick my tongue over her, working her tight pussy with my fingers. Slow and steady strokes until she is a bundle of sweet sounds and cries that will keep me rock-hard for months.

I suckle her clit and add another finger.

"Hudson," she begs, her grip turning feral in my hair.

"Mhmmm?"

"Ah, Hu—" She tightens around me, hips bucking with every wave as she comes undone.

Her hands ramble through my hair when she all but goes limp on the log, pulling my head into her stomach, cradling me against her. "How do you always get that so right?"

"Because, Adeline, I was made for you, and you were made for me." The words slip out before my smart brain has a chance to censor that shit.

I mean it. I fucking do. But . . . . I'm also not supposed to be getting involved. And we are way past that point, if I'm honest with myself. Way fucking past it.

I guess what Harry doesn't know, won't hurt him.

"Your turn on the log, gorgeous man."

The throbbing between my legs is almost unbearable. Addy slips off the log and into the water. She ushers me onto the log and her eyes rove over my body. She starts at my collarbone, her hands pressing against my pecs. She trails a finger down my stomach before letting it wander sideways, moving over the V of my lower abdomen.

Her touch is light, warm, too much, and not enough. When she finally drops it to my cock, I have to slam my eyes shut to stop the flood of sensation. Feeling and seeing her between my legs . . . It's fucking poetic. Her mouth finds my head, and I groan, hard. She sweeps her tongue around the wide tip, sending electricity up my spine.

I run my hands behind her neck, but she takes one, shoving it into her hair. "Jesus, Addy, you have no idea how much I want to fuck your sweet mouth."

She pops off my cock. I open my eyes and drop my gaze to those deep brown pools of hers. "Do it, Huddy. I want to feel every inch in my mouth. Give me every drop; don't you dare hold back."

"God, girl. You are fucking perfect."

She holds eye contact as she slides me back into her mouth with a subtle nod. I grip her hair, cupping her face with the other hand. I thrust into her mouth, and she closes her eyes. Her hand disappears beneath the water, and she releases a little moan.

"Fuck me, Addy."

I thrust in deeper, and she tightens her mouth around me, adding a little suction. Her tits bounce with every thrust. Her eyelashes flutter as she looks up at me, wet hair dangling over her shoulders,

"Good girl. A little more?"

She nods, humming. It's too much. I thrust into her deeper, harder. Her eyes water, and she moans around me. She must be getting close again. Her breathing shallows out.

I stroke her face, trying to slow my pace, but the need to fill her mouth with my seed wins, and I pick up the pace again. She snaps a hand to my thigh, gripping hard. A string of little moans hum over my cock. She arches her back, writhing in the water as she comes undone again.

Good girl.

I follow her, losing seed into her mouth. She opens her eyes, swallowing with every thrust. Goddamn, sweet girl. Fucking perfect. Said it before, will say it again.

Perfect.

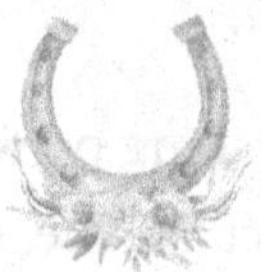

Mack is in the barn when we make it back. Addy did brilliantly, even loping ahead by herself on the way home. She has no idea how damn proud I am of her. Her riding is barreling along. I swing down out of the saddle.

"Hudson, you're with me." Harry doesn't mince words.

Fuck.

I glance back at Addy, but she smiles at me before dismounting and taking Rocket's reins. I follow after my father, feeling like a little kid about to be on the wrong end of an ear chewing. Did he somehow find out about the river, the camping trip?

When we walk into the kitchen, Ma is chopping veggies, something bubbling on the stove already. Smells amazing.

Pa stalks into the study, snapping up the phone from the desk, where it has been sitting off the receiver, waiting. He folds a hand over the end that picks up sound and turns back. "Justin. And he ain't happy."

I guess navigating business partners is my job now, too. I take the receiver from him.

"Morley," I grunt. I've never liked this little upstart. Went off and got a degree; comes back and thinks he is better than the folks he grew up with. It doesn't sit right.

"Hudson? Your father said you were handling the clinic now? That was quick."

"Is there a reason for this call?"

"Yes, I am calling to talk about the prospect of letting the current equine vet go and finding another, more suitable one."

My hand whitens around the receiver.

"Why the hell would we do that?"

Harry shakes his head at me.

"I mean, why?"

"She's not performing. Her work is okay, her methods are off script sometimes, for around here, at least. You know what I mean. Clients expect their vets to behave and work a certain way and she is a little too . . . modern."

"So, what I am hearing is that you have a problem with Dr. Howard because she follows the most up-to-date practices and has good bedside manner? Is that really what you're going with?"

"Well, yes, but there have been . . . Complaints."

"Who's complaining, Morley?" I grit out.

"Well, some of the other ranchers and—"

"There isn't anyone who's complained apart from you, is there? Afraid of being showed up, is all. Stop wasting my fuckin' time."

I slam the receiver on the cradle, sucking in a long, steadying breath. Fuck Justin Morley. Fuck his whiny, stupid, little-man syndrome. Addy has done nothing wrong. She earns her keep and more. We have had many equine vets over the past twenty years; she is the best one yet.

Harry opens his mouth to say something, probably about to ream me out for flipping on a business partner. I hold up a hand. "Don't, Pa."

I stalk out of the study. Ma's gaze snaps to me, closely followed by Harry.

"What did you tell him, Huddy?"

It sounds different when she says it. But that nickname will always be tied to Adeline now. Fuck me—if this doesn't work out with her, I'm going to be a shattered man.

"Nothing. Morley being a little bitch."

"Language!" she scolds.

"I'm not eleven, Ma."

"No, but you have a pretty girl in orbit. Behave yourself. No woman wants a foul-mouthed redneck for a husband."

Harry grunts, throwing her a side glance. I school my face, partly because of Pa's current scowl and partly because my mother is trying her hardest to have me hitched to Adeline Howard, scolding me like some school-boy. *If only she knew.*

"And you, Harrison Rawlins, you butt out. Our children come before your business interests." She is pointing with her chopping knife now. Poor man doesn't stand a chance.

"Yes, ma'am," he growls.

She gives him a cheeky smile. But the glare he gives me is a reminder that he expects me to uphold his order to not get involved. Period.

"Now, you two. We need to get to organizing my birthday party. It ain't gonna happen all on its own. Can Addy and her friend help? They are invited, after all."

"I'll ask, Ma."

"Good. Have them to stay for dinner so we can iron out the details."

"Sure thing."

I tip my hat at her and walk back outside, leaving a reprimanded Harry alone with his knife-wielding wife. I chuckle. Reed was right—it might be Harry's ship, but Ma's the captain, no two ways about it. Poor man's simply along for the ride. Lucky for him, he wouldn't have it any other way.

Addy is leaning against the barn, talking with Reed, Ruby, and Mack. Charlie ignores me, still getting attention from her when I walk over.

"Everything okay?" Addy asks.

"Yup." I eye Charlie. "Happy, buddy?"

"Pretty sure at this point he thinks he's Addy's dog. Sorry, Huddo," Mackinlay says.

"I see that." I tug his little ear playfully. "Ma wants you two to stay for dinner, if you can. She wants help planning her birthday party."

Ruby claps her hands together, jumping on her feet. "Yes! We are so doing that."

"Sure, we can stay a while," Addy says, smiling at me like a woman who had multiple orgasms an hour ago.

Mack glances between us, raising a brow. Reed clears his throat. "Milady." He crooks his arm for Ruby. She giggles and hooks hers through his. He leads her toward the house.

Mack takes Charlie from Addy's arms. "Catch you inside, then."

He wanders after Reed and Ruby.

"Rubes will be stoked; she practically plans events for a living," Addy says.

"Ma should have an awesome party, in that case."

"Do I get an elbow, too?"

"How about a piggyback?"

Her eyes light up, turning my insides upside down, and she wastes no time jumping up on my back. Her body against mine has my cock hard within a second. Maybe this wasn't the best idea. "Horses squared away okay?"

"Yes, Mack helped. He's a sweetheart, your brother."

"Well, hold on to your panties, Howard, you'll meet the last Rawlins brother at Ma's party."

"Lawson is coming?"

"Ma would drive to New York and hunt him down herself if he didn't show up."

"He's in New York?"

Her voice is excited.

"Did I leave that bit out? Sorry. Yep, the Big Apple. The home of the Statue of Liberty and Adeline Howard, both national treasures."

She swats my head with a scoff. "What's he like?"

"Laws? He's the book smart one out of the four of us. Works in HR in some enormous PR company. He's got the muscle and the smarts. You might wanna jump ship, pick a different brother."

She strangles her arms around my throat, and I mock a choke, staggering around on my feet and pretending to be half passed out. She squeals. I chuckle, my Adam's apple rubbing the soft skin of her wrist. And her head sinks into my neck.

"I don't want a different ship, Huddy."

The apple turns to a stone. And like that, Adeline Howard steals what was left of my breath.

Chapter Eighteen

ADDY

R uby stands at the white gate, Reed behind her. She is practically buzzing. Fairy lights, fire torches, and party decorations are strung around the homestead yard. I kill the engine and jump out, carefully lifting the cake box from the back seat and making my way to the gate.

"Ruby, this is beautiful."

It really is—it's like a wonderland. All themed in the aspects Louisa told us about the night we stayed for dinner. Every old oak and willow has twinkly lights wound up the trunk and around the branches, illuminating the old trees. I wonder which one of the brothers was sent up the trees for that task. Knowing Rubes, probably all three of them.

Hudson stands by the grill with a guy that has to be Lawson. They're so similar. Okay, four of them into the trees, then. The same brown hair, broad shoulders—even their stance matches. The only difference is the clothes. No Wranglers on this one. Levi's and a button-down charcoal shirt, sleeves rolled up to his elbows. He laughs at something Hudson says, sipping a beer.

Hudson.

My stomach flips.

Reed is grinning from ear to ear, his blue eyes full of excitement. He rests his chin on Ruby's head, slouching so his arms dangle at her sides like a total goof. If I'm not careful, my spot as her best friend might be up for assessment with this new contender. He shifts his head to her side and whispers something to her. She slaps the side of his head, like you would a sibling. He winces, chuckling, and rubs his head, glancing sideways at her with narrowed eyes before opening the gate for me.

"Keep your comments to yourself, Reedsy." She scoffs.

Reedsy. Okay, that's new. In my hands is the birthday cake. One enormous yellow cake box. And if I drop this, I might crawl in a hole and wish for death. And when Reed takes it from my hands, I sag with relief. The breeze is cooler than a few days ago when I was out here. The pale blue boho dress I chose for the party tangles around my legs. The cinched waist and sweetheart neckline mold to my curves well, and it has pockets, but now I am regretting not bringing a cardigan. Or a jacket.

My phone buzzes, and I slip it out of my pocket, glancing at the message. Adam. Again. He got a burner phone just to piss me off? I lock the screen, ignoring him, and slide the phone back into my pocket. I wish he would give up.

I push through the gate and wander around the yard, taking in the decorations, before making my way to the kitchen to find Louisa. I have a small gift for her. A bracelet with a ship's wheel and a few other nautical charms, her four boys' names on a charm each, and behind the wheel charm is Harry's.

I hope she gets a chance to wear it. This family is so close. And it's something so precious. Something I wish for myself one day. The kitchen is buzzing with women, most of whom I don't recognize, preparing dishes, chatting, and pouring wine. Louisa stands by the kitchen table with Ruby.

"Addy! Come here, sweetheart," she calls out.

I close the space and fold her in a tight hug before handing her the small ribbon-adorned box. "Happy birthday, Louisa."

"Oh, honey, you shouldn't have!"

I beam at her. "I really, really wanted to."

Shaking her head as emotion fills her eyes, she gently removes the bow and lifts the lid. When she takes out the bracelet and turns it over, a sob chokes her, and she slaps a hand over her mouth. Hudson and Lawson peer through the door, checking on the noise, beers still in their hands.

Louisa's silver-lined eyes find mine. "Addy, I don't know what to say . . ."

I try to respond but the words are lodged in my throat. Hudson walks over, studying the bracelet. Ruby beams at him and glances to me.

"Nice work, Howard."

I scoff a laugh. "Thanks, Huddy."

Louisa's eyes widen as she glances between Hudson and me. She clears her throat. "Her name is Addy, Hudson Andrew Rawlins."

He walks away, taking a sip of his beer before looking over his shoulder. "I know, Ma." The cheekiness that lights up his face has Ruby and Louisa gaping.

"Where does a girl need to go to find some wine around here?" I ask, hoping both women will snap their mouths closed and forget that look he gave us.

"I can set you up, Adds. Follow me," Ruby says, taking my arm.

I am dragged into the heart of the kitchen, to where the wine fridge is packed full. She opens the door and grabs a sparkling white before uncorking it and grabbing two glasses. The girl appears to know her way around this kitchen better than I do. But I guess she has been here all day setting up, organizing, etc. Reed appears by her side like he has been doing for the past week, and she glances up at him. "You need another beer, Reedsy?"

"Nope. Addy, Lawson wants to meet you."

"Oh, sure. I was getting there, I promise, but I wanted to see your ma first."

Reed glances to where a gathering has now blossomed

around Louisa. She is holding up the bracelet. I guess she likes it.

"I'll be out in a sec," I tell him.

He pats the counter, glancing at Ruby's back as she sorts through the cupboard, trying to find what, I don't know. He turns and walks back to his brothers. I haven't seen Mack yet, or Harry, come to think of it . . .

Curious.

I sip the wine. Cold and refreshing. I press a hand to Ruby's arm. "See you out there, hey."

"I'll be out in a bit; hors d'oeuvres start soon."

I wander to the patio door. Hudson is flipping steaks on the grill. Reed has turned toward the yard, chatting to some more people who are only now arriving. Hudson is wearing a navy button-down shirt, sleeves rolled up to his elbows like his brothers. His hair is neat and his face freshly shaved. *God, he is gorgeous.* He looks up and drops the tongs on the side of the grill.

"Lawson, this is Dr. Howard. Our new vet."

My mouth gapes a little, and a gigantic smile cracks over his face. "Laws, this is Addy."

I choke out a laugh. Lawson holds out a hand, formal, dry. Still not sure if this is part of the joke, I raise a hand and slip it into his. He tugs me into a hug. "Hey, Addy."

When he releases me, I am all warmth, and Hudson's eyes are lit with so much adoration that my throat closes over.

"Thanks for putting a smile on the cranky asshole's face."

"Whose, Harry's?"

Lawson howls a laugh, throwing his head back. "I like this one, Huddo. She's a keeper."

Hudson smiles and gives me a wink before Lawson grabs my hand and drags me away to meet more people. I turn back. Hudson is watching us. A steak flares behind him, and he curses under his breath and turns back. I am swallowed by family and friends and introduced as Hudson's friend to anyone who will listen. No mention of being the vet. Of being a short-term member of the community. Not some city girl who will go back to where she came from when her time is up.

When we run out of people to talk to and my stomach rumbles, Lawson grabs a platter and ushers me to a bench seat. We sit quietly for a moment as people mingle, laugh, and chat, and the sun disappears completely. Hudson has left the grill and gone inside.

"Which part of the Big Apple are you in?" Lawson asks.

"Northern outskirts, actually."

"I'm Long Island. It's another world entirely."

"Isn't it."

"You been there?"

"Yeah, my old boss has a house out there. Montauk."

"Oh yeah, the beach."

"It's fine. But I think your parents have the better spot."

"It sure is pretty out here."

"Do you miss it? All the mountains, open spaces, and slower-paced life?"

"Is this your way of asking me if you're gonna miss the city lights, constant smog, and rat race?"

"What, no—I mean . . ."

"Relax, Addy, it's all good. Whatever you decide will be fine by this family. My father may come off as a harsh man, but he always does what's best for his family."

I frown. I'm confused.

"Huddo told me what Harry said about you guys . . ."

"What?"

Lawson's face slackens. "Fuck. Shit, I'm sorry. I thought that dipshit would have told you."

"Told me what, Lawson?"

"It's not my place to say if Huddo hasn't told you, Addy."

What isn't he telling me? I don't understand what Harry has to do with what happens between Hudson and me. Lawson runs a hand through that perfect hair, messing it up. He looks as stressed out as I feel. The phone in my pocket vibrates.

"Adds, I think your creep of a boss is here." - Ruby.

Shit.

Could this get any worse? *Breathe, just breathe. It's fine.*

Whatever is going on between Hudson and his father, I am sure he will tell me when the time is right.

I take three calming breaths and stand. "I should go help Ruby out."

"Sorry, Addy."

God, all these boys are so different, but all such sweethearts. Reed the joker, Mack the everyman, Hudson the grumpy protector, and Lawson the brains. Louisa and Harry did good.

Ruby meets me halfway across the yard. She tilts her head to the side, and I track my gaze to where she nods. Justin stands with Harry. They are talking. Justin is dressed up like a cowboy—pale blue Wranglers, a darker blue shirt, and a white hat. It's ridiculous. Everything about him gives me the icks.

Hudson walks out of the house, looking around the crowd. And when his eyes land on mine I give him a little wave and smile. Reed is fussing with the speakers and a stereo. There's a squawk and crackle and slow country music starts up.

"Oh, that's my cue. Sorry, Adds. Stick with Hudson, babes."

"It's fine. I can handle Justin."

She kisses my cheek, and Hudson comes to stand by my side. He leans down and his hand lands on the small of my back. "Hey, Addy."

He smells divine. All masculine and crisp. His aftershave is addictive.

"Hey, Huddy," I rasp.

"Your boss invited himself."

"That's not the real Justin. That"—I wave a palm toward my boss—"is some cowboy Ken doll."

Hudson pulls me a little closer. Harry glances in our direction and Hudson's hold fades, his hand slipping. Hudson's face is pulled between staring at his father and something pained. When Harry looks back to Cowboy Ken, Hudson pulls me along by the hand and into the house.

We wander into his room, and he shuts the door. His hands are on my face a heartbeat later, his mouth over mine. I don't even hesitate. I couldn't even if I wanted to. This thing between us has a life of its own. Like the two of us are only along for the ride. The insane chemistry pulls and pushes before smashing us together. I grip his shirt, walking my fingers up to his collar, letting them wander over his throat and into his hair. He groans.

"We should be at the party, Huddy."

"We will, in a bit. I have missed you, beautiful."

Well, when he puts it like that . . .

I slam my mouth to his. He picks me up, dropping me on his waist. I push and pull my fingers through his hair, thoroughly messing it up. He deepens the kiss, and I open for him. His tongue meets mine. I whimper. He spins and locks the door before walking to the bed and sitting on the end. I settle over his lap, and his mouth finds my neck.

"God above, Huddy. Look at you."

He chuckles against my neck, and heat floods to my core. His hands cup each breast before he tugs the dress and bra down and they spill into his hands. I arch my back, and he claims what I offer up, teeth snatching up a nipple. I stifle the moan that rushes up my throat. His cock is rock hard underneath me. I wiggle and he groans. "You want me to ruin this pretty dress, sweet girl?"

I'm almost breathless.

Fire has consumed every inch of me. Desperation is taking over my mind, traveling through my body.

When his hand traces the inside of my thigh, my breathing shatters. He slips my panties to one side and sinks a finger inside me, rubbing his thumb over my throbbing clit. I grip his face with both hands, kissing him hard. He opens for me and my heart almost cracks. Now hungry and insatiable, I taste him.

Tracing a thumb over my nipple, he breaks from the kiss. "Addy, come for me. I wanna see that beautiful face of yours turn desperate. It's my favorite fucking thing." His voice is gravel.

And I desperately need to give him what he wants. Whatever he wants. He drops his mouth to my breast, flicking his tongue over the hard peak before sucking it. He releases it with a pop. I cry out. He smiles and gently puts a hand over my mouth. I grab it and suck his fingers, closing my eyes.

"Jesus, Addy," he rasps.

"Huddy, I'm going to—"

"Good girl. Let me watch you."

He intensifies the movements of his fingers, sweeping his thumb over my clit. He kisses my neck, and when I release the first whimper as I constrict around his fingers, his heated gaze finds mine. Whimpers turn to moans and his hand readjusts over my mouth.

God, all I want to do is eat him.

Starting with his long, strong fingers and making my way to the head of his gorgeous hard cock. Oh god. I ride out the waves of one of the most intense orgasms I've ever had. When I settle and my breathing slows, he adjusts the top of my dress. He kisses my nose, planting one on my lips before he withdraws his hand from my panties. I gasp and he smiles. I shuffle off his lap and sink to my knees, very much wanting to repay the favor. He sucks his fingers clean before offering his other hand to me.

"Come on, Ma will be waiting for us to start the food."

"Are you going out to the party with that?" I nod to the enormous bulge in his jeans. "I can take care of that."

"I know you can, Addy. But I got what I wanted." He tugs me to my feet and traces a hand over my cheek. "Come on, let's wash up and get back out there."

We walk down the hallway to the bathroom. Hudson washes his hands and fixes his messy hair. I stare at him in the mirror. At the two of us. And when I find his blue eyes, my gut flips, my heart aches, and tears burn. He dots a kiss to my head and walks out. My chest caves as I realize I am completely and irrevocably in love with Hudson Rawlins.

Eyes falling shut, I grip the edge of the sink and fight back the tears that swell. In a few short months, I will have to leave him and all this behind. I give myself exactly five minutes to have a pity party before I pull my big-girl pants on and go back to the actual party. Tonight is about Louisa.

Happiness, Addy. Radiate goddamn happiness.

For Louisa's sake.

Absentmindedly, I make my way back to the yard for the meal. Everyone is mulling around the long tables, finding seats. I find Ruby and Reed and they point me to the other end of the table where Hudson stands waiting, a chair pulled out. Harry's stern focus tracks me as I walk to where Hudson stands.

"Sit with me, Howard."

I smile at him and drop into the seat, rising slightly as he lifts it and edges it toward the table. Mack is opposite me at the table. "Where have you been?" I ask.

He pulls an innocent face and tilts his head to Louisa, who sits by Harry a few seats down. Secret, right. My lips are sealed. I purse my lips and pretend to lock a key and throw it away over my shoulder. Now I am intrigued.

Mack smiles. "You got it, Addy. Just wait."

Chapter Nineteen

HUDSON

Food lines the center of each table. Piles of roasted meats, grilled steaks, chicken, and sausages. Salads, rice dishes, creamy potato bakes, and so much more. Every place setting is topped with a napkin wrapped elegantly around silver cutlery. Fairy lights and candles are strewn through the dishes of food, along with small glass vases of Ma's favorite flowers and baby's breath. Ruby has outdone herself. She really is amazing at this.

I lean over to Addy. "You're flushed, Howard."

She gives me an incredulous glance.

"I like it. We will have to put that color on your cheeks again later."

"You first, Rawlins."

I straighten and slide a hand into hers under the table;

her fingers lace through mine. My cock hardens. When someone clinks a glass, chatting fades to silence, and Harry stands.

"Thank you all for coming to celebrate my Louisa. I know we do this every year. And there is a reason why we do." Ma looks up at him, and he runs a hand behind her neck. She grabs his arm, leaning into him. "It was a little while after our youngest, Reed, was born, and we were up all night again. Exhausted, walking the halls with the little devil who wouldn't stop crying. We swapped shifts in some wee hour of the morning, and she took him from my shoulder. I asked her then what she wanted in exchange for four sons. I felt so bad for the weariness written all over her face. The pain she went through with feeding, labor, the lot. It was supposed to be a little joke to lighten the mood, but she stood there staring at me for a moment. Then she said she wanted a birthday party every year for the rest of her life. Now at first, I thought that was an odd request for a woman who doesn't do fuss. But then I realized, only a month or so later, that it wasn't about the birthday. It was about seeing her boys grow. Marking every year that passed like waypoints on a map. She was strategically ensuring we had memories of each of their years. Of the milestones our family made throughout the decades. Smart woman, my wife. And it worked. We know that at least once a year, all our boys will come home. And that means something else entirely now." He tracks his gaze to Mackinlay before glancing around at the rest of his sons. Addy squeezes my hand in hers and my breathing shallows out. I swear there isn't a dry eye in the whole damn yard. "Anyway, happy birthday, my love. Here's to many more milestones." And now his eyes fall to Addy.

Talk about mixed signals, old man.

Ma catches the silent exchange between him and Addy and beams up at him. He drops his gaze to her and raises two fingers to his forehead in a subtle salute before he leans down and kisses her briefly.

"To Louisa!" someone yells, holding their glass up.

"To Louisa!" we all shout. Every last person raises their glass or bottle and takes a sip before the clatter of glasses and bottles being set back down cues the ruckus of chatter, plates and cutlery clinking. One of our neighbors, Brian, starts chatting to me about the mares. "How's ya herd comin' along?"

I turn to face him, swallowing. "Good, they should be foaling not long after we come back from the roundup."

"All twelve of them this year?"

"Yep, they're trackin' along well."

"Hear you have a new vet at your clinic. She taking care of your girls right?"

Addy stiffens and Mack catches her attention. My fork is suspended halfway to my mouth.

"Dr. Howard. Yep, she has done a brilliant job with them all. An asset to the clinic."

Mack smiles at her then shoves a forkful of food into his grin.

"Got the same feedback from a few other folks with their horses. I should give the clinic a ring and see if she can come and check over my herd this year."

I turn to find Addy stifling a laugh, and Mack's shoulders trembling. Pair of idiots. "You takin' new clients, Howard?"

"Sure." She tries not to laugh, as if not wanting to offend the man. Brian's eyes widen when he realizes who she is.

"Sorry, love. Brian Lovett. Nice to meet you, Dr. Howard." His hand shoots past me.

I lean back, and Addy says a quick hello to the man, confirming he should call the clinic and book in. "I'd be happy to come and check your girls over."

He raises an eyebrow to me and goes back to his food. Mack is back to talking to the woman beside him. And I lean over and whisper, "Eat your food, sweet girl. We're not stayin'."

When I straighten, her mouth gapes. "We're not? What about your ma?"

"Think she has enough company."

I finish my meal and stand. Addy pushes up out of her seat, and I manhandle the chair on the grass, stuffing it back under the table. "Say a quick goodbye to Ma; I'll meet you at the truck."

She closes in on me and whispers, "I have to make a quick pit stop first."

"See you in a minute."

She walks toward the house as I make my way to the other side of the table and tell Ma I have to take Addy home. She protests, but I kiss her forehead as her face deflates. Absolutely smitten, this mother of mine, with the woman I want and can't have. At least, not for much longer. And I intend on making the most of her time here. Showing her exactly how I feel.

I sit in the truck. When five minutes have passed, I wait another five minutes. The pit of my stomach twists.

Fuck.

I jump from the truck and walk back inside.

"Get off me, Morley," Addy seethes from somewhere in the hallway.

What the fuck?!

I rush through the kitchen, and as I round the corner, I find Justin holding Addy up against the hallway wall. One of Reed's fists is around Justin's collar, the other bending his arm back around behind his back. I fly into the mix and throw the asshole onto the ground. I spin back to Addy.

"Fuck, Addy, you alright?"

She nods, shallow and quick.

Reed folds her into his chest, and Justin clambers to his feet. "So, it's only the Rawlins boys you fuck, then, Howard? I see how it is. Little slut."

My fist smashes into his face faster than Reed can stop me. Knuckles burning, I slam into him again and again. Rough hands pull me off when Mack flies in through the front doors.

"For fuck's sake. Not at Ma's party, you idiots." Then his gaze swings between Addy and Morley, and realization washes over his face.

"Get him out of here, Mack," I seethe.

Reed holds Addy like a porcelain doll with one arm wrapped around her.

Mack pulls Morley to his feet, slaps the back of his head, and escorts him out the back door. I step over to Addy and my little brother excuses himself.

Every breath burns. "Did he hurt you?"

"No," she whispers. Her eyes drop to my reddened knuckles. "I'm fine. I could have handled it."

Fuck, what a way to screw up the things I have planned.

"I promise I am fine. It's not the first time a guy hasn't taken no for an answer."

Jesus, that's fucking worse.

"Addy?"

"Not like that far. But I have fended off my share of delusional guys, Rawlins. Don't overthink this, please."

"Are you sure he didn't hurt you? I will gladly make the other side of his face match my hand."

She huffs a laugh and her cheeks flush. "No need to

damage your hand any further. Let's go. I'll say a quick goodbye to your ma."

She slips past me, and I slump against the wall. The feeling of being helpless only moments ago comes rushing back, catching up with me now that the moment has turned quiet. The raging red that flooded my vision when Morley opened his fucking mouth. I pinch the bridge of my nose, sucking in a long breath, and rub my hands over my face. Moments later, two fine hands gently wrap around mine, lowering them from my face.

Addy's dark brown eyes find mine. "Take me wherever you want, Huddy."

I remind myself that our time together is limited. And I don't want to waste another second of it with Justin Morley in my mind. I sweep Addy into my arms, and she squeals, her curls bouncing as she laughs with her head back a little over my arm. I walk toward the back door. "Where are you taking me?" Her words are soft, intimate.

"You'll see."

"That's what Mackinlay said. You boys will be the death of me."

"Now you sound like Ma."

"I will take that as a compliment."

I smile down at her when I lower her to her feet by the passenger-side door of the truck. When I open it for her, she climbs in. We drive a little way, around the back of the furthest barn, and I kill the engine and jump out. Addy gets out of the truck, eyeing the rows of fireworks Harry and Mack set up earlier. I lower the tailgate of the truck and grab some blankets out from behind the driver's seat. This might take a while, and I don't want her getting cold.

Addy winds through the rows of fireworks. All positioned and ready to ignite. If it was daylight, she would be able to see all the different colors they claim to be, according to the wrappers on their canisters. All the colors of the rainbow. When Reed mentioned fireworks as an inside joke from when we were kids, Ruby took it literally, and here we are. Maybe she wanted to fulfill something from Reed's childhood wish list. Who knows?

I sit on the tailgate and pat the spot beside me. Now we wait for Mack to send the go-ahead text. If he isn't still dealing with that loser Morley, that is. That fucker better not have ruined Ma's big show.

Addy comes to sit by me, and I wrap her in a blanket. She presses a kiss to my jaw before resting her head on my arm.

My phone lights up beside me.

Mack

Now, Huddo.

"They're ready, Addy."

She throws the blanket off and jumps off the tailgate. "Show me how to light them."

I grab the two gas lighters that Harry left by the first row and hand her one. The long, bendable wands of the lighters keep you far enough away from the spark when the fuse catches. "It's pretty easy." I bend down, click the lighter on, and hold the flame on the end of the fuse of the first one. It catches and sparks.

I step back, and Addy lights the next one. "Oh, I love this."

"How about we take opposite ends so the colors mix as they go off? Then I'll meet you at the truck."

"Sounds good," she says and walks to the opposite end of the row and starts lighting the back row. I step through the first row and light every fuse, leaving a minute or so between them so Addy's shoot up between mine. The first one fizzles as the fuse hits the base of the canister and it shoots into the air. The air around us is rank with the tang of gun powder, the hiss and crackle of dozens of fuses.

One of Addy's takes off and she snaps her head up, watching it. Some fuses are longer than others. We finish our rows and scramble back to the truck to watch the show. I wriggle back when she wedges between my legs, resting the back of her head on my stomach. I drape my arms over her shoulders, and she grabs my hands. I fold mine around hers, letting them fit inside, as I nuzzle her hair for a moment, breathing her in. A man could get used to this.

Color bursts over us and she gasps, looking up as the most beautiful blues light up the dark night sky. Her eyes glitter under the sparkling crackles above us. I glance up, but if I'm honest, the view below me is much,

much more beautiful. Her smile stretches her face; her perfect scattering of freckles pop on the apples of her cheeks.

"Heavens above, Addy, you are gorgeous," I whisper into her hair. She turns and pulls my face to hers, her hands planted on either side of my jaw, and claims my mouth.

"Take me somewhere, Huddy."

She moves out of my hold, and I slip off the tailgate, shutting it behind me. Addy is sitting in the passenger's seat by the time I'm behind the wheel. As we drive into the darkness, her gaze hasn't left my face since I started the truck. I smile and glance at the fireworks in the rearview mirror when we're far enough away.

Happy birthday, Ma.

Forty minutes later, Addy is quiet, leaning against the window of the truck. I pull up out front of my half-built house. "Wait here."

Checking that everything I organized earlier today is still in place, I walk in and stride through the house to the master bedroom. And to be honest, I'm stalling. My heart thunders. Everything is raw. I light the candles that I have scattered around the house, hundreds of them. It takes a solid ten minutes.

I check the water is running. No electricity, but at least we have rainwater tanks installed already. A flushing toilet and a shower. Even if there's no mirrors, doors, or furniture. Or kitchen. But the cooler that I packed after lunch today and packed full of ice has enough food to carry us through.

I realize that every date-type of occasion Addy and I have had has been out of a picnic basket or cooler bag, if you're not counting the Italian restaurant. Gonna make up for that. Mental note—done.

"Huddy?" Addy's voice is soft but lined with wonder.

I spin back from where the cooler bag sits against the wall where the oven will stand. Her shoulders are wrapped in the blanket from the back of the truck. Her hair is disheveled, eyes reflecting the flames of the candles between me and her. When I close the space between us, she drops the blanket, taking my collar in her hands.

I claim her mouth with mine, grabbing her up and onto my hips. Her legs wind around my waist. This, right here, is my version of heaven. Nothing else will ever come close.

I break from her hunger, and she rests her arms over my shoulders, breathing heavy.

"You want to go to bed, Adeline?" The words are no more than a rasp.

"With you, always."

"Oh, good. I am kinda tired."

She slaps my chest, and I release a hearty laugh.

"Don't you dare go to sleep on me, Hudson Rawlins."

"Never."

"Always you and me, never sleeping. We're off to a good start," she whispers before her mouth finds my neck. The stretch in my jeans is almost uncomfortable, but I'm going to take this as slow as I can. If this takes hours, it will still be not enough time. When I turn and head down the hallway, Addy is busy exploring my neck and face with her mouth, her hands.

I make my way into the master bedroom and set her down, spinning her around. Her breath stills and her head turns as she takes in the room. The mattress on the floor is adorned with white linen and way too many fucking pillows. A small wooden box is to one side, and hurricane lanterns sit around the walls of the room with dozens of candles in between.

Yellow wildflowers from the first hill I took her to are scattered over the mattress and the floor between the candles. They reminded me of the sundress she wore to Sunday lunch. That dress gave me a rock-hard cock. So damn beautiful.

She glances back, a hand landing on my chest as she tracks her gaze up, eyes lined with silver.

"You did all this for me?"

"Absolutely, sweet girl."

"Hudson Rawlins . . ."

I sweep the hair from her neck and nip her throat before sliding my arms around her waist. She chokes through a sob.

Fuck.

I slide around her until I'm facing her. "What is it?"

She huffs a tangled laugh. "No one has ever done anything like this for me."

"That's fucking criminal, Addy."

Or maybe it's because the only one who was supposed to do this was me. But I can't say that out loud. I know our reality. If tonight is all I ever have with Addy, it will be a memory this man will never forget. And, if I am completely honest, this is it for me. I have no delusions that there would be anyone else. Not after Addy.

"What are you thinking?" Her hand is pressed over my heart.

"How much you mean to me, Howard."

"You know, your ma is right, you should probably stop calling me that." A cheeky smile pulls up on the side of her face.

"Adeline, the last person I want to think of right now is my mother."

She laughs, bubbling with hysterics. I can't help but laugh with her. When she settles and catches her breath, I open my mouth to say something smart, but her finger lands over my lips.

"No more talking, Huddy. Stand still while I repay you from earlier."

"Jesus. I'm supposed to be loving you."

"Ut! Shhhh."

Her finger drags over my lips, and she works on the buttons of my shirt. When the last one pops, she slides it off my shoulders and down my arms, letting it hit the floor.

"Boots, cowboy."

I pull them off and toss them behind me. "Socks, too?"

"Nope."

Her fingers trace the curves of my shoulders, along the veins that have long since popped, down my biceps, and over my forearms. "I love these," she whispers.

When one elegant finger slowly edges toward the V at the bottom of my stomach, my breath hitches. Not like we haven't been naked in front of each other before, but tonight is different. More intense. More like a defining life moment that neither of us will come back from.

She undoes the buckle on my belt, letting it loose before sliding it through the loops.

"Addy—"

"Ut!"

Chest cycling through each ragged breath, I try to rein in the burning need to claim her mouth with mine, her face with my hands, her body with every part of mine. She opens the button and pulls on the zipper of my jeans and pushes them down. Her gaze finds mine. Her face shifts, caught between desperation and desire. Her bottom lip sucks in between her teeth, and I scramble to suck in a breath. I step out of the jeans pooled at my feet, and she closes the space between us, pulling my lips down to hers.

Thank fuck.

I claim her face with my hands, my tongue sweeping into her mouth. The fire in my core rushes my veins, head light from the burning need for her.

When her finger slips behind the waistband of my boxers, I groan. She whimpers against my mouth.

"Huddy—"

"Mhmmm."

"I don't want this to end."

This kiss, this night, this thing we have created between us that feels like the ember of a life. A beautiful fucking life that could unravel into something I would die to keep safe.

"Me either, sweet girl."

Chapter Twenty

ADDY

When I hit my knees, Hudson groans. What I wouldn't trade to keep that sound in my life. His hands push and pull through my hair when I take him into my mouth.

"Sweet Jesus, Addy."

Swirling my tongue around the head of his cock, I sweep it over the glistening tip. He tastes so damn good. My core is liquid at this point. Flammable liquid. One strike and I would burst into flames. I take him deep and come back up, releasing him with a pop. I run a hand up his hard stomach and his legs tense up, his arms flexing as his hand moves quicker in my hair, almost frantic. He is so wound up, it's beautiful.

I take him deeper, one hand gripping the base of him and moving in time with my mouth. When his hands still in my hair, I look up. His face is twisted, and he's almost breathless.

"Stop, Adeline."

A second later, I release him, and he is pulling me to my feet, mouth devouring my neck, chest.

"Too many clothes, Huddy," I pant.

He gathers my dress and pulls it up over my hips, shoulders, and finally off, letting it hit the floor with his jeans. I stand in my black bra and panties, and his face turns feral. Seeing that expression will never get old. And knowing I put it there is *everything*.

"As much as I adore these on you, they need to go." He slips a finger behind the lace of my bra and the breath leaves my lungs. He reaches around. The clasp snaps open and the lacy black piece slides from my body. His mouth finds my hard peaks, and the fire low in my belly surges. By now, my panties are soaked.

Every inch of me vibrates, strung out waiting for him. Aching, throbbing, a blissful agony only he can ease. My breasts are heavy, and now with his teeth scraping over the other peak, I can't help the whimper that tumbles from my lips. His hands grip my ass. I rock my hips as he kneads me with both hands before kissing a path down my stomach to the waistline of the black lace.

"And these, too," he rasps. A finger slips inside the band on each hip as he drops to his knees. "These go, Adeline."

When I can't piece together a single syllable, I nod.

He looks up at me, those blue eyes darkened, swallowing me whole. I run my hands through his hair and close my eyes, trying to steady my breath. Trying to make the moment last. When I open my eyes, Hudson stands with his head dipped, eyes burning into mine. He lifts my chin with a finger and kisses me, deep, hard, and hungry.

I open for him, and he sweeps me up, one hand under my shoulders, the other under my bottom. When his feet hit the bed, eyes still closed, he sinks to his knees, lowering me onto the bed. He breaks the kiss, and his voice is gravel when he says, "Make yourself comfy."

Everything is so soft and warm as I shuffle back on the bed and lie on the pillows. The angles of his face, his jaw . . . Looking at him has my heart aching. When I meet his gaze, he crawls up the bed and over me, nuzzling my neck, kissing and sucking his way down my chest. His tongue swirls around each hard peak, one hand cupping the soft flesh.

I arch into him. "Huddy." But his name is barely a whisper with the last of my air gone. He tracks down my stomach, moving backward on his knees, hands gripping my hips. When his warm mouth meets my throbbing apex, it takes everything I have not to lose it. He growls. "Jesus, Addy, I don't even know who I was before you."

I whimper, arching off the bed as he drags his tongue through my wet center and suckles the peak like a man starved. Everything is heightened. More than it has been before between us. So much more intense. Sweet ecstasy tangled with torment. Each touch from his hands, his mouth, the pleasure he gives me with the slightest pass. And my heart twists with the agony of this moment I know is fleeting.

He sinks two fingers inside, and I cry out. He licks me, strong strokes over my throbbing apex, and I spiral, gripping the linen underneath us. Every inch of me trembles. Each too-shallow breath sears in my lungs. When his thumb finds my peak and he rolls it, I explode around his fingers.

"Hudson!"

He stays the course through each wave. When I melt back into the bed, he crawls back up to where I lay breathless. I pull his mouth to mine, tasting my release all over his lips, his tongue.

"You sure about this, sweet girl?" He sweeps a rogue curl from my cheek and pushes it behind my ear.

"Yes, Hudson, very."

He leans to the side of the bed, reaching for the small wooden box. He's organized this time. But I grab his wrist. "No, we don't need it. I'm on contraception. Have been for years."

He raises an eyebrow, as if saying *now you tell me*. I can even hear the *Howard* that he would tack on the end of it. But he only says, "Yes, ma'am."

I can't help the smile that cracks over my face. But it fades as I study his face, now serious, hungry, and desperate. "I want to feel you, Huddy."

He groans and drops his forehead to mine. "God, Addy. How did I have to wait thirty-four years for you?"

"No more waiting." I shake my head. "Please."

He nudges his tip against my entrance. He is so warm, so large. I lift my hips and he sinks inside, and I gasp. He stole my air with just the tip. I stretch around him. He kisses my mouth, then my nose, cheeks, and neck. I run my hands through his hair. "More, Hudson."

He pushes up on his hands and sinks in further. His face twists as he closes his eyes. "Damn it, Addy," he rasps. He leans his head back, stilling. "I'm gonna have to take this so damn slow."

I smile up at him. He traces a finger over my lips, still propped up on one hand, his muscles flexing. I take his hand and hold it in place as I take two fingers into my mouth and suck them. He groans, and it sounds like a warning. I remove his fingers from my mouth and release them to my breast. He works over the softness before finding my peak. And instantly I arch and tighten around him.

"Addy, slow down." He is breathy, desperate. He plants his hand back to the pillow beside my head and kisses my mouth, taking up the rhythm between us, inching further inside with every slow, languid stroke. When he fills me completely on the next thrust, I grab his hips and hold him there, letting the stretch take me under. He is the perfect fit. I widen my legs and, somehow, he sinks in a little further.

And I know his wrecked face mirrors my own now.

"More, sweet girl?"

"God, please."

He pulls out and thrusts back in. Fire ripples through my core. I lift my hips, needing him. Again, he pulls out, slow. When he sinks back down, it's torturously slow, gentle. "I want you above me, Adeline."

He braces and flips us over. I push up and come to rest over him, sinking deep as I straddle his hips. My hair falls around my shoulders. Hands on my hips, I tilt my head back, savoring the feel of him deep inside.

"God, look at you," he growls.

I lean down and claim his mouth. He props up on his elbow and dips his head, claiming my nipple with his teeth, his tongue. I rock a little, seeing what he can tolerate. When he looses a small groan, I press my palms against the wall and push up until only his tip is still inside me. His grip lands on my hips, tightening. He liked that.

Good.

I push up again, and he stunts my movement a little as his body starts to tremble underneath mine. I sink down hard and whimper as he fills me up so good, the heat surges in my core. He pulls me up and pushes down in quick, short movements. And I barrel toward release, every short stroke sending me higher. "Huddy."

He pushes me down. "Not yet, sweet girl. If you go, you send me, too."

I lean down, pressing kisses to his collarbones, neck, and jaw. Gentle hands lift my mouth to his. This kiss is soft, gently teasing.

"Kneel by the wall, Addy."

I release him. And the absence is almost too much. I whimper, fingers splayed against the bare, paneled drywall. He moves in behind me, lifting my hands a little higher before covering them with his. Sweeping my hair to one side, he nips my ear as his cock presses into my lower back. I widen my knees, desperate for him inside me.

"Huddy, please."

"Always, sweet girl." He nudges my entrance before thrusting up, and I cry out. With one hand, he takes my chin, sliding his hand down my throat. I lean back onto him, closing my eyes, and breathe him in as he rocks us toward the jagged edge. The one that will splinter us to shattered pieces. His other hand unfolds from mine and his fingers find the throbbing apex of my heat, thumbing over it with every stroke inside me. I reach back and run my hands through his hair. Pushing and pulling.

It's too much, and I am too close. "Now, Hudson."

He picks up the pace, and in a few motions, he turns frantic. Breathless. I ignite around him, tightening. Sparks flood from my core, sweeping through my veins. With every wave, my core constricts around him further. "Hudson. Huddy!" Whimpers turn to breathy cries with each wave he pulls through me, still giving me every part of him, hard, hungry.

"Right behind you, beautiful," he rasps, and the words turn into a growl.

When his hands hit the wall in front of me and his head dips to my shoulder, I huff out a laugh. So satiated, my whole body still buzzing. Soft, warm, and pliable.

He groans and wraps his arms around my belly, not lifting his head. For the first time in my life, I feel loved and safe. Treasured.

"Thank you," I whisper into his hair.

Something tugs at my heart, something that smarts. The bridge of my nose prickles and I suck back a sob, trying to not let in the thought that these arms will have to let me go, eventually.

Right now, I am so high on his touch, the adoration in his eyes when his gaze meets mine. And my purchase on this elevated place is rickety. Too high. Up this high, there is a damn long way to fall.

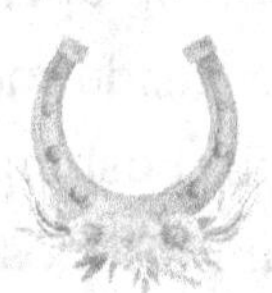

Dawn's first rays splinter the hazy air around us through half-built walls and exposed rafters. Hudson is wrapped around me. The deep and steady rise and fall of his chest sends breathy puffs into my hair from behind. I turn in his arms and nuzzle into him. He groans in his sleep. I want so badly to touch his gorgeous face, trace his lips and jaw with a finger. But I resist and lay watching him, a palm flat on his sternum.

"It's rude to stare, Addy." A grin pops over his face.

I slap his chest. He chuckles, his Adam's apple bobbing. I kiss it and work my way across his jaw until his hands claim my cheeks, and he covers my mouth with his. I wriggle closer, finding his hard cock as it hits my hip bone. He rolls me over until I'm under him and trapped, fingers laced in his as he nips kisses over my neck. "Shower time, sweet girl."

"You have water here?"

"Yup, went in last week."

"Thank the heavens."

He releases me and scoops me up and wanders out into the hall to a bathroom. And I really need to pee.

Shit.

"Um, I really have to pee."

He lets me down and wanders back out into the hall. "You have five minutes, then we are getting clean."

After relieving myself, I flush and wash up. There is no mirror. Probably just as well. The oversized shower has two showerheads, light grey tile, and modern silver fittings. It's stunning, and the room isn't even finished yet. I'm slightly sore, but mostly aching for more. More Hudson. I round the doorway to find him standing there, hands gripping the doorframe above him.

Naked and ready, he crowds me back into the bathroom and toward the shower. When I slip into the glassed space, he flips on the water, and we wait a moment for the solar-heated water. Hudson guides me into the shower's tiled wall. He puts my hands in his against the tile above my head. I want to touch him so badly.

No fair.

He tracks kisses over my neck before nipping at my peaks. And after last night, my body responds to his even faster, as if primed for what he gives me.

"I want you to ride my cock, sweet girl. So fucking desperate for you now. Jesus, Addy, last night was—" His words choke out. His hand slips from mine, and he runs his fingers through my wet heat before sinking two fingers inside.

I arch off the tile, and he grins at me.

"Fuck me, Addy."

"Always."

"So wet."

"I don't stand a chance around you Hudson, none. You look at me and I'm wet."

"You have no idea how much I love that. I'm going to fill you up every fucking chance you give me."

"You better."

"Insatiable. I love it." He stills a little, as if something dawned on him.

"Don't you dare stop."

He smiles. "Never, sweet girl."

His thumb sweeps over my clit and I explode around him. His mouth finds my peak, like he's saying his prayers and my body is his place of worship. I fucking love it. Every wave, I buck on his fingers, and he groans, sending electricity through my lungs, burning out the last of my breath. When I slump against the wall, he flips me around and pulls my hips out. I spread for him, aching to feel every incredible inch of him.

"Slow, Huddy."

"Yes, ma'am."

His tip stretches my entrance, and I tilt my hips so my ass perks up and I take him in further.

"God, more." The words are a growl, and his hands tighten around my hips, rough.

I changed my mind—I don't want slow like last night. I want him to slam into me. Rough me up, claim me as his. Because as of last night, I am ruined for anyone else.

Utterly wrecked.

"Harder, rougher, Hudson. Take what you need. I'm yours."

"Jesus, you are mine, Addy. Don't you ever forget it."

"Never, Huddy. Now, harder, deeper."

He pulls out and slams in so damn hard that I meet the tile with my face. I have never been so full. And every time he pulls out agonizingly slow, he thunders back into me. And I crawl higher and higher with every rough, damning inch of my Hudson.

"I'm almost there. Jesus, Addy."

"Take me with you," I beg. His fingers find my apex and sweep frantically as he pumps into me, and I tighten more and more. When he slams a hand beside my head, I grip his fingers with a hand and cry through the biggest orgasm I have ever had. It steals my breath. My fingers and toes tingle. I gasp for air, choking through sobs of pure pleasure. He growls beside me, and his seed spills inside me, hot and fast.

Hudson Rawlins, you are the undoing of me.

Chapter Twenty-One

HUDSON

The winter winds and chilly days are officially there. And Addy is late for her Tuesday lesson. I flip my phone out of my back pocket on my way over to the barn to saddle up Sergeant. No texts. No calls. I barely use my phone, and Addy is the only one who has been lighting up my phone since the party. And it's deathly quiet.

My gut sinks like a stone in stagnant water. Addy isn't the fickle type—if she hasn't arrived by now, she has good reason. Or good reason has her caught up.

With that thought, I stalk back to the house and call her phone. It goes to voicemail.

"Fuck."

"Huddy, can you come here?" Ma calls from the study.

I pull off my hat and drop it on the kitchen table and make my way to the study. Ma sits at the computer. A video is paused on the screen. When she turns back to me, her eyes are narrow, her mouth is a little gap, and her hands are on her glasses.

"What is it, Ma?"

"It's . . . It's Addy."

"What?" Heat floods my insides when I glance back at the screen. A video of Addy riding. Show jumping, by the looks of the colorful setup in the blurred background. "She's riding; let's see it."

Ma doesn't say anything. She swivels the chair back around and drags the little black dot on the bottom of the video back to the start. "I had to watch it a few times to make certain it was her," she whispers.

Why is she whispering?

A stone develops in my throat. I move to stand next to her. She tilts the screen up and glances at me with an agonized expression. Her finger slowly clicks the mouse, and the video starts. Addy sits on an Arabian-type horse. She's stunning. A real competition horse. Shiny, bay, her hooves polished.

Addy leans forward on her mare when the buzzer sounds, and Jewls takes off toward the first jump. They clear the first half of the course easily. She turns the mare to the hedge jump. And it's like watching a car accident in slow motion, knowing what comes next.

Ma grabs my arm, her grip tight. I grind my jaw tight as they sail over the hedge. Jewls flinches. Addy heads her toward the next jump and they sail over it, but the mare shakes her head, faltering a little. The triple comes up.

I can't help the choking sound that steals the air from my lungs with every breath. Ma hides her face with her other hand. Helplessness gutters through me. Jewls goes down, crashing into the jump. Addy screams for her. Poles fly from their cradles. The ruckus is too loud.

I grip the edge of the desk in horror as the horse falls. Addy's hands fly above her. Her head bounces on the sand. The horse jerks and rolls again, squashing Addy under her. She screams and stills. That must be the moment her hips were smashed. Bile crawls up my throat.

Ma's shoulders shake and I slam my eyes shut, trying to block out the god-awful sight of the woman I would sell my soul for being thrown around like a rag doll.

Sick to my stomach, I groan, low and heady. "Turn it off, Ma."

She smashes a hand over the mouse. The screen goes black, and she pushes the chair back. I brace against the desk with both hands.

"I'm so sorry, Huddy. I thought maybe you'd seen it? That Addy had already showed you."

I blow a long breath and wait for the dizziness that threatens to swallow me whole to subside. I knew her accident was bad. I wasn't prepared for how I would feel watching it. I slide to the floor.

Ma sits back in the chair. "She is a tough girl, your Addy."

I huff a strangled sound. *My Addy.*

Ma checks her watch. "Where is she? It's five o'clock."

"She didn't turn up. No texts, either."

"Why are you sitting on the floor? Go and make sure she's okay. God, if that low-life Justin made her stay back late—"

"Shit!" I bolt up from the floor and rush from the study. I swipe my hat up and jog to the truck. Starting her up, I slam the stick into drive. It takes ten minutes less than usual to make it into town. I head to the clinic, but the lights are off and the doors are locked. Reversing out of the parking lot on screeching tires, I head to Addy's townhouse.

Her car is in the drive. *Good start.* I park beside her Cherokee and kill the engine and race up the steps. The last hour still running through my head, I knock. The house is quiet. I knock again, louder.

No answer. Ruby went back to the city after Ma's party, and I wish I had her number now. Maybe Reed has it. I round the house and try the back door. It's unlocked. I walk in and remove my hat.

"Addy?"

No answer.

I walk through to the kitchen and living room. Nobody there. "Adeline!"

Something moves upstairs. I fly to the stairs and bolt up them, taking two at a time. When I swing around the banister and head for her room, she stands, gripping the doorframe. Swaying. Her face is far too pale. Hair a mess, and she is in stained pajamas.

Fuck, sweet girl.

"Huddy?" she utters. Her eyes are glassy and strung out.

"Yeah, beautiful, I'm here."

I press a hand to her forehead. She's burning up. When I scoop her into my arms, she cries out. Shit, she must have the flu, aching everywhere. I lay her back in bed.

"Addy, where's your thermometer?"

She points to the floor. Downstairs. "I'll be right back, okay?"

"Okay," she whispers.

She probably hasn't been to work today, possibly not yesterday either. Jesus, I wish she had told me she was sick. She was unwell and all alone. Nobody here to take care of her. I hurry back downstairs and rummage through the kitchen cupboards until I find her Tylenol and ther-mometer and grab her a glass of water.

I pull out all the drawers until I find a tray and head back upstairs. Shivering, she reaches for another blanket. I take the blanket and remove it from her hands. She whimpers.

"You are burning up. You need medicine, not a ton of blankets."

I set the tray on the bedside and sit beside her. "Can you sit up for me, darlin'?"

She moans and I help her up, cradling her body against mine as I rearrange her pillows.

"You smell nice," she croaks.

I chuckle. I smell of horse and sweat. "That's the fever talkin'."

"No, you always smell like this. I love it."

I lay her back on the pillows, slightly elevated, and take her temperature.

One hundred and two.

Fuck.

I peel another layer off her, and she objects, grabbing at it with trembling hands. Gooseflesh washes over her skin. I pop the pills into my hand and hold them out to her. She wraps fine, shaky fingers around them and slides them into her mouth. I raise the glass to her lips. She drinks enough to wash the pills down and then shakes her head. Probably dehydrated, too, then. I stand and close the curtains to block out the streetlights. She needs to rest.

"Huddy, don't go."

"Never, Addy."

I sit back by her side, and she closes her eyes. I pull out my phone and text Ma. She will be worried. She texts me back a second later with a blue heart. Addy's hand closes around my wrist. "Stay with me, please."

"Do you need something to eat?"

She shakes her head no.

I slip off my boots and walk to the other side of the

bed. A heartbeat after I lay down, she rolls over, nuzzling into my chest. "I'm so cold."

I wrap an arm around her and dot a kiss into her hair. "Close your eyes, Addy. I'll be here when they open."

Her hand presses against my neck. Her breathing slows and steadies twenty minutes later. I feel her forehead. The heat has almost gone. I pull one layer over her. There is nowhere else I would rather be. And when I close my eyes, the sight of her trapped under her horse replays incessantly in my mind. I tighten my hold on her. This precious woman who has turned my hard heart on its head.

I have no idea where anything is in this kitchen, but I am making her breakfast if it takes me all fucking day. So far, I've found eggs and bread. So, I cut the crusts off and cut out a shape like Ma used to do for us boys when we were little. But a flower for Addy, instead of the star Ma did. It's a little corny, but it might make Addy smile. And I will happily exchange corny, or anything else for that matter, to see her smile.

Butter sizzles as I drop it into the hot pan, and I spread it around before laying two slices of bread into the bubbling mix. I crack an egg and hold it over the flower-shaped cut out. It plops into it filling the space. I crack the second egg and it does the same. I wait a while before I flip them over and make coffee.

On second thought, juice would be better. Fuck it, I'll grab both. I turn off the stove and pull a plate from the overhead cupboard and flip the toast from the pan onto it. Assembling the plate, glass, and mug on the tray, I make my way upstairs. She is asleep on her side when I sit on the opposite side of the bed, resting the tray on the duvet.

I touch the back of my hand to her forehead. Her fever hasn't returned. Hopefully it has broken. Her eyes flutter open when I remove my hand, brown eyes finding mine. A small smile blooms over her face. "Hey, Huddy."

The air leaves my lungs. I feel like it's the first time I have seen her since I saw her fall on Ma's screen. And the overwhelming emotions snag my voice, rendering it useless. I clear my throat. "Morning, Addy."

She pushes up to sitting. "I feel better, thank you."

"I didn't do much, you—"

Emotion clogs my throat, so I stare at the wall, and she frowns.

"What? Did I say something in my sleep?" She feigns a laugh.

I pick up the tray and place it in front of her and shuffle off the bed. Her gaze drops to the contents of the tray. "Wow, thank you."

She runs a hand through her hair and tucks it behind her ears, leaning forward to grab a slice of toast. I have to leave. She's so delicate, so small with her legs tucked underneath her, wrapped in a blanket. *So fucking precious.* Fire burns in my lungs, my breaths too shallow.

I walk into the hall and lean on the wall, head back, eyes closed. The image replays, her underneath that damn horse, the agonizing sound that filled the stadium when the horse crushed her. I slide down the wall, knees up, letting my head drop. I suck in every burning breath.

Something hits my foot then rubs the top of my socked toes. I rub the heels of my palms into my eyes, trying desperately to dislodge the horrific replay that has been haunting me from the moment I saw Jewls go down during that jump. Fine fingers pry my hands from my face. My legs part and Addy wedges herself between them. Her hands land on my face, eyes tortured and searching.

"Huddy?"

My face cracks. I fight the choking feeling crawling up my throat and fail.

"Oh no, what is it?" she whispers, hands searching my face like she can find what's broken there and piece it back together. "You can tell me."

Schooling my face back, I shift my focus to the wall behind her. I can't look at that beautiful face if I want my words to have any chance of forming right. "I saw your fall. Ma found it online. She showed it to me."

She stiffens and leans back on her heels, hands dropping from my face to her lap. I'm an ass for bringing it up when she's sick. For watching the video at all.

Fuck.

"I'm sorry, I didn't realize what I was watching until it happened."

I know that's not an excuse, but her reaction isn't what I expected. Her eyes turn vacant.

Fuck, fuck, fuck.

Shit, I shouldn't have said anything. I shouldn't have watched it; that I knew even before I saw her reaction. Watching her fall and be crushed under a horse is not something I can unsee. "I'm sorry, Addy."

She shakes her head, and her gaze hits the floor. "I—"

I reach for her, but she doesn't move. I drop my hands to the floor beside me. "Jesus, sweet girl. I had no idea," I rasp.

She forces a small, sad smile, and my whole body aches to hold her. To wash that memory from her mind, to take away the pain that must haunt her.

"I let her down . . . " She starts with shaky words. "I didn't listen. I was so focused on our time . . ."

"It wasn't your fault, Addy."

She whimpers, tilting her head as her eyes crinkle. I lean forward and lift her, pulling her into my lap, folding her into my chest. She sobs, her grip tight around my t-shirt. God save me, I'm an ass.

"Seeing you underneath your horse—"

I swallow past the stone in my throat that cuts off my words. She nuzzles her head into my neck, her breathing ragged through a constant stream of sobs. And I can imagine she is reliving it right now.

Because of me.

But still, the words pour from my ridiculous mouth. "The sound of your scream . . . It broke my fucking heart, Addy."

Her breath hitches and a shattered cry crashes into my neck. I tighten my hold on her for the second time since I watched that goddamn video. It will never feel like enough. And the fact that she is back on a horse after a fall like that makes her the strongest person I have ever met. Hands down.

When she pushes away and her hands find my face, she composes her face and sucks in a breath. Her chin trembles as she traces a thumb over my lips before holding my face. "Thank you," she whispers.

I didn't expect that, either. Tears burn behind my eyes. The air in my lungs turns to lead. "What for?" I choke out.

She forces another sad smile. "For giving me back that part of my life."

I huff a strangled groan, letting the tears run down my cheeks. "I don't think bringing up your accident was the best thing I've ever done for you, Addy."

She shakes her head and presses her forehead to mine, thumbing the moisture from my jaw. "For getting me back on a horse, Hudson. I thought I had lost that part of my life. That huge part that was like half of me."

"I think Sergeant did most of the work . . ." But I have to know if she's okay. "Do your hips still hurt from the injuries?"

"They ache a little when it's cold, sometimes when I've been sitting too long in one place. But it's not a big deal. It doesn't stop me from doing anything."

I doubt anything could.

She huffs a laugh and sniffs before pushing back and wiping her face. "Ugh, but now my head hurts."

"You should be back in bed."

"Yes, sir." A cheeky smile curls up on her lips and she winks.

And when she stands, I push to my feet and pick her up, letting her wrap her legs around my waist. "Doctor's orders, Adeline."

"If you say so, Hudson."

"I'll even let you finish your breakfast before I take off."

"You can't stay?"

"I have to help ready everything for the roundup. And you need to rest before we start Monday."

"What, are you my boss now, Rawlins?"

I stare at her. When I don't respond, she rests a hand on my jaw. And I feel like a creep at that throwaway mention of being her boss and telling her what to do. How the fuck does Justin sleep at night?

"Nope, definitely not. But at the risk of having to share my tent with Morley for a week, I would really like you to catch some rest and get better to save me *that* particular torture."

She giggles and drops onto the bed. The coffee

splashes a little, and she turns and picks it up, taking a sip. "I'll be there. Can't have you rolling over and hugging Justin in your sleep instead of me, Huddy."

I chuckle and dot a kiss to her forehead. "Absolutely not."

She swallows her mouthful, and I tuck her hair behind her ear. My gut flips, like it hasn't already done it a thousand times before when I get close to her. "Get some rest. Call me if you need anything, please."

"Uh-huh."

She puts the coffee down and pulls me down to her, but then hesitates. "I don't want to make you sick."

I turn my face and she kisses my cheek, then my jaw, then my neck. I might not catch her cold, but I definitely have a hard-on now. I groan, torn between not caring if I get sick and remembering she is and needs rest, not what's currently occupying my bloodless brain.

"Bye, Huddy."

I linger by the doorway as she settles onto the bed and bites into the toast. She looks so much better than she did last night. Walking down the stairs, I am fully aware I left my heart behind with her.

Chapter Twenty-Two

ADDY

I'd be lying if I said I wasn't nervous. Actually, that is also a lie. I'm more than nervous—I'm anxious, kind of terrified, to be honest. After a few long hours in the truck, pulling the goosenecks, we are gathered at the base of the mountains. The ones that I wondered at from the hill by the vista. They looked so majestic from there. Now, looming above me and capped in snow, they are plain intimidating.

Sergeant moves under me, chewing at the bit. At least he's not chomping it. I have a horse loaded with supplies tied up beside Sergeant. I am to tail behind and go where needed over the next seven days of this roundup. And the air is cold.

Hudson says it is colder in the mountains where we are heading. Great. Potential frostbite and fear—what more could a girl want in her career? So, I am bundled up with a parka, Wranglers, long boots, and thick socks that are under my jeans, and three layers under the coat and gloves. Dry ones in my small, condensed pack on the back of my literal packhorse. It's a surreal feeling. I feel like I'm in the middle of a *Yellowstone* episode.

Hudson assembles the crew of ten riders. Harry, Reed, and Mackinlay are amongst them. Six of the men I have seen around town but don't know. Louisa will be coming in five days' time, in the truck, bringing food and keeping up with our progress every few days. Being so remote, it is smart to have her drop in. She has a satellite phone and first aid supplies.

"Right!" Hudson says. Rocket is a live wire on his feet, anticipating what happens next. *He* is literally chomping at the bit. Hudson sits steady in the saddle. "We split up. Covering the most northern, western, and eastern boundaries of the ranch. Nothing beyond the river on the other side. Harry takes the northern end. Mackinlay and Reed, the eastern. I will take the western boundary. Two men with each party. In two days, we herd them to the ridge, and push them down the mountain. Back here in five days for a rest, then push them home. Any issues that need attending to, we deal with then. Search every pocket, every valley and peak. The estimated head count for this roundup is around a thousand. I want no beast left behind. Any questions?"

None.

They have done this every year for who knows how

long. The men mutter and split between Harry's party, Mack and Reed's, and ours. Hudson shifts the reins against Rocket's neck and sidesteps closer to where I sit on Sergeant. "You okay, Addy?"

"Yup. Keen to start." The words are forced, and Hudson gives me a knowing look. I'm a trillion percent happy that he didn't assign me to another party. The two men who are riding with us say polite hellos and dip their hats.

"Hi," I offer back.

"Right. Be safe, make sure you don't leave any stragglers. We will catch you all in five days." Hudson tilts his chin toward the mountain.

Actual yeehaws crow as most of the men push their horses into a lope and head for the ascent of the mountain in front of us, each one of them with a bedroll and supplies tied to the back of their saddle. A lariat hanging from the side of each man's saddle. And Mack, Harry, and Hudson all have a rifle slung over their backs. I don't even want to think about what that's for.

I can imagine Reed loving this wild adventure. He stands in the stirrups as he and Mack gallop toward the thick mountain forest. The two men with Hudson and me eye the mountain like they want to gallop off into the wilds like the other two parties did. But with a glance from Hudson, they mill about on their excitable horses.

"Addy, this is Ned and Mick. Mick, Ned, this is Dr. Howard. The vet."

"Please, call me Addy."

"Addy," Ned says dipping his hat. He is grey-haired, possibly a little older than Harry.

"Howdy," Mick mutters, not meeting my gaze.

Awesome. At least Ned seems nice.

"Let's go!" Hudson exclaims. He takes off at a steady canter toward the western rise. The two men burst off the spot after him. Squeezing Sergeant into a lope, I cluck my tongue and the packhorse, Mira, follows along. I'm assuming our time will be a little slower since I have two horses to wrangle.

I don't want to be left behind or let them slip out of sight, so I push Sergeant a little faster. The cool breeze whips past my cheeks and they burn. I suck in deep, satisfying breaths. This right here is freedom. It's priceless. And for a second, I understand with deep, guttural instinct why this is the life cowboys choose.

The moment the frosty mountain forest swallows Sergeant, Mira, and me, a shudder snakes through my body. The men are already ahead a little way. Hudson yells something to Ned. Rocket sinks on his haunches and spins back. His mane follows, slapping his neck as he springs into a canter and heads for me.

The pure bliss over Huddy's face takes my breath away. This is him. Raw. The heart of who he is. And he is spectacular. His white hat, navy jacket lined with cream fur, Wranglers, boots, spurs, and the biggest grin wrapped on his sweet face I have ever witnessed.

He is *literally* lit up.

And my heart almost explodes at the sight of him. When he reaches my side, he lopes around us and comes up beside me.

"This is something else, Huddy."

"My favorite week of the entire year."

"I bet it is. Have you seen your face?" I laugh, and he throws his head back with a hearty laugh that rattles right through me.

"We can't really slow down. Can you ride along with us?"

"Oh, when Harry said trail behind, he actually meant keep up?"

"Don't take my father's words literal. You ride beside me, Addy, never behind."

I roll my eyes at him. But he stares at me. He actually means it. And I try not to overthink the meaning of that. After all, it's only a few short weeks and I will be back in the city. And this stunning place and this incredible man will still be here. That closes my throat up real quick.

I scan the spaces between the trees. Snow is dusted over everything. It's so stunning. Like no place I have ever been before. Then again, when I look into Hudson's eyes, I see that there, too.

"Hup," I rasp to Sergeant, leaning forward. He takes off up the ascent. Mira follows close behind. We lope between the trees. Hudson and Rocket catch up, and he grins at me. God that face—happiness personified. He rubs his jaw and tracks his focus ahead again, his Adam's apple bobbing as if something stole his breath. And I'm sure I know what it was. Because it's the same thing that stole mine.

Something so big that it has both of us enthralled. Captivated. Unwilling to break away.

Something that makes my chest swell and my heart ache.

After almost an entire day of riding, we are only halfway up the side of this ancient mountain. And the sun is dazzling us with its light, piercing the snow as it sinks further and further. The three men are building the tents. We have found a total of twenty head so far. They are corralled in a makeshift yard between trees with the fallen dead wood that lays around under the snow. I tend to the five horses.

They are tired, and I make sure they all drink and eat some grains to hold them through the night. It's going to be cold. I bundle them up the best I can with the few blankets I could fit onto Mira. I hope the others are doing as well as we are so far.

"How are our trusty steeds coming along, Doc?"

Hudson says behind me. The lilt in his voice makes me smile.

I turn back. "They're okay. Tired. Like their riders."

"We're only getting started. Come on, Ned got the fire going, the pot on."

"Great, I'm frozen through." I rub my hands together, clouds curling from my mouth with every word I say. Goddamn, it is cold. "Can I ask why you do this roundup in these conditions? Why not wait until spring, at least?"

"We work to the seasons and the calving season of the cattle. Spring is calving season. Trying to herd calving cows never ends well for anyone, 'specially up here."

"Oh, how?"

"You ever tried gettin' between a cow and her calf in the open? Cowboys come out worse off. Plus, we would prefer the wolves not take a quarter of the calves before we can wrangle them down off the mountain."

"I didn't think of it like that. Makes sense."

"Plus, when it's cold it's easier on the horses. We ride hard. And . . . It gives us an excuse to snuggle up."

"Who did you snuggle up with last year?" I feign a shocked look and he laughs.

"Definitely not Morley. This is the first year that I won't have to freeze." The smile that cracks his square jaw lights up his blue eyes.

"Is that why Mick is in a bad mood? Ned wanted to be big spoon?" I can't keep the grin from my mouth. And then instantly I regret my words, thinking Mick will hear me.

Hudson cracks up, his laughter echoing through the trees. "You should probably keep that theory to yourself unless you want some type of wildlife ending up in your tent, Addy."

"Oh shit! God, I hope he didn't hear me."

We make our way to the fire, and three tents are set up close by. The aroma of fresh coffee and something that smells like stew wafts around the frigid air of the camp.

Ned rolls over a stump, dusts off the snow, and pats it, gesturing for me to sit. "Thanks, Ned."

It's hard and cold, but the fire is warm and delicious.

"New York, hey, missy?" he says.

"Yup. Lewistown, hey?"

He chuckles. "Born and raised, sweetheart."

Mick grunts, shoving the end of a long stick into the fire. Embers fly up into the air, fizzling out as they touch the snowy canopy above us. "Didn't do you much good, either."

"Speak for yourself," Ned says, pointing a finger.

"You're not from here, Mick?" I try to break the ice with him.

"Sort of."

"Mick's a man of few words, Miss Howard. He'll warm up to you, about ten minutes out from home, in about a week, I reckon." Ned tosses a twig at the other man. He swats it away and gives him a scowl.

"That's okay; so was Hudson, once. And please, call me Addy."

"This one?" Ned shakes his head. "Never shut up as a kid. Now he's a chip off the old block."

Hudson meets the old man's gaze. "Easy, Ned, you say it like it's a bad thing. Harry might hear you."

"That old bastard clues onto everything. You're probably right. If there's one man who can read people like nobody else, it's your old man. Knows what most people need before they do."

I stare at Hudson, and his eyes find mine as his jaw feathers. I mull the words over in my mind and pull back the memory of the day I met him. The glance between us that Harry took. His insistence that his son help me back onto a horse. The mandatory ride-along-vet gig. Was Harry reading me or Hudson—or both? Or was it the way Charlie responded to me, like he hasn't to anyone else except his master?

Hudson is still staring. Is he only now figuring this out, too? Harry knew Hudson wouldn't deny him the request to make the vet 'roundup ready.' It was an easy play. It's like all the pieces of the puzzle were sitting on the table, and Harry was the one to connect them together.

Oh shit.

He may have read both of us right, but the timing, the situation is wrong. I'm not staying. My contract ends. And

I can't throw away my career and be penniless. I shake my head, breathing faster.

"You okay, missy?" Ned asks, resting his hand on my arm. Hudson is staring into the fire, his throat working up a storm.

I stand and turn to Ned. "I'm sorry, I'm going to go to bed."

He simply tips his hat, eyes searching mine, as if reading what I've figured out. Something like regret and hurt, fueled by the embers of desperation, wraps around my heart and tightens its surly grip.

After a while, the tent flap moves. I pretend to be asleep. But it's too early, and any fatigue I was feeling a moment ago is washed away by the thoughts galloping through my head. Thoughts about Hudson, me, and my veterinary career. Harry's goddamn stinking intuition.

Hudson sits on the end of the blankets and takes off his boots and hat before lying next to me. But he doesn't touch me, only lacing his hands behind his head and staring at the peaked top of the cream tent.

"Addy, about what Ned was talking about—"

"It's fine. You know what, Harry was right. And that's the part that scares me the most."

"I can see that. Harry can be scary."

"Your father isn't scary, Hudson; he's direct, smart, and loyal. Like his oldest son."

"Yeah, well . . ."

"I—"

"Tell me, Adeline."

"Tell you what?"

I don't dare look at him or roll over to face him. My heart hammers in my chest. I have no idea what he wants me to say. I hold my breath.

"Tell me your plans for your veterinary career. What are your dreams? You must have them. I know you well enough now to know you would have a plan *and* a backup plan."

A soft smile blooms over his face, but it never reaches his eyes. I blow out the breath. I can't be anything but honest with this man. "After my internship, the plan was to take six-to-twenty-four-month contracts in various equine clinics and sectors and grow my experience. One day, I was hoping to have my own clinic. But the backup plan was always returning to the clinic outside New York. Some of my friends are there. My parents still live there. And Joe, he was such an amazing mentor. Possibly had a lot to do with him being my dad's best friend. But still, I was happy there."

"And now? Are you happy now?"

Now I roll over and face him. I trace a finger over his jaw and push up a wobbly smile. "Right now, I am."

He nods and closes his eyes.

"Hudson?"

"Yeah."

"It's kind of early for bed . . ."

He smiles and cracks one eye open. "What did you have in mind?"

I push up on one elbow and kiss the side of his mouth and cup his jaw with my free hand. He rolls quickly and pulls me over him. I stifle a squeak, and he chuckles. "You are going to have to be really, really quiet."

"With you? Never, Hudson Rawlins."

"Addy—" His breath hitches and something like grief flashes through his eyes. "I'm not going to make you choose between me and your dreams, sweet girl."

He pulls me down to him and claims my mouth, the weight of what he said not getting a chance to sink in before the words fly from my head. The cold that has sunk into my bones from a day of riding through the snow melts.

God, the things you do to me, Huddy.

Chapter Twenty-Three
HUDSON

The snow drifts through the sparser canopy as we ride higher and higher. Addy is doing brilliantly. Ned is a huge fan already. Mick has always been quiet, so I don't expect him to warm up to her. And to be honest, I have been preoccupied by the task at hand. This has to go well.

Harry needs every last head of cattle to have the funds to buy out the clinic and purchase the next property on his acquisition list. Reed will need a ranch of his own one day, as will Mack. I'm assuming he won't be a soldier for the next forty years. I pray for Ma's sake that he won't.

We always talked about the properties we would run when we grew up when we were boys. But life takes you in different directions, and while Lawson is good at making decisions and left after high school to go to college, Reed, Mack, and I hung around doing various apprenticeships and jobs between working on the ranch.

And staying, making this life your own, is a lifelong commitment. I've never wanted anything else. I know what it is to have a dream that you have held onto your entire life. I won't let mine slip away. And I am going to make damn sure that Addy gets to keep hers.

Rocket falters on the icy ground, and I steady him up. Ahead is the mob of cattle, grazing on the few green shoots they can find poking through the snowy ground. Spread out, their woolly winter coats make them look like moving boulders between the trees. And I count around one hundred, at a quick estimate. With the twenty we have plus these, I am hoping we find an even bigger mob in the hollow, a dip before the mountains' last peak. Every year I take the western sector, and every year that's where we find most of them.

Addy rides up alongside me. "They're warm, at least."

"Like furry boulders." I chuckle.

"Where will the last two hundred-odd be?"

"Hopefully in the hollow a little further up. Then we drive them across the top and down to meet the others at the rendezvous point."

She nods, running her gaze over the animals. "How do you think the mares are getting on back home?"

"Ma is keeping an eye on them."

"I hope we make it back in time."

"We will; we do every year."

"You guys really have this ranching thing down to a fine art, don't you?" A smile blooms on her face.

"Would be pretty outrageous if we didn't by now, Addy."

She adjusts her reins. "It's some life you have here, Hudson." Her words are soft, almost longing. Something aches in my chest. And for a split second, I let myself think about what it would be like to have this life with Addy. The whole thing—the ranch, the horses, the farming, the house, the babies.

Air lodges in my throat.

"Should we keep moving?" She breaks my reverie.

I swallow. "Yup."

I squeeze my heels into Rocket, and he breaks into a trot up closer to the herd. Ned and Mick have already gotten around them, and we start tracking back east and upward to the hollow. We ride under snow-laden branches, ducking and weaving through the trees until every beast is gathered with our twenty from the first find.

I take the lead, riding in front of the mob while Mick and Ned flank them. Addy brings up the rear of the mob. Her sweet little "hup, hup" encouragements have turned into absolute business after the first day. She's just as useful as Ned and Mick. Quick learner, my girl.

As the sun sets on the side of the mountains behind us, we spill into the hollow. Rocket and I move side to side at a brisk trot at the front of the herd, trying to keep them from rushing. The last thing we need is this lot setting the larger mob off.

I am not galloping down the side of an icy mountain after them. Even in broad daylight, it would be stupid. In the fading light when the horses are tired . . . Straight-out fucking dangerous.

"Woah." I hold up a hand and slow the herd as we reach the larger mob.

As predicted, a little over two hundred head are milling about, grazing on the easier pickings, the snow cover almost nonexistent in this spot. It's stunning in summer. Right now, it's a much-needed reprieve after days of ice and snow and climbing. Rocket relaxes as the cattle mingle and settle. I ride back to Addy at a lope. She throws a giant smile at me in between turning her head every which way. Wonder lights up her eyes.

"Huddy, this is something else. And the view." Her voice is light, raspy. Fog puffs out of her mouth with every word. She is looking out over the treetops, and from here the surrounding mountains sprawl until they reach the heavens. Like we're in another world.

"It's one of my favorite places. We camp here tonight and then back down the mountain."

"I should check the horses. Make sure everyone's alright."

"Whatever you say, Doc."

I ride beside her as we make our way to a small clearing. Mick and Ned are already waiting, leading their horses around to cool them down. I swing a leg over and dismount from Rocket, handing Ned the reins to help Addy with Mira and Sergeant. Mira nudges my arm as I lead her toward the others, and Mick takes her, talking to her softly. At least he talks to the horses.

When I turn back, I catch the wince that washes over Addy's face as she shifts in the saddle. "How those hips holding up?"

Not answering, she stretches her lower back, sinking her hands into it and closing her eyes. She leans forward and kicks her foot out of the stirrup. When she swings out of the saddle, it is awkward and stilted.

Fuck.

She groans, and when her feet hit the ground, she stifles a hiss, hands gripping her left hip for a second.

"Addy?"

"I'm fine. Long day."

"You tell me if you are in pain, please?" I say.

"I'm not in pain. Just a little stiff. Please don't." She walks away, heading for the spot where Ned is now pulling out the tents and Mick is tending to the horses. But my gut sinks. We pushed too hard. And she is going to pay the price for Harry's stubbornness. The last half of the roundup is the hardest.

An hour later, after a walk around the mob, I return to

the camp site. Ned has the fire roaring and the stew bubbling away. And Addy . . . Has Mick talking to her.

Well, fuck.

"So, you did a stint in the Navy? That's amazing."

"It was a long five years, that's what it was, Addy."

Addy? Is there anyone this woman can't charm? I stifle a chuckle and school my face before sitting beside her. "Mick."

"How come you never told us Addy was a show jumper?" Ned asks.

Addy goes quiet, eyes tracking to the fire.

"Not my story to tell, Ned. Besides, I am almost one hundred percent certain you would have many tales to entertain us without Addy having to offer up her life stories."

"Well, that is true."

"They asked why my hips were bothering me," Addy says absently.

When she turns back, there is only happiness and fatigue in her eyes.

"Oh." I hold my hands toward the fire, hoping to thaw them out after walking around in the freezing night air for over an hour.

Addy takes the bowl of stew Ned holds out for her. "Thanks, Ned. I'm starving, must be the cold."

"Nope, that's the mountain air," Mick offers.

Ned hands me a bowl and a spoon. "I'm sure it is."

It warms my fingers instantly. When his gaze lingers

on mine, I wonder what he is trying to tell me. Something, no doubt. Old man wisdom is no foreign concept to me. I live with it every day. Harry. Reed.

"Can you check on my horse, Addy? I think she might have a stone bruise. Her gait was a bit stilted when we got up to the hollow."

"Sure. What about your horse, Mick?" she asks.

"No change that I've noticed. Thanks."

"You let me know if you want me to give him a once-over. I'm happy to be of assistance. I'm starting to think I'm only a tagalong at this point."

"We are happy to have you along, Addy. Lord knows you're much better company than that smart-mouth Morley. Can't stand that little shit," Mick says.

Ned hollers a laugh, and I can't help but chuckle. Addy laughs, soft and light. It is a stark contrast to the rough men she sits with. And warmth wraps a soft hug around my heart.

She grins, taking in the faces of the older men that sit in front of her. Her freckles pop on the apples of her cheeks. Her curls tousle in the cold breeze where they flow from beneath the beanie she has on.

Ned glances between us then slaps his leg. "Well, this old man is done. I'm turning in." He rises and dips his hat to Addy and nudges his friend beside him with a foot. "Mick, you going to bed?"

"Oh, yeah." He startles, and when Ned tilts his head in

a not-so-subtle gesture our way, Mick clears his throat and stands. "Night."

The fire crackles. The only sounds are the lowing of the cattle and the rustling blankets and groans of the two men in their tents as they relax their weary muscles. And when soft snores come from Ned's tent, I turn to Addy. But she rises and moves to the horses. She runs a hand over Ned's horse before checking each hoof in turn.

When the mare doesn't show any signs of a stone bruise, she takes to feeling each leg from top to bottom. I rub a hand up the mare's face and she nickers into my side, lowering her head. When I look back up, Addy is standing in front of me. Sliding her beanie off, she runs a hand through her hair.

I force air into my lungs. "You feelin' okay?"

"Yes, Hudson," she drawls and moves closer. "Mick is lovely."

"Only you would be able to get that old grump to talk, Adeline Howard."

"He's lovely, had a hard life. But I don't really want to talk about Mick . . ."

"Aren't you tired, sweet girl?"

"Nope." The word pops off her lips. Those brown eyes light up, swallowing me whole. Her hands press to my coat before slipping inside it.

I crowd her into the side of the horse and take her hands in mine. They're cold. I rub the backs of them with my thumbs while I dip my head, mouth by her ear, breath brushing her neck. "We are gonna freeze out here . . . That tent is calling our name."

"I don't hear anything," she coos, arching into me.

Jesus, Addy.

My cock is stretching the small space it has in my Wranglers. Blood disappears from my brain, filling my head with nothing but the image of her naked in my house, against the wall. What I wouldn't do to be there right now. "You realize you are going to end up with frostbite being naked out here, right?"

"But this view and you naked would so be worth it, Huddy." She nips my ear, and her mouth travels down my neck.

"Addy," I growl.

She really will get frostbite. And that isn't something you want so far from medical help. I scoop her up and she squeals.

"Shhhh, you want to wake the old men?"

She giggles and nuzzles my neck. I walk us back to the tent and set her down on the blankets. When the zipper is thoroughly closed, I turn back to find Addy peeling off her clothes, one by one. Slowly.

I stand by the tent flaps, chest heaving. Cock rock hard. Hands curling, aching to touch her, to hold her. To make her say my name like a prayer.

But when I take a step toward her, she shakes her head and holds a finger to her lips.

Fuck.

She steps out of her jeans.

Unbuttons her shirt and lets it fall to the blankets.

Her thermal knitted undershirt, she tugs over her head and tosses aside.

In only her underwear, she stands with those *come here* eyes. So I take a step forward, and she shakes her head again, gaze dipping to my coat. I pull off my hat and toss it to the wayside. Boots follow next.

"Come on, Huddy. I have been thinking about you all damn day. Watching you working the cattle, you and Rocket. God, I was so damn wet."

My breath shallows out.

I unbuckle my belt and lose the jeans, standing in my button-down shirt and socks. A gorgeous smile claims her face and her breath is ragged. I run a hand through my hair and start on the top button. Addy appears in front of me, and her hands close over mine. "Let me."

Her fingers work the buttons, one at a time, slow, as her eyes hold mine. It's torture of the best possible kind. I raise a hand to touch her face and she bats it away. "Ah, no."

"You have no idea how much I wanna touch you right now."

Her lips part. "I have a pretty good idea."

When the last button is released, she slides my shirt off, revealing the t-shirt underneath. Her nails drag down my neck and over my chest, splaying out around my ribs and down to the hem of my shirt. A heartbeat later, it hits the blankets. And now I stand with the world's hardest erection in nothing but socks. I try again, one hand moving toward her hip. Swatting it away again, she whispers, "Nope, not yet."

I groan and she huffs a sweet laugh, dropping to her knees. She taps my foot and I lift it. Her fingers sweep the wool from my feet. One then the other. When both feet are unsheathed and I stand trembling, she rises to her feet, resting her hands on my shoulders.

I search her gaze. "Addy."

She pulls my mouth to hers and I am putty in her hands. I'm a man broken. Shattered into pieces that will never go back together the same way. Never.

She pulls me around, and I walk backward over the blankets to the center of the two-person tent. Pushing me down to sit, she straddles my lap. "Now, Huddy. Now you can touch. You can be mine for a little while."

I drop my mouth to her peaks, palms cupping each perfect, soft mound. She arches into me with a small moan. I don't even care if the men hear. Fuck, that just makes it better. Turns me on more. Her fingers push and pull through my hair. Heat melts in my core, spreading through my veins as she wriggles in my lap.

"God above, Adeline. You have me, I am yours."

Her head drops to mine, her mouth finding mine, and I deepen the kiss. She opens for me, and I savor everything she lets me have, my tongue inside her mouth, over her pretty pink lips. Hungry for any scrap she will give me.

"Hudson, please." She rises on her knees, and I line up my throbbing cock with her hot, wet center. Emotion claws at my heart and lungs, wringing out the last of my breath as she sinks onto me with a whimper. The sweetest fucking sound I will *ever* hear. I search her face. Her wrecked face. And I hang on every ragged breath that comes from her lips.

Wanting her to take her time to feel everything. To give her everything she wants. The bridge of my nose prickles and something burns behind my eyes. I tighten my grip, now on her hips. The ache in my chest turns hollow, and I gasp for air with a realization: I am so far gone, it's inconceivable. Adeline Howard has dusted off my hidden heart and claimed it for her own.

And she can't stay.

I can't let her give up everything for me.

I . . . can't.

Sweet Jesus, this one is gonna hurt.

She pulls up and my body shakes with every tiny move she makes. I nip her peaks, running my hands behind her neck and through her hair. Every stroke upward drags a moan from those elegant lips I can't take my eyes off. She arches her back and tightens around me.

"Huddy," she breathes, eyes closed, fingers digging into my shoulders as she comes. Her beautiful waves pull me from my trance and send me over that jagged edge right after her. Like I'm not already falling from the highest cliff known to man.

Fast.

Hard.

If I'm honest with myself, this started the day Charlie killed that snake and I kissed her in the tack room. It's the same feeling. And I don't have a chance in hell of getting out of this unscathed.

Wouldn't want to, even if I could.

Chapter Twenty-Four

ADDY

The descent down the mountain has been vastly and utterly understated. It's rugged, hard riding, and the cattle have to be continually pushed back to stop them from racing down the side of it. Foam drips from Rocket's mouth around the bit as Hudson spins him back to steady the mob for what seems like the thousandth time since we broke camp this morning.

Sergeant is faring a little better with us bringing up the tail like the previous days. But I can feel his steps shake a little every so often. My heart would break if something happened to him. So, I hold him back, take it even slower, and thank the heavens I'm the tail today.

Rocket is strung out. Hudson more so. Ned is trying to be helpful, shouting advice over the ruckus of the bellows, hooves, and branches snapping. Everything echoes through the mountain timber forest around us, amplifying the hustle, ratcheting up the tension all around.

Hudson is incredible.

Whoever says cowboys have laid-back lives is grossly naive. I am stressed for him. The herd is huge. The mountain is too steep.

When we finally come to a flatter spot on the mountainside, Hudson calls us to a stop. Rocket is sucking in huge breaths. His sides flare with every forced gulp of air. He needs a break, badly. I dismount, ignoring the pain that lances through my hips.

I make my way to where Hudson is walking him in a small circle, trying to get the horse's breathing under control as he wipes sweat from his forehead with his arm, hat in hand. It's freezing, and this man is sweating up a storm.

"You need to swap him out, Huddy."

His gaze snaps to mine.

"Let me take Rocket for the next few hours. You take Sergeant."

"You sure that's gonna be okay?"

"I'm more worried about Rocket than anything else."

"Sure, we'll break for a bit."

"Are you sure there isn't anything else I can do?"

"No, this is what it is. The descent is always the hardest part. We'll make it."

But his words aren't reflected in his worry-filled eyes. I know he is under pressure to bring every beast home.

Harry's orders. And the ranch needs the income. Nobody talks about it, but it is evident in everything that they do, every penny counts. Especially when they are in business with other people, such as Justin Morley.

I hope Harry knows what he's doing with that one. Morley is not what I would call a stand-up guy in any field. But Harry is nobody's fool. He's probably been waiting for the day he can afford to buy that shithead out. Wouldn't that be *something*.

Ned and his mare appear by my side. "She's doing good today. You have the magic touch, Miss Addy."

"Actually, I didn't find a stone bruise. Maybe it was a small rock or something under one of her shoes, but it worked its way out. Either way, there was no damage I could see."

Ned gives my arm a squeeze and walks off to sit on a log. It must be a hard job for the older men.

I pluck the canteen from the side of my saddle and suck down a few mouthfuls. I hold my water out to Hudson. "Drink."

He takes it and guzzles it, letting water spill and run down his throat, eyes closed. Butterflies take flight in my belly, and I can't keep my lips from turning up into a smile. God, this man. When he swallows, he wipes his jaw and hands me back the canteen. I touch his jaw and dot a kiss to his lips. "Relax, Huddy, you're brilliant at this."

He huffs a strangled laugh and shakes his head. "Tell that to Harry."

"Hudson," I whisper but he walks away, taking Sergeant's reins from my hands. I wrap my fingers around Rocket's reins where he let them swing and rub a hand up the gelding's face. "You're amazing, you know that, Rocket? Look at you two go." His breathing is a little slower. Walking him in another small circle, I wet his muzzle with my canteen. He laps at the water, and I drop my forehead to his cheek. "We'll take it steady for a while."

When Mick whistles, we are off again. With the stirrups adjusted to my length, I swing into Rocket's saddle. It's softer than mine. Worn to Hudson's seat. The gelding walks on as we follow the rear of the herd. I secure Mira's reins around the pommel, and she falls in beside Rocket. I make a point of rubbing his neck as we go, talking tenderly to him, hoping he settles from the pent-up state he was in before.

When a smaller beast straggles behind and wanders off to the west, I trot through the trees and head it back. Rocket negotiates the forest well and Mira is all but glued to his side. "Hup, hup." I wave my hand to the side, pushing it back into the mob. An ache settles in my hips.

Keeping a keen eye on the animals at the back of the herd, I'm always looking for stragglers. This roundup means everything to Hudson. Every beast makes it down this mountain. Period. Only another night until we are back to the rendezvous point. And I am looking forward to seeing Mack and Reed. Not to mention Louisa. And her cooking. It's worlds better than the rations we have been on.

But I wouldn't trade this experience for anything. It has me wondering if it would be plausible to take my vacation time and come and help on the ranch every roundup time. And then the thought that if I was visiting once a year, that would mean Hudson and I were no longer a thing. Are we even now? He is . . . His life is here.

Mine isn't.

At least, it isn't what I planned for myself. For my career. Working on cats and dogs day in, day out isn't where I wanted to be. And it's definitely not where my specialization lies. Another few head straggle over the timbered forest floor, and I push them back into the mob with Rocket's help. "What do you think, Rocket? What would you do, hey, boy?" I lean forward but pain shoots through my left hip and I sit back with a hiss.

His head dips with every steady, grueling step down the mountain, putting a whole new meaning to the word workhorse. I search the front of the mob to find that white Stetson bobbing in front of the cattle. It stills before sliding sideways and I watch in utter fascination as Sergeant works, cutting back and forth, holding the hairy cattle back every time one of them gets the idea to run ahead. He is precise and so quick. God, he must be so damn bored with my quaint riding sessions. Patience in spades, that sweet horse. Like his owner.

Stifling the ache in my chest, I search the timbers on

either side of me, making sure no herd member has been left behind. It will not be for lack of focus on my part that Hudson loses a single head of this mob.

Mick is yelling to Ned when I glance back to the noisy herd. A beast breaks away on Ned's side.

He flies off after it, weaving between the trees 'til he rounds it and herds it back. His mare is agile and alert. These working horses are as in their element as their riders. It's brilliant to witness. And I can tell, this life is something that would suck you in and hold you hostage. And men like Harry and Hudson wouldn't have it any other way.

Or maybe they never stood a chance.

The sun has reached her apex when we clear the tree line of the world's hardest mountainside and the rest of the mob, horses, and cowboys come into view. Ned whoops, throwing a hand up. Mick growls something that sounds like "about fucking time." One hand on my stiff, painful hip, I sway with Sergeant as he takes us down the last steep section. When we finally reach the flat, I sigh. Ned halts his horse as the mob reaches the bigger one and waits for me. "How you holding up, Miss Addy? Sergeant taking good care of you?"

I swallow, hoping he doesn't notice the heat in my cheeks from the pain in my lower back and both hips now.

"Your mare is doing so well. You're an amazing team, Ned."

He tilts his head, smiling. Apparently not missing the fact that I deflected his question at all. "We have been together a long time. When you spend this much time with someone, you can practically read each other's minds."

I smile back. I know that relationship between horse and rider, the intimate connection that time affords you both, well. I had it with Jewls. Hudson dismounts and hands Rocket over to Mack. He spins back and walks my way. I shift and my hips are locked up. Stiff beyond movement without pain.

Shit.

"Ready for a hot meal and a turn in the camp tub, Addy?" he says, beaming up at me. He takes his hat off and runs a hand through his hair. If I wasn't in pain, that alone would have me off this horse in a heartbeat. But I can't even lift my leg over. My joints are frozen. When I don't move from the saddle, he searches my face, his slackening with concern. "Addy?"

"Addy! I need you over by the main tent; Reed's horse needs seein' to," Harry barks.

We both flinch and snap our gazes to where he is striding toward us, all business.

"I—" I clench my teeth and try my right leg. Blinding

pain shoots up my hip and through my side. "Fuck." Tears burn behind my eyes.

"Now, please." But his tone is no less demanding.

Hudson takes a step forward, as if putting himself between Harry and me.

"What's going on?" Harry snaps.

"She will be there in a moment," Hudson says, but his voice lacks conviction. Will I be able to walk in a moment? Dismount? Oh god. This is beyond mortifying, painful, and plain fucking stupid.

"You have three minutes." Harry turns back and walks to where Louisa waits, arms folded over her chest, watching her husband. He stalks into the tent. Clearly, Harry is stressed out from the roundup. He has never spoken to me like that. His boys, sure, but never me. I don't have time to mull over it as Hudson turns back and comes to a halt at Sergeant's shoulder. "You can't get down, can you?"

I shake my head, and a tear streaks down my cheek.

"Jesus, Addy. How long have you been in pain?"

"Since yesterday morning. But it wasn't that bad. Not like it is now."

"Can I help you down? Would that work?"

I drop the reins and lean forward. Hudson grips my waist, lifting me from the saddle. I can't stop the cry that leaves my lips. His face contorts, worry turning to fear and desperation. He takes my hands. "Dammit, Addy."

I huff a strangled laugh and wipe my face with the back of my hands. "It's not your fault."

Reed and Mack walk from the tent to where I sit astride Sergeant. "Adds, what's going on?" Reed's face crinkles when his gaze meets Hudson's. "Oh shit."

"If you can't come down, Sergeant will have to do it for you, okay?" Hudson says softly.

Mack and Reed exchange a wide-eyed glance.

"Okay?" I whisper.

"You trust him, right?"

I nod. "Yes, of course."

"Good, hold onto the pommel. He's gonna sway a little but then you will be down, and I will lift you off, okay?"

"Alright." But my chin wobbles.

Mack appears at my side by Sergeant's other shoulder and holds up a hand. "Hold my hand, Addy, Hudson will need to hold the horse."

I take his hand, and he offers a small, warm smile. I feel tears burn again. Harry comes over, standing by Reed. The youngest of the brothers throws a warning glare the old man's way. If I wasn't in pain, I would have a chuckle at that. Hudson moves to Sergeant's head and takes the reins at the side of the bit. He drops to one knee and guides the horse's head down.

"Down, buddy," he says.

The gelding moves forward a little and he rocks as he drops, folding one front leg until his knee hits the grass, then the other. I whimper as the movement tenses the muscles in my core. Mack rests a hand on my leg. My grip around his hand tightens.

"Easy, boy." Hudson holds his head as the gelding lowers his haunches, coming to rest on the ground.

When the rocking stops, Mack drops his gaze to me. "You alright, Adds?"

I nod.

Hudson stands and moves to where I still sit, immobile. "I'm gonna lift you off, okay?

You tell me if you want to be carried or to be let down, once you're off."

"Uh-huh." I scramble for a deep breath. Trying to mentally prepare myself for what comes next. Hudson hugs me and leans his head against mine. "I've got you, sweet girl."

"I know," I breathe out on ragged breaths.

He wraps his arms around me, and he whispers, "Three, two, one . . ."

The moment my butt leaves the saddle I grind out a cry through gritted teeth as fire streaks through my stiffened joints. "Keep going," I choke out.

He pulls me up from the saddle, and my legs drag over the saddle and swing into his. I hold onto him for dear life. His throat works as he steps back from Sergeant. Mack clicks his tongue and Sergeant pushes back up and onto his feet, nickering and shaking his head, mane tossing about his neck.

"Down or carried, Addy?" Hudson asks.

"Down, I think."

He lowers me to the ground. Louisa walks over, wrapping an arm around Reed's shoulders, her face pulled with concern. When my feet hit the ground, my hips clunk, aching something fierce. I take a step and whimper.

"Nope." Hudson's arms have my feet off the ground and me huddled against him a heartbeat later. I rest my head on his coat, breathing through every lungful, desperate not to cry in front of Harry.

"There are animals that need tending to, vet care required." Harry steps forward despite the warning written all over Louisa's face.

Hudson grinds to a halt and turns back to face his father. "Fucking drop it, Harry."

"The whole point of her riding along was to tend to the needs of the horses and cattle. You have ten minutes to sort yourself out, Addy."

Hudson growls, then . . . "I'm sorry about this, sweet girl."

I glance between Harry and Hudson. Hudson lowers me to the ground and strides to where Harry stands. "Screw your fucking animals. Everything is about the bottom line with you!"

"Someone has to make sure this family is taken care of."

"Really? 'Cause from where I'm standin', you're more worried about your cattle and workhorses than an actual person right now," Hudson growls.

"You decide, then. Make a decision, Hudson. Because right now, you're not taking the reins on anything, just following orders, as always."

Always.

That word is always followed by never with Huddy and me.

"You know what? Here is a decision for you, Harry. Addy comes before your precious fucking herd."

Louisa fights to hold back a smile. Reed and Mack fist pump like absolute kids.

Harry's eyes narrow before he turns on his heel and walks away. Hudson stands, watching him leave, hands balled to fists, shoulders shaking.

God, Huddy.

Louisa moves to where I stand. "Hon, I have a hot bath that will fix those sore muscles and stiff joints of yours right up. Can you walk?"

Desperate to see Hudson's face, I nod, waiting for him to turn around. And when he finally turns back and closes the space between us, he is shaking. Hands cupping his face, I plant a kiss over his lips. "I'm so damn proud of you, Hudson Andrew Rawlins."

He groans and drops his forehead to mine, closing his eyes. "Then why do I feel like a complete ass?"

I chuckle and cup his jaw. His eyes find mine. "Nobody said decisions were easy, Huddy."

He forces a small smile and traces a finger over my cheek. "Bath time, smelly."

"Hey!" I slap his shoulder, and he picks me up and walks into the tent. Over his shoulders, I glance at Louisa. She winks at me before turning back to her husband who now stands, arms crossed, his expression unreadable.

What is going through your mind, Harry Rawlins?

I guess, in time, we will know.

Chapter Twenty-Five

HUDSON

I have never been happier to see the homestead come into view as I am now. On the home stretch, and what a week it has been. Addy rides beside me on Sergeant. She insisted. Saying that she wouldn't be a burden or a flake. Strongest fucking woman I have ever met. I think she is worried what Harry thinks, but I wish she wouldn't. Harry can go take a flying leap if you ask me. Not that anyone has.

Things have been oddly quiet in the Rawlins' camp since Addy was stuck on Sergeant and he had to go to ground for me to lift her off. I know Ma is quietly pleased that I finally stood up to the old man. But I can't help feeling that I have overstepped. And I am fully prepared for an ear chewing when we make it home and the dusts settles.

"What are you thinking, Huddy?"

God, when she calls me Huddy, I feel like a stupid teenager, all giddy and shit. Not a grown-ass man who will be thirty-five in a matter of months. Not a man running a ranch and building a house. A needy pup that hangs on her words, on every look she gives me. "Nothing much. Possibly the ass chewing Harry's gonna give me when we're back."

She laughs, throwing her head back.

I raise a brow. "How is that funny?"

"I would be more worried for Harry than you. Honestly, you were brilliant this week. Thoroughly impressed, cowboy." She smiles, big and wide, and so fucking beautiful.

"Huh . . . You did pretty good yourself."

"I really loved this. Being in the mountains and all. It was hard going but so satisfying. I understand why you love it here so much."

"Yeah."

That's all I can say. I have to bite my tongue. 'Cause what I want to say is that I wish she would stay if she likes it . . . loves it. But that is selfish, and not what she wants. So I return my focus to the homestead and dream about what a hot shower is gonna feel like after a week in the outdoors.

One bath in seven days doesn't cut it. Better than nothing, I guess. It was Addy's saving grace after her rough dismount. And I am glad Ma had it organized. God knows what we would have done without it.

The herd is noisy, funneling into the yards by the homestead. A few nights here and some work through the pound and they will be set out into the fields between here and my place. Close, so we can keep tabs on them during calving. *Every beast counts.* Harry's motto since the beginning of time, I suspect.

The men ride around the stragglers. Addy rides beside Ned, waving her arm and calling out sweet hup hups as she steers the last of the cattle through the double gates, her seat rising and falling back into the saddle as she paces along with Sergeant. She's a fucking natural at this. And, well, that burns a little.

When the last of the herd is safe inside the main yard, I ride through the herd, taking a last look. I check for any signs of injury. When none seem distressed, I walk Rocket to where Addy is chatting to Mick.

"Good-looking herd this year, Hudson," Harry says, trotting up to me.

"All accounted for."

"Are my eyes on the fritz, or is Addy actually getting conversation out of old Mick?"

I huff a laugh. "Has been for a few days now. You should give her a break, Harry. She more than earned her keep this week."

"I've never had a problem with her work or work ethic, son. But you haven't upheld my instructions where Addy's concerned."

I stare at him. What the hell am I supposed to say to that?

I hear the familiar yapping before the small streak of white makes it halfway across the yard. Charlie flies through the cattle toward us. Ma leans on the rail on the other side of the yard, a huge smile on her face. She would have heard him whimpering and felt sorry for him and let him out. He scoots between two cows, and one spins on him. The other kicks out.

Snap.

Charlie cries out, sliding on his side in the dirt in the center of the yard.

Fuck.

Sergeant lopes past me, with a distraught Addy. She reins the gelding to a sliding stop and the cattle scatter. She jumps down and hovers over Charlie. I swing out of the saddle and run to where she is kneeling between the herd of cattle, heads down, their sights on the dog. Mack trots over, ushering the mob away from us.

"He may have a broken leg," she says as I drop to my knees on the other side of Charlie. He's panting, whimpering every other breath. "Shhhh, little man. Stay here with him, will you, so I can grab some painkillers before we move him?"

I nod, and she takes everything in stride. A moment later, she is back in the dirt beside me, syringe in hand. She administers something into his skin by his shoulder and sweet-talks him. When she rocks back onto her heels and wipes her forehead, I can't keep my eyes off her.

"He will be numb in a moment and then we can move him into your truck and into the clinic."

"Sure thing."

Her brows are stuck down tight. "He'll need an X-ray, and then we'll go from there."

"Yup, tell me what you need me to do."

When Charlie has settled, I lift him from the ground, and Addy leads Sergeant back to where Harry and Reed stand watching us. Harry takes Sergeant's reins and walks the horses back to the barn. Addy pulls some gear from Mira, and we make our way to the truck. She holds the door open for me and I lay Charlie in the center on the bench seat. Addy hops in and I round the truck, jumping into the driver's seat. I fire her up and we head into town. Addy is quiet.

"You alright?" I ask.

"Yeah." But worry lines her face as she checks the pup every other minute.

"He'll be okay. He has a brilliant doctor."

Forcing a sad smile, she stares out the window.

The clinic is closed when we arrive, and Addy unlocks the doors as I carry in a very sleepy Charlie. She hits the lights, and we head to the X-ray room. She takes the picture while I wait outside.

When she walks back out, she holds up a tablet with

Charlie's images. "It's not too bad, only a cast and painkillers, thankfully."

"That's great. Do you do that now?"

"Yes, if you can help hold him still?"

"Anything you need."

Addy walks into a treatment room, and I follow her. Charlie is on the floor on a bulky blue blanket. Addy goes about pulling out supplies. She drops to her knees and clips away the hair on his injured leg before wrapping it up in a soft bandage. When the plaster comes out, she selects a navy color and gets to work. "Hold him still, Huddy."

"Sure."

When the cast is finished, she leans against the wall with a sigh. She looks exhausted. A week on a horse will do that to a person. Addy's phone buzzes on her desk. She ignores it.

"Talk to me, Addy."

She closes her eyes. "I'm just tired and really, really need a shower."

Her phone buzzes, inching closer to the edge of the desk, and she snatches it up and slides a finger over the screen. She rolls her eyes, muttering something that sounds a lot like "leave me alone" before locking the screen and tossing her phone onto the desk. If someone is harassing her . . .

"Addy, is everyth—"

"Hello?" Pa's voice comes from the waiting room.

Why is he here?

"Huddy?" Ma, too.

I push up and wander out to the waiting room. "What's going on?"

"We wanted to make sure you two were okay." Ma squeezes my arm.

"Addy back here?" Pa asks, already walking down the hall. I hear as she stands and says hello before explaining Charlie's injury.

"Walk with me, Huddy." Ma heads for the doors. *What on earth?*

I follow her out the doors and into the street lit with streetlights and shop fronts. She doesn't say anything for a block.

"I hope Charlie will be okay, I feel bad for letting him out."

"He'll be fine, Ma. What's with Harry?"

She smiles. "He has clinic stuff to talk about with Addy, that's all."

"Now?"

"Your father waits for no man, or woman, apparently."

"Do I need to be in there? Aren't I supposed to be taking over this sort of thing?"

"Let your father handle it; besides, both of you are exhausted."

"Yeah well, having to prove your mettle to Harry Rawlins is no easy feat."

She tilts her head, stopping on the sidewalk. I stop and meet her gaze.

"Who said you had to do that?"

"This roundup was supposed to be me showing Harry I could make decisions."

She laughs a little. "Coming from the yes-man himself. His father was the same. Always going on about him taking the reins instead of doing only what he was told. Old habits die hard, even when you know better."

"I would rather earn the ranch than have it handed to me, Ma."

"It was always yours, but he was right that we needed to make this roundup count. We have business financing to take care of and two more properties in escrow. One for Reed and one for Mack. But that pressure isn't yours, it's ours. Your father's and mine."

I huff a small incredulous laugh. Ma always has it figured out. Right now, she lives up to her endearment of captain.

"You and Addy should get some rest tonight. We will see you both for lunch Sunday."

"What about the herd?"

"Your brothers and your father have that under control. Take a moment for yourself—you earned it." She squeezes both of my arms and her smile wobbles, but she releases me and crooks her arm like Reed does. I wrap mine through hers and escort her back to the clinic. She waits outside for Pa while I go inside. Harry and Addy are still talking shop when I find them in the treatment room.

Harry stops talking as I lean on the doorframe and Addy yawns. This girl is good and worn out. Time to go home. "You two done?"

"I think so. Addy, catch you Sunday," Harry says and walks out of the clinic, the glass double doors swooshing behind him.

"Can I take you home?" I ask.

Addy closes the space between us and drops her forehead to my shoulder. "You can take both of us home. To your place, Huddy."

My gut flips in the best way possible. And when she pushes away and heads for the double doors, I scoop up Charlie and follow her to the truck. Charlie sleeps most of the way home and Addy checks him every fifteen minutes. She's a fucking awesome vet. Lewistown will be worse off without her. When we finally reach the house, I park and shut off the engine. Addy opens the door and slowly climbs out, as if her muscles are too sore to go any faster. My girl needs a hot shower. And a good rest.

I pick Charlie up and carry him inside, settling him by the fireplace. Addy appears by my side and smiles down at him. "He's content there."

"Don't go gettin' used to it, buddy. Once that leg is better, it's back to being a ranch dog."

"He's all talk, Charlie. He's really a big, big softie."

"Only with you." I wrap my arms around her waist and drag her backward. "Shower time, Doc."

Spinning in my arms, she pushes me toward the hallway. "Absolutely. You are filthy, Hudson Rawlins."

She plucks my buttons open as I walk backward to the shower. By the time we reach the bathroom, I'm naked, and she is still fully clothed. I cluck my tongue and she holds her arms above her head. I make quick work of her shirt, undershirt, and jeans and we slip into the steaming water.

Addy sighs as the water washes away a week's worth of dirt, sweat, and grime. I take up the soap and lather it over her body. She tilts her neck to the side and moans when my hands rub over her hips. They must be sore. Dammit.

Next, I squirt shampoo into my hand and massage it over her head. The moan that she makes sends my cock rock hard. But we are both far too exhausted to bother with anything else right now. I tug the shower hose down and rinse out the shampoo, repeating the process with the conditioner. The fragrant apple scent that reminds me of her is the one I chose when I stocked the bathroom before Ma's party.

When she is all washed and her hair is clean and hanging in tangled curls around her shoulders, she spins and takes the soap from the holder. Her hands glide over my tired muscles. My chest, arms, abs, legs, and then she moves and does my back. Her fingers crawl through my hair a moment later, lathering it with the apple shampoo.

This time I groan. She giggles behind me, but it disappears into another long yawn.

Once she's clean, dried, and comfy in one of my light blue t-shirts, I sweep Addy up and carry her to the bed. She doesn't protest, only rests her head against my shoulder, eyes closed. I'm pretty sure she is asleep before I even make it to the bedroom. I lay her down and pull the blankets over us. I have barely wrapped an arm around her soft body before sleep drags me under like a raging torrent.

I roll over as my phone vibrates by the bed.

Dawn's light splinters the dark outside.

It's Ma.

I slide to answer.

Huddy, the mares. It's started.

Chapter Twenty-Six

ADDY

Two petite hooves poke through toward us from the pliable opening of the mare on the ground. Foal number nine is moments away. Hudson is anxious. Like a doting first-time dad. It's the sweetest thing.

I chuckle as he pulls off his hat and runs a hand through his hair for the twelfth time in the last ten minutes. It's adorable, the way he worries for his mares. So far, so good—nine foals, and three to go. The hard ones, apparently.

"You always like this for the births?" I ask.

He stops dead and shakes his hands before shoving them into his back pockets. I smile and he bends down, lips brushing my ear. "Thank you for being here, Addy."

"It's my job, Huddy. But I wouldn't have missed this for the world."

Birthing a baby is hard on most mammals, but with horses and cows, the chance of prolapse and a breech birth is high. So, I take my time and monitor for any sign of distress or trouble.

But I'm distracted. My conversation with Harry has been twisting around in my mind since we left the clinic. Now, for the first time since I made my grand veterinary career plan all those years ago, I am weighing up the possibility of changing course. And twelve foaling mares is a handful for two vets, let alone solo, all going well. I am going to need help. I pull out my phone.

A missed call from Adam.

God, that is the last thing I need right now. I had five text messages and two missed calls when I got home from the roundup. All asking if I'm alright, and can he visit. I don't even want to consider that possibility.

But if I'm being honest, his skill and expertise wouldn't be unwelcome right now. I am wholly in over my head with a dozen foaling mares all in labor at once. And the man is a brilliant vet and has a knack with horses that most don't. The one and only thing he has in common with Hudson.

I tap out a message to Justin, asking for his help. He replies straight away.

> Off duty doing paperwork, but I will send someone soon.

Great. Just great. He couldn't care less, that guy.

I dump my phone onto my bag and push to my feet. With a minute between contractions, I check the other mares, one by one. All twelve of them in the barn. It's better than being out in the cold and haze of snow that has started falling.

The bag vibrates. No, my phone is ringing.

Justin.

I swipe it up from the bag on my way past to check Vanity, two stalls down.

"Justin, I really need a hand here."

"Hello to you too, Adeline. I can't be out there today. Would a nurse be enou—"

Something bangs in the background where he is. Is he at the clinic?

"Sorry, someone is pounding at the front doors. All the locals know we are closed Sunday. Must be some out of towner. Call you back in a sec."

Beep, beep, beep.

Fuck.

Even a nurse would be okay, if that's all he can spare today. If this is one of his plays to set me up for trouble, I am not taking this one lying down. These are Hudson's mares we are talking about. The phone buzzes in my hand.

Sending someone out now.

Thanks.

I have no idea why I'm still polite to that giant donkey's ass—my parents' civilized ways imprinted on me, no doubt. Hudson is talking to a mare in the stall. When I hear him shift in the hay, he calls out, "Addy!"

I fly into the stall. Two feet, legs, and a slick head spill from Vanity. She groans, rocking as the contractions take her hostage and the foal slips from her. Hudson clears away from her, still talking to the mama mare. A bay foal scrambles to his feet and face-plants in the straw. I chuckle and Hudson slips through the stall door and shuts it before leaning on it. I check Vanity over, making sure there is no excessive bleeding and her vitals are stable. I rub her face as she looks around for her foal. "Well done, Mama."

Hudson's gaze follows the foal before tracking to me. The broad smile on his happy face is everything. The afterbirth hangs when Vanity finally stands and starts to clean her baby. I wait, making sure it falls away.

When I walk toward the stall half door, Hudson lets me out. "She did so good."

"Always does. It's Whimsy we need to watch," he says, and we track to the mare's stall. She's weaving against the barn's half door when we reach her.

Shit—she's distressed.

"Hold her head, Huddy. I need to check her."

I run a hand down her neck and over her back and rump as I move to check her over. She swishes her tail urgently, and I try to hold it aside to check on her progress. I pull a long glove from my back pocket and stand close as I slip a hand in to check the foal's position. When my fingers find a little rump instead of a nose and feet, my stomach plummets. She's breech. Dammit.

This far into the labor, turning the foal is almost impossible. "This one is gonna hurt, Mama."

"She's breech?"

"Yeah. I can't turn the foal, either."

I pull my arm out as another contraction starts. Poor Whimsy, I can't imagine how painful that must be. Peeling the glove from my hand, I slip out the barn door. I could really use that backup right about now.

I wander back to the bags and double-check I have everything I need to stitch her up after a bad delivery or to make the delivery easier. When I have organized everything I will need for whichever way this turns out, I do another round of checks on each mare.

Louisa walks into the barn carrying a tray of steaming mugs and a plate of something. "Thought you two could use something warm."

"Thanks, Ma," Hudson says, taking the mugs from the tray and handing me one. I wrap my hands around the hot cocoa and sip it. It travels all the way down to my stomach. Mmmm.

"Thank you, Louisa. We needed that; it's going to be a long day, and most likely a long night."

"Oh?"

"Whimsy, again," Hudson offers.

"Every year without fail, that poor girl. Next year she gets a break, Hudson. There is only so much a woman can take."

Hudson chuckles and nods, sipping the cocoa. But the humor slips from his face when his eyes meet mine. I'm not happy that she is breech and there are only the two of us. Far from it. I finish the cocoa and replace it on the tray. Louisa leaves with the tray but insists on leaving the cookies behind. I set them down on the bales of hay and head to check the first of the foals.

He is getting cleaned still when I lean over the barn door, and I take in the beauty of Mother Nature's design for a moment. A low whinny, followed by thumping hooves, breaks me from my short respite. I turn to track the sound. Whimsy. She whinnies before dropping to the floor of her stall. God, here goes.

Hudson beats me to the stall and has the door flung open and is by her side a heartbeat later. I round her rump and move her flicking tail away the best I can. The foal is close. His rump appears with every contraction but sinks back down. *Damn it, where is our help?* I rush back to the bags and decide to pluck up both before running back to her stall.

I fling it open, snatching up a syringe, a numbing agent, and a scalpel. I draw up the medicine and inject it into the area I intend to cut. After waiting two minutes, I make a cut to widen the foal's exit. We wait for the next push. Whimsy groans, her head nodding up and down against the bed of hay she lies on.

When the foal edges closer to the exit again, I don a glove and take his tail in my hand before he can slip back again. I pull as Whimsy pushes. The contraction is huge. His little rump clears the exit and stays when the contraction stops. *Good. Good work, Mama.* The skin around the exit starts to blanch, over stretched. Whimsy is panting hard. Only the section where I cut is numbed. Everything else must be so painful right now.

Tires on the slushy gravel drive outside the barn track closer and stop, and I look to Hudson.

"Must be your help, Addy."

"Good. I'll take anything at this point."

Another contraction, and Hudson strokes her face as I tug on the foal's tail. He slips out past his hips as the contraction ends.

"Hello? Help is here, Addy girl."

Hands tight on the foal's tail, I freeze.

The familiar voice.

The very *British* accent.

Hudson raises an eyebrow and wire twists in my belly, my breaths shortening. I force my eyes shut for a heartbeat, sucking in a long lungful of air.

This is not about me.

He is here to help with Huddy's mares.

"In here, Adam," I call out.

"Marco!"

Hudson's face has slackened. His eyes burn into mine.

"P-Polo," I force out. When Adam comes to fill the stall doorway, he is loaded up with medical bags. His neat, gelled brown hair is fixed as it always is, to the side. His blue eyes are lit with excitement, his crooked smile pushing the happiness around his face the way it always has.

He is wearing loafers, Calvin Klein jeans, a button-down shirt, and a vest that probably cost more than my phone. He is immaculate and put together, as always. Hudson glances between the two of us. He has disheveled hair, a muddy and bloodied t-shirt tight over his chest that has ridden up over his wrangler-clad hips. His cowboy boots are covered in muck. And the contrast between the two is staggering.

Whimsy, ignorant of the tension that landed like freshly poured cement throughout her stall, groans as she contracts again. I snap my attention back to the foal in my hands and pull with everything I have. This time, it's a big one, and the foal shoots out. He slips from his mother and onto me, and I fall backward with his rump squarely on my stomach. Afterbirth, fluid, and blood soak into my shirt.

I move him to the side as he starts to flail around and stand. Hands hanging by my sides, hair in my face and covered in muck, I stand staring at the man who broke my heart more times than I can count. And the only emotion I feel is relief. Thank god he is here. Because I cannot let *anything* happen to Huddy's mares.

Hudson stands and holds out a hand, but his jaw clenches. Adam glances down to it before shaking it tentatively. "You look happy, Adeline. But then again, you always were happiest playing around in the muck and dirt."

I open my mouth to say something, but Hudson ushers him out of the stall. Snapping from my daze, I drop down by Whimsy's head and rest a hand on her chest. Taking the stethoscope from the bag by the door, I check her heart rate and breathing. I will have to stitch up that cut. But when I turn back to gather the gear, Adam walks in, sleeves rolled up and vest off. "I can stitch her, Addy. I think your friend needs your help with another mare, three stalls down."

"What are you doing here?" I utter.

"You didn't answer your phone. I got worried. So, I came out to make sure you were alright."

"But why are you *here*, here?"

"Your boss said you needed a hand. I told him I was the best equine vet for the job. Literally. So, he gave me the directions. Lucky I got here when I did, baby."

"Don't call me that."

"Oh, come on, Addy girl."

"Nope, no Addy girl. Just Addy. The only thing I need you here for is to keep these mares and their babies safe. End of story."

He throws his hands up as if to say *don't shoot.* "Okay, if you insist. Here to work. Now, off you go and let me fix this poor girl up."

"Fine." I grab up one of the bags and walk three stalls down, torn between hating Adam right now and being desperate for his help. Hudson is leaning on the side of the stall three doors down, chewing a piece of straw. And when his blue eyes find mine, they are consumed with concern.

"I'm sorry, I didn't know he was coming."

"It's alright, Addy. You said we needed help. Here it is."

"At least he is a brilliant vet. I'll give him that."

When I'm inside the stall, Hudson pulls me into his arms and drops his head into my hair.

"God, Huddy, I'm filthy. You don't have to."

"I also need a long, hot shower, sweet girl." But the last two words fade out a little. When the mare behind us starts pacing, we uncouple. She twitches, pawing the ground as Hudson clips a lead to her halter. Something's not right. Plucking the charts from the bag, I flick through them until I find Cherry's.

Healthy heartbeat, size was a little small, but the last ultrasound was fine. A bit hazy and all legs but . . . I snap the images out from last time. And then I see it. Six legs, not four . . . No, is that? Eight! How the hell did I miss twins!? Fucking hell.

"Shit."

"What is it?"

I look up at Hudson and he reads my face, rushing to my side to grip the folder and scan the page.

"Twins. I have no idea how I missed it. She should be in the clinic. I should have monitored her better."

"It's fine. We deliver them one by one like human babies, right?"

"Actually," Adam says from outside the stall. "The odds of both twins being viable in horses are much less than in humans."

"Jesus." Hudson pinches his nose, slamming his eyes shut. "And what about Cherry? Will she make it through this?"

"She has Addy and I; of course she will." He is so confident. Cocky. But he backs it up by helping work her over while Hudson stands outside. We run a baseline set of vitals between contractions. Make a plan and a backup plan. Plan A – deliver each foal naturally, one after the other. Plan B – Cherry isn't coping or one of the foals goes into distress, then we deliver them by caesarean.

Working with Adam is like clockwork. Everything is routine. Automatic. We are so used to working together that we easily fall into the roles we had for four years in the clinic together. I stand and walk to the barn door and fill Hudson in. He nods and steps back. He stares at Adam, then drags his gaze back to me. "Can you two do all that here?"

"Yes. Ideally, she would be in a clinic environment, but this will suffice."

When Cherry starts kicking her belly with her back foot and her tail is switching erratically, we know it's time to intervene. She isn't instinctually laying down. As if she knows something is wrong.

When I do another internal assessment, I find out why. The first foal is tangled with the second. There will be no Plan A. No clean birth followed by another. They must have shared the same sack. Dammit.

Hudson paces outside the stall.

"Plan B, Adam. It's a TTTS and . . . Tangled babies."

"Shit, okay. Twin-to-twin transfusion is rare. I'm surprised she made it to term at all . . . I'll prep the gear. You get her ready."

Seeing Adam flustered is rare, and I stare at him for a heartbeat before glancing at Hudson. We cannot lose either of these foals. I am kicking myself for not noticing the twins on one of the other visits. Internal exams only ever felt like two feet and a muzzle, and I guess the second foal was underneath at that point in time. Now, however they are so entwined there is no way she can birth them naturally.

I clean Cherry the best I can with the surgical wash and draw the incision line on her belly. When Adam has the anesthesia set up and my instruments laid out, I call Hudson over. "Hudson, can you help Cherry down when she gets dozy?"

He is by her head in a heartbeat, talking to her. He's nervous, glancing between Adam and me every few minutes.

"It'll be okay. She will be okay," I say when he glances at me.

I slip a gown over my mucky clothes and scrub my hands in the bowl full of antiseptic solution as I would in the clinic before surgery. Adam does the same, and when he secures a cannula and administers the drug into Cherry's vein, it is only minutes before she sways on her feet.

Hudson guides her down, as he did with Sergeant when I was stuck. Something aches in my chest at that memory. Once Cherry is on her side and Adam has her set up with a manual breathing apparatus, I clean her belly again with the solution before making the long incision.

Thirty minutes later, two small foals are huddled tight in the straw on the opposite side of the stall. And we have a crowd. Mack, Reed, Harry, and Louisa lean over the stall's half wall, watching as Adam runs vitals on the twins and I stitch Cherry up.

"Well, that's a first for Rosewood Ranch," Louisa says brightly.

I tie off the last stitch and clean up the site one last time before pushing to my feet. Hudson is still by Cherry's head, manually feeding her oxygen with the pump. I come to her head and rest a hand over his. He stops the pump.

I wait, making certain Cherry is breathing on her own.

When she takes her own breaths, coming out of the anesthesia, I pull the gear away from her and drop a hand to Hudson.

He looks up at me, but his gaze is far away as he stands. "Thank you."

"Always, Huddy."

He slips out of the stall and walks out of the barn.

My stomach plummets.

No doubt he is angry I missed the twins. I missed the second foal. It turned out okay in the end, thirteen foals instead of twelve.

Louisa watches him go and then turns back, glancing between Adam and me.

Jesus.

When Adam is done with the foals, he turns back, peeling off the gloves and gown. He pulls off the hat and mask and walks over to shake Harry's hand, as if he was the one who pulled off thirteen foals in twenty-four hours. Always so cocky. Must go with the hair.

"Adam Hervey. Lovely to meet you." He smiles at Louisa, and she shakes her head.

"Are you one of Justin's vets?" She glances to Harry. The old man's face is pulled tight.

"No, actually, I work at the equine clinic in New York. Only visiting. I'm Addy's boyfriend."

Louisa's shocked face finds mine.

Air lodges in my lungs like a stone.

Chapter Twenty-Seven

HUDSON

I lean against the side of the barn in the falling snow, letting it drift onto my shoulders, into my hair. I can't feel a thing.

"What the hell?" Reed grinds out from inside where he and the rest of my family stand, witnessing the downfall of any slim chance Addy and I ever had.

Mack stalks out of the barn and turns on me. We stand in the falling, powdery snow, listening to the conversation inside.

"You are *not* my boyfriend, Adam." Addy's voice is strained.

"Well, you know what I mean. When you're not gallivanting around the countryside having a quarter-life crisis, or whatever this is."

Reed appears through the doors next. "Did you know about this guy?"

"I know he is her ex, and he's been harassing her, messaging and calling."

"Seriously, does she need our help then?" Mack pushes off the wall ready to go in guns blazing to Addy's rescue. Always the hero, my little brother.

But all I can feel is devastation after watching her and Adam work together. He is more her type. Seeing the way they worked in unison like clockwork, refined and automatic. I know that comes with time spent together. And if Addy is to have a great career as an equine vet, he is the type she should be with. Not *him*. But someone like him. Someone with the same ambition and field of work. Someone who is already living the life she wants.

Not this.

Not me.

I can't be the reason she doesn't have a shot at her dreams.

I won't.

"Why are you out here, if he is in there with her?" Mack snaps.

I swallow past the lump in my throat. "Watch the mares for a while will ya, you two? I have to get outta here for a bit."

I track to the truck and start it up. As I pull away, Addy flies through the barn doors, hands in her hair. Hurt twists her face, and I tell myself this is for the best. We both knew our time was limited. At least now, we can both go our separate ways. I force my gaze to the road. White covers everything, and the wheel tracks that make up our dirt road blur as I stifle the sobs that claw up my throat.

I drive slow, not caring about the cold that is seeping into my bones deeper with every minute that passes. Reed said if you love something you should set it free. Wise ass. Regurgitating goddamn clichés like he's Gandhi or some shit. But now, that phrase is too fucking raw. Addy deserves the life and career she wants, that she dreams of. After all she has been through, it is the least life owes her. So, that is exactly what I am going to do.

Let her go.

That's my decision.

When my newly lit-up house comes into view, I'm so glad to have power. The house is so close to being done. And the irony of my house finally being a home as the love of my life walks away is not lost on me. Not one iota. I will be the world's most magnificently housed king of broken hearts to ever live. I might be in goddamned agony, but I will do it in my ranch homestead, refined rustic style.

I park by the steps and kill the engine. I let my head hit the steering wheel and breathe through the ache in my chest. It's like a fire I can't put out, because every breath has turned too shallow, and I couldn't even if I wanted to. Pushing off the cold plastic, I slam a hand into the wheel.

Fucking hell, Hudson.

I open the door and walk up the stairs and inside. The

house is cold. Funny, my heart feels the same right now. I toss timber into the fireplace and shove kindling under it, lighting it with a match. I could drag the mattress out here so I don't freeze. But before I have the chance to mull that life choice over, a vehicle rolls up the drive and comes to a stop beside my truck. Reed's truck.

Addy jumps out and runs up the stairs. But she stops short when her gaze finds mine. "Huddy?" she whispers.

I shake my head.

"Please, I . . . He's not—" She strangles a cry.

My heart cracks.

"It's alright, Adeline. It's better this way. You can check on the mares in a few days if you want. Or not. I've handled it all before."

She steps forward, her hand raised like she wants to touch me, but drops it when I don't respond.

"Go home, Adeline."

"What? Hudson, no . . ."

"Harry was right; we shouldn't have got involved."

Her face buckles with devastation. "Because you always do what your father says."

"This here is exactly why. He was right when he told me not to—"

She folds her arms across her chest. "Harry told you to stay away from me?"

My eyes fall shut.

"Hudson?"

"Yes," I breathe.

She huffs a breath. "Oh."

"Addy, I had no intention of following that particular order."

"Why not?"

I open my eyes. "What d'you mean?"

"I mean, I'm leaving in a few weeks. Harry was right." Her words are sharp.

And they fucking hurt.

"You can't be serious, Addy?" Every syllable burns up my throat. But it's the truth—she's leaving. She won't have a job after the contract. There is no way Justin is going to sign off on an extension—he fucking hates me, and she barely tolerates him. "It was because I am taking over the ranch and the business. That includes the clinic. I never wanted to be your boss. And being involved would have complicated things."

"Well, I don't want to be some city girl who strung you along and broke your heart."

I stare at her stunned for a heartbeat. She thinks this was all some defensive move? What the hell? How fucking good has that douchebag worked her over that she thinks all this is some fancy charade to blow her off? And am I okay with her going back to the city with him? No. Definitely not. But here with me is not her best option, either. She should have better choices than a ranch life and no career to speak of.

"Right," I utter.

"So, this is it. Your roundup is over, you have your foals. I'm supposed to leave like nothing happened here?"

I can't say what I want to . . . Just can't.

"You probably should."

Her chin wobbles but she nods. "I'll be back in a week to take out Charlie's stitches and check the mares and foals. Text me if anything comes up."

I nod and stare at the fireplace. If I look at her, I'm gonna lose it. Most likely beg her to stay, and I'm not a begging man. Won't make a scene. She deserves better.

"Good night, Rawlins."

I grind my jaw shut. Fuck. Why does that hurt like nothing else?

She turns and heads for the door. When she crosses the threshold, she glances over her shoulder. Silver lines her eyes.

Jesus Christ.

I'm a fucking asshole.

But it's for the best. And Adeline Howard deserves nothing less. When Reed's truck door slams and he pulls away from the house, I take in this big old house that I'm gonna have to knock around in by myself. I watch my heart leave in my brother's truck. And I am never getting it back.

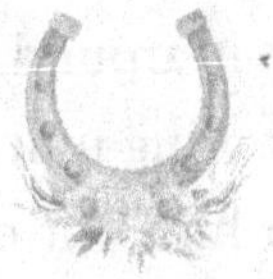

Charlie wags his tail so hard, I swear that furry little butt will pop right off. Addy walks up the steps and her gaze finds him straight away. He huddles into her lap when she kneels on the porch and extends her arms to him. His little heart will be shattered on the ground next to mine when he realizes she ain't coming back after this visit.

Addy doesn't look at me . . . That's how I know this is over.

I set my face in stone and walk back into the house. I can't be around her right now. Or I'll say something fucking stupid, like *stay*. If the last seven days have been anything to go off, after this visit and she is out of my life forever, I suspect simply breathing in the mountain air is goin' to be painful.

I busy myself with the kitchen install. The cupboards, sink insert, and stone countertop lie around the living room floor. I slide another cabinet into place and screw the batons in the wall. It's the design Addy drew up, with the finish that I have imagined since I started this project.

Now the heart of my home is now tied to her. Fitting. Another blow. I close the doors and stand up before setting the drill down. The counter section with the sink goes next. I manhandle it into position by the cupboard. I put in place and shuffle it around until it is flush against the back wall and neighboring unit.

"He's all good. Keep him out of the mud and the like so the site doesn't get infected." I turn back. She is studying the kitchen progress and a small, sad smile blooms over her sweet lips. Most likely she has figured out the design is hers. The layout is exactly the same. "I like your choice of finish. It suits the house." Her words are weak, and she tucks her hair behind her ear, breaking eye contact.

"Charlie's alright, then?"

"Yeah," she whispers. She rocks on her feet, looking like she wants to say something else.

And when the silence doesn't end, I say, "Reed's probably waiting. See you around, Addy."

"Sure, see you around."

She turns on her heel and walks out the door. When the car door closes, I turn back to my work, flinging the new doors open on the sink unit, grabbing up a bunch of screws to secure it to the wall. The front door opens, and I freeze.

"What the hell is wrong with you, Huddo?"

"Leave it alone, Reed," I say from the depths of the cupboard, drilling in a screw and then the next.

"Nope, no can do. Why are you doing this? Letting her leave, for fuck's sake?"

I inhale and blow out the breath. The ache in my chest that appeared the second Addy walked up the steps intensifies.

"You can't seriously be okay with her leaving and going back to that Adam guy?"

"Addy's a smart girl. She's not going to go back to him." I back out of the cupboard and push to my feet. "She is going back to her life, Reed. Her career. Adam isn't a factor. That much I know."

"And what about you? What do you get?"

I glare at him.

I get the ranch.

I get "the empire," as Morley put it.

I get nothing.

Absolutely fucking nothing. I swallow, my throat almost closed with emotion.

"Huddo, I know you. I know her. This"—he waves his hands wildly between me and his truck—"is not what either of you want!"

"What I want doesn't matter, Reed! *Addy* matters. And what she needs is to get the hell out of dodge before she loses everything she has ever dreamed of and gets *stuck* here. End of story. Now get out of my house."

"You're one stubborn motherfucker, you know that, right?"

He spins on his heel and walks out, shaking his head. But when his truck pulls away, all I can do is stare at the floor. I always knew Addy was mine. But I never thought letting her go would be this goddamn hard.

I move the next cupboard into place. But my head is

fuzzy, too big, the air too thin. A vice tightens around my heart. Staggering through a handful of breaths, I grip the side of the unit. I turn and slide down the unit and rest my head back on the smooth finish before slamming the heels of my palms over my eyelids.

Her stunning brown eyes are all I see. And the hurt that lanced through them.

What the fuck have I done?

Chapter Twenty-Eight

ADDY

Justin stares at me. "No."

"Fine, can I at least finish out the week?"

"Fine, but no more equine visits. Only in-house clients."

I have no idea what the hell he is playing at, but my contract isn't up for another week and a half. And now he wants me gone early? Did Harry have something to do with this? Did Adam showing up make them think that I was dishonest with Hudson?

Because I told him everything about Adam and me. And that Adam and I have been over since before I came here is a fact Hudson is well aware of. It is also not like him to cause drama or share personal information with other people, especially the likes of Justin Morley. He barely tolerates him.

"Can I ask why?"

"Why what?"

"Why do you want me gone before my contract is up? I don't understand."

"It's not me who wants you gone, it's New York who wants you back, Adeline. I got an email from the guy who runs the equine clinic you were working at before you came here. For god knows what reason, they are desperate to have you back."

"Oh," is all I can say.

Joe emailed? That's unlike him. He was onboard with my *garnering experience* plan. Unless . . .

Adam.

He would have been in his ear about this. Sweet-talking him. He probably told him I was flailing, not coping. That absolute fucking asshole. This is not the first time he has done something like this. Why does he always do this? Always swinging in like a wrecking ball to anything good in my life.

This time I am not standing for his bullshit. He thinks he can manipulate me into coming home and straight back to him. Since I have been so caught up in the roundup and other priorities, mainly Hudson, I haven't fleshed out any job opportunities after Lewistown. I could take Joe up on his offer, for six months at least, until I can find another contract somewhere.

"I have a nine o'clock," I say and walk out of his office and to my treatment room. A little old lady, greyed hair and light green cardigan over a pale-pink dress stands with a cage housing a cat.

"Morning, Mrs. Johnson. What's Felix up to today, hey?"

"Well last night, he was acting strange and this morning he threw up everywhere in the kitchen . . ."

I listen as she recounts Felix's last twenty-four hours as I coax him out of his cage. But I'm not even listening. Not really. Everything is out of whack.

Like I have changed irreparably.

Everything I thought I knew about myself, my world, and my place in it has shifted. I feel unhinged and less certain.

I know where my anchor is.

In a half-built house on a ranch that is the first time I have felt at home and alive in over a decade.

"Dear . . ."

The word is muffled, the sounds only just audible.

"Dear? Are you alright?"

Mrs. Johnson's hand blurs in front of my face. She waves it side to side.

I stutter through a burning breath.

Tears burn my eyes. "Not really," I utter.

"Maybe you should sit down, sweetheart?"

A fine, papery-thin hand guides me to the rolling office chair by my desk.

"I'm sorry."

"I'll find Sally."

"No, please, I'm fine. I . . . I—"

She peeks back to her cat, now roaming the small treatment room like a tourist. "You know what, I think Felix ate one too many lizards. I am sure he will be fine."

"No, I will check him out, give me a moment."

"Oh honey, I know that face." She offers a sad smile and pats my hand.

I work my way through a handful of deep, steady breaths. "What do I do about it?"

"There is only one choice. You follow your heart, no matter the risk."

I huff out a strangled laugh. "I was afraid you would say that. And that's not an option."

"Then time and distance always help." She gives me her best condolence face. I push from the chair and scoop up Felix. I feel his belly. It's soft and pliable. No obvious hard lumps or anomalies. I check down his throat, listen to his heart and lungs. A little on the thin side, but he is fit as a fiddle. Will most likely outlive his owner.

"Felix is fine. You were probably right, one too many lizards. Some more food, a little more if you can. And he should be fine."

I steer Felix back into his cage and secure it tight. "Well, I guess this is goodbye. I won't see you before I leave next week. It has been lovely getting to know you and Felix."

She presses a thin hand to my cheek. "You are a gem. We're sorry to see you go, sweet girl."

The smile falls from my face. My gut twists, sending pangs through my chest. Oh, fantastic—every other thing now reminds me of Hudson. The man who gave me back half of my life. The half that I thought I'd lost for over eight years. The part of me that lived and breathed in my soul. The part that felt like joy and freedom bundled into one.

Every time I look at a horse, swing into the saddle, it will be bittersweet. And that is going to be one hell of a problem for this equine vet. I walk Mrs. Johnson out to reception, and she waves goodbye. When I turn back, Sally is standing in my way. "Another appointment?"

"In the spare treatment room. He's waiting for you."

My heart thunders and I walk around her. Sally's gaze tracks me, and I have to shake out my trembling hands. But when I open the door, my gut plummets. No Hudson.

Harry.

I close the door and lean against it, bottom lip between my teeth. When he turns back, it is all I can do to steady each burning breath and hold back the burn of tears that prickle the bridge of my nose.

"Addy, still here."

I release a breath. "Yep. I have 'til the end of the week."

"Have you thought about the offer I made you?"

"I didn't think that would still apply after the foaling."

"Why would you think that?"

"I missed the twins on the lead-up examinations. And Hudson—"

Harry holds up a hand.

I wait for the reprimand.

"You know, I have been working alongside equine vets for over twenty years. And in all that time, you are the first to own up to a mistake and to correct it. With a successful outcome, I may add. That takes skill, knowledge, and a whole lot of gumption. I'm impressed, not annoyed."

I don't know what to say.

"Hudson—he's a stubborn, strong man. But he does what he thinks is right for his family. Always."

I suck in a breath on that last word.

Did we subconsciously pick up our *always* and *never* from Louisa and Harry? Hudson, my ship. Me, his captain? No, he told me to leave. So, he can what? Sail aimlessly, lost at sea. Find another captain . . .

What?

"My son has it in his head that he will never be good enough. For the ranch. For the people he loves. It's why I challenge him every day, why I spent the last four years trying to get him to take the lead. He is beyond capable and a better horseman than I will ever be. But he is missing one thing. The one thing that is the makings of every man. And when the two of you figure it out . . . However long that takes, or if you ever do. My offer, the business partnership that we spoke about for the mobile equine veterinary clinic, will be there. That particular demand in this area is never going to dry up."

All I can do is nod. Louisa was right. Harry is up front, he is honest, and he knows what his family needs. I stifle a chuckle. Usually, he knows before they know themselves. And having my own practice is my end goal, what I've always wanted. But he is missing one crucial part. Hudson doesn't want me to stay. It doesn't matter if he needs me; he doesn't want me. A stark contrast to Adam, who always wanted me but never needed me.

The way I see it, by telling me to leave, he gave me two choices . . . To live a career life and dive headfirst into what I love doing by following my plan of accumulating experience all over the horse industry. Or to return to New York and hone my surgical skills. Back to the life I had before this.

Nowhere in those choices was the word *stay*. Or the idea that we could build a life together.

"Actually, I am going back to the clinic in New York. They have requested I return, so I will take them up on their offer."

"I see. Well, if things don't work out, please know you have a place here. At least within our community."

A consolation prize.

"Thanks, but I don't—"

Harry closes the distance between us, and I see every feature of his that he gave his son. His brilliant blue eyes, his defined square jaw, and his brown hair that has started to thin, unlike his son's. He pulls me into a hug, and I clench my jaw tight to fight back the tears. "Never say never, Adeline. Life will laugh in your face and give you what you least expected but *always* what you need."

God, now I know where Reed gets his philosophy lines from. I huff a laugh, and he releases me. His blue eyes search mine. "You are always welcome in our family. Bye, Addy."

"Bye," I whisper, but he walks out the door and closes it behind him.

After the last box of things I own is squeezed into the back, I slam the trunk shut and walk to the driver's side door. With a last glance at the townhouse that has been my home for the past six months, I drop into the seat and pull the door closed. I start the engine. As I shift the car into drive, Reed's black truck wheels around the corner at an alarming rate.

Butterflies explode in my belly. And . . . Then they fizzle out as I recognize Mack in the passenger's seat. They park across the driveway, blocking me in, and spill from the truck. I push out of my car and Mack has me in a rough hug a heartbeat later. "You were gonna leave without saying goodbye, Adds?"

I huff a strangled laugh past my swollen windpipe. And he releases me and dips his head. "Bye, Addy. Know you will be sorely missed. Ma says see ya later, *her words*."

Reed steps into my space and hugs me around the waist, lifting me off my feet. "See ya later," he whispers. I stifle a sob and slam my eyes shut to stave off the burn of tears.

When my feet hit the ground, I have to wipe my face, and Mack tousles my hair with a hand. "Safe travels, Adds."

"Thanks."

Reed stares at me for a moment as his brother gets back in the truck. "I know Hudson can be a stubborn ass—"

"Is he—is he okay, Reed?"

"He went out on Rocket this morning, early. Haven't seen him since."

"Oh."

"You know where to find us . . . You know, when we *see you later*." He winks and dots a kiss to my cheek before jogging back to his truck. My hands gravitate to my chest, shaking over the pounding heartbeat. When Reed's truck roars back around the corner, the horn beeping like a loon, I huff a breathy chuckle. God, I will miss those two.

I slip back into my car and shut the door. Forehead hitting the wheel, I moan. I can do this. I can move on to my next chapter.

I set my shoulders back and put the car in drive.

My phone buzzes.

Ruby.

Turning onto the street, I let the car roll to a stop at the lights. Everything seems to shrink around me. And by the time I pass the city limits heading east, tears stream down my cheeks, dropping onto my jeans. Now I need to get out of here.

I smash the power button for the music and the last channel I had tuned in blares some slow country song. I bawl, letting the road in front of me blur. Sobbing hard, I chug for breath and have to pull over.

I've never felt this distraught over a guy. But Hudson is not *some guy*. He was so much more to me. He touched every facet of my life. Of my heart.

A crushing weight thunders through every inch of me. I grip the wheel and cry until my throat is raw. And my ribs ache with every inhale.

An hour later, I dry my face and fix my mirrors, pulling back onto the highway. Every mile, the tears flow. It's going to be a long, long four days by myself. I pick up my phone with one hand and tap speed dial for Rubes. She picks up on the second ring.

"You okay, Adds? Reed called."

Of course he did.

"No, not one bit."

"Fuck, Adds. Come home, babe. I got you, boo."

I chug another sob, nodding. When I remember she can't see me, I choke out, "On my way."

"Good, I will have everything ready when you arrive. You're staying with me until further notice, alright?"

"Sure," I rasp, and a raspy chuckle slips out at her bossiness. Always organizing people, our Ruby.

I fall into the loving arms that wait for me as sirens wail around us and the filthy air of New York City reacquaints itself with my senses. Ruby hugs me tight. It takes everything I have to not fall apart on the sidewalk of her street.

"Come on, let's take you inside." She wraps an arm around my shoulders. "I have ice cream, chocolate, and reruns of Friends . . ."

"I wanna crash. Ain't got an ounce of energy for nothin' else."

"Listen to you, Montana small-town speak just falling out of your mouth." She laughs and squeezes my shoulders. But I have to swallow past the stone that grows in my airway. God, even my own words stab me in the heart. Everything is a reminder of Hudson. We cross the threshold to her apartment. It's modern, clean, and organized within an inch of its square footage.

"Tomorrow night, you and me are going out for dinner. After that, we have a full calendar. You know what they say about getting back on the hors—" She drops her arm. "Fuck, I'm sorry, Adds."

"It's okay," I utter, wrapping my arms around myself as tears spill over, running down my cheeks. She is folded around me a second later. All these people hugging me, I swear, it makes everything so much harder.

Let me be heartbroken in solitude, please.

"I think I'm going to turn in." I make sure the words are whole, even if my heart feels like it never will be again. Ruby leans in and grabs my shoulders. "Let me know if you need chocolate. That's what I'm here for, hey."

I nod and wander toward the spare room that I've crashed in more times than I can count. I guess now it's my short-term room until I find another place for however long I am working at the equine clinic. The second the door is shut behind me, I flop onto the bed. But I roll over and stare at the ceiling. Nothing matters anymore. My phone pings.

Louisa.

My heart cracks.

And I have to grit my teeth as I slide to open her message.

> Just checking you got back to the big apple okay, darlin.

The last of my resolve dissolves and I chug out a sob while I text back.

I'm at Ruby's. Thank you for everything. Addy xx

It was my pleasure, hon. Take care.

You too. xx

I send Mom a text letting her know I'm back and can visit on the weekend. She sends back a smiley face emoji; she must be at work. Crawling under the blankets, exhausted, I curl up and pull my knees to my chest.

And when my eyes fall shut, I imagine being amongst the snow-laden trees, riding Sergeant, Hudson beside me on Rocket. Sobs come hard and fast. For the life I never knew I always wanted. Until sleep finally drags me under. But my dreams are full of those blue eyes and snippets of a life that will never be.

Chapter Twenty-Nine

HUDSON

Ma stares at me over her coffee. Her face is tight, her usual smile nowhere to be found. I wait for Pa, Mack, and Reed to file into the kitchen after feeding out hay. I'm the only one who is on the receiving end of Ma's scowl, if the smile she beams at Mack is any indication.

"Right, now we're all here, we should talk ranch and business before we're busy with the rest of the chores." Harry pulls out the chair at the head of the table and drops into it, palms coming to rest on the shining hardwood.

Ma glances between him and Reed, to Mack, and then me. I run a hand through my hair, stirring the sugar in my coffee, if only to avoid her glare again. I know what it's about. But she is way off the mark. This is how it was supposed to be. Even the old man thinks so. Why else would he have told me to stay away from Addy?

"Come on, Harry, I have chores to do," Reed pipes up.

Harry continues. "Right. Hudson. The final numbers are in for the roundup and the contracts that have already come in from the sale of the first six foals. We have enough equity finally to buy out Justin, so that was sent over yesterday. And we are booked in to do a walk-in inspection for two other ranches next week. Without your hard work this year, Hudson, none of these things would have been possible. So, on that note . . ." He glances to Ma, and she suppresses a small smile, holding his gaze. "This ranch is officially yours. I will have the documents drawn up this week when we're in town. And the company, which now consists of three businesses and six half shares, will be divided and managed between all four of you boys. Lawson, we have already talked to last night."

I don't know what to say.

Ma looks to me. "We were hoping you didn't have to do this by yourself. But—"

I hold up a hand, knowing exactly where she is going with this. She rests her coffee on the coaster in front of her.

"Thank you both. I will continue to earn what I have been given. But Addy's life is not mine to influence. I won't have her give up her life as an equine vet so I can be happy. Unlike all of you, I'm not that fucking selfish." I push out of the chair but as I walk away, Harry gives Ma a look.

"Well, I for one am glad to be moving out," Reed says. He is trying to lighten the mood. It falls on sullen hearts. Nobody responds. I push through the back door and stalk to the table under the weeping willow.

I didn't mean to be disrespectful after all my parents have done for the four of us. But this team effort thing is grinding my fucking gears. Laying down on the bench seat closest to the tree, I shove my hands over my face, blocking out the dappled sunlight.

Ma sits by my feet a moment later. "Loving someone this much could never be selfish, Huddy."

Charlie appears by my head and jumps up onto my belly. God, he's a heavy little mutt. I sit up and he curls up in my lap the way Addy let him every time. So much for a working ranch dog. My sweet girl has spoiled this little man. The air lodges in my lungs and won't budge.

Not my girl.

Not anymore. I grind my jaw shut.

"Oh, my boy." Ma slides closer to me on the bench.

"Think I'm a bit old for that, Ma." I rub a hand over the stubble on my jaw.

"Your children never outgrow what they are to you."

I grunt. Words hurt. Everything hurts.

I usher Charlie from my lap and walk for my truck. "Later, Ma."

"Hudson, I wasn't finished."

When I wave a hand, she mutters something under her breath.

At home, I sit in the truck for a moment. The quiet is too loud. Charlie paws at the door and I lean over and open it, letting him out. I kill the engine and walk inside. The house is all but finished now, the kitchen in and functional. The fireplace crackles behind me. The rooms are mostly bare, but more furniture should arrive next week. How much stuff does one man and a spoiled dog need, anyway?

I wander down the hall. Something yellow and small catches my eye near the bedroom door. I pick it up. It crumbles between my fingers. One of the flowers I spread around for Addy the night of Ma's party. My back hits the wall and I slide to the floor, gaze stuck on the dried yellow petal in my fingers. It falls to the ground between my legs, and I grip my hands in my hair until it burns. Sobs chug from my throat.

I pound my head into the wall behind me and scream, long and raw. Dropping my face into my hands, I choke on the ragged sobs that crawl from the too-heavy space in my lungs. Charlie appears by my side and sits, whimpering. When he lies, resting his head on his paws, worried little eyes watching me, I lose it.

"I'm sorry, buddy. She isn't coming back."

Charlie whimpers, closing his eyes.

She isn't coming back.

And I realize in this moment, that there is no coming

back from Adeline Howard. My heart is in pieces. I wouldn't even know where to start to find every last one to put it back together.

Pain floods my chest and steals the last of my breath.

If you had told me a year ago that Hudson Rawlins would find the love of his life, as well as his heart that had been stowed away forever after the last woman, I would have said you're a fucking idiot. But the only idiot here is me. This . . . This thing between Addy and me, should have gone either of two ways, as far as I can tell.

One, it should have never happened. Not keen on that idea, to be honest.

Two, it should have eclipsed everything else, for both of us. But I screwed that up . . . .

And here we are.

Miserable and sitting in the hallway, with a sleeping dog in my lap, contemplating every single damn life choice I have ever made. When tires crunch to a stop outside, I don't even bother getting up. Charlie doesn't stir. Maybe they will do me a favor and fuck off. Or burn the house down around me. The feeling in my heart wouldn't change, that much I know.

"Hudson Andrew Rawlins, front and center."

Ma.

"Do as your mother asks, son."

Pa.

Charlie snaps his head up with a growl. The only person he has ever been happy with inside this house is Addy. I drag my weary body up the wall and pad to the kitchen. I don't even care that I'm a mess. Or that Charlie is snarling at Harry, who is now leaning against the new center island.

Harry drops papers on the counter beside him. He wants to do this now?

"It can't wait 'til tomorrow?" I say.

"Nope."

Harry's brows pull down as he taps the papers. I sigh and pull them across the counter and in front of me. Deeds, partnership agreements for the businesses. I flick through them and sign where my name is. I turn to the next bundle of papers. *Partnership between Harrison John Rawlins & Adeline Grace Howard.*

What the hell?

I flick to the last page.

There are two spots to sign: one for Harry, one for Addy.

I snap my gaze up. "What is this?"

Harry points to the papers in my hand. "That is the contract I offered Addy."

Why didn't she mention this? Why didn't they tell me?

Ma taps the papers. "And it still stands. Always will—she is a brilliant equine vet."

"But she left. I don't understand. Why didn't anyone tell me about this?"

Harry pushes from the counter and folds his arms over his chest. "We didn't need Addy to ride along; Justin would have done fine. But you did. We didn't need Addy to get back on a horse. She needed that for herself. We don't need another business. But you two need a way to make this work." He glances at Ma. "When I told you not to get involved with her, I needed to see for myself what you thought was worth fighting for, Hudson. I couldn't care less who you fool around with. But Addy was different." He swallows. "I needed you to show us how much you were willing to work for her. Every order I have ever given you, you followed. Every single one, *except that one*. You see where I'm going with this, son?"

He rubs a hand over his jaw. "Hudson, I am going to make this real plain for you. When you find your captain, you do everything in your power to keep them, because without them, you will wander the sea like a lost sailor, second-guessing every choice you ever make. Alone and bitter. Your mother is mine. And I wholeheartedly believe Addy is yours. Hell, even that mutt hound of yours knows it."

"It was a test?"

"Bless your father's cockeyed methods. And after Jemma . . ." She tilts her head, her mouth a thin line, silver lining her eyes. "We can all see who Addy is to you, Huddy."

"But she still left."

"Isn't that what you told her to do? After everything, you were hell bent on *not* giving her a reason to stay?" Ma's words are soft.

"She deserves to have her dreams. I'm not gonna be the person to take that away from her, after everything she went through . . ."

Harry shakes his head. "And thank god she did. Otherwise, you two never would have met. You never would have had reason to work together. Not one moment of this was coincidence, Hudson. But now, you can give her what she wants, what you both want." He points to the contract with Addy's name on it.

"What if she doesn't want it?"

"I have a feeling it will all work out fine." Ma pats my shoulder and walks out.

"Don't just stand there, son. This ship ain't gonna steer itself." Harry winks at me and follows Ma.

I stand stunned in the kitchen. The fire crackles and pops, filling the space around me that the ringing in my ears miss.

Four days.

I have four days to figure out what to say to Addy.

To analyze every memory that I have of me and her.

No time like the present . . .

"Charlie, pack your shit."

He chases his tail before faltering and tumbling with a whelp. His leg is probably still sore. Looks like he gets to pay his doctor a visit. Hope fills my heart, and I suck in a breath.

After a rushed packing job, one quick shower, and closing up the house, I pull out of my driveway and settle in for the long haul. This cowboy is going to New York City.

Chapter Thirty

ADDY

"Fuck, shit. Stay here, Adds. Be right back." Ruby springs from her seat and rushes from the Italian restaurant like it's caught fire, and the firemen are standing outside shirtless. Never seen the girl move so fast. Her phone buzzes. Reed. Those two are always talking. It's sweet.

I draw mindless patterns on the red tablecloth. I might not be hungry, but she insists we eat out. Something about getting back on the horse. That phrase will never be the same or stop haunting me. I check my phone. A message from Mom. Nothing else.

When Ruby walks back in, she mouths *sorry*. And when Adam slips around her and leans down to kiss my cheek, I freeze, eyes wide and on my best friend.

"Who wants drinks?" Adam asks, upbeat, as if he's welcome and this is simply a happy coincidence.

"No thanks," I utter.

"Gin and tonic, Hervey. Take your time."

Ruby sits down, stare burning into Adam's back as he weaves through the crowd near the bar before tracking her wide eyes to mine. "Sorry, Adds. I had no idea he would be on this side of town, I swear."

"It's fine." I force a smile.

She shakes her head and taps her phone. Muttering, "Reed is going to kill me."

"You two get along well, still."

"Who, Adam?"

I huff a laugh. "No, *Reedsy*."

"Oh, yeah, we kind of clicked, I guess. He's a goof. Like a big brother or something."

When I raise an eyebrow, she stares out the window and I mutter, "Or something."

Adam appears with three drinks, and I roll my eyes as he sets down my favorite drink and takes the seat beside me. I shuffle a little way away. And Ruby suppresses a smile. "If I wasn't starving, Hervey, we would have abandoned you." Ruby nods to the drink I didn't ask for.

"Drama isn't your color, sweetheart," he coos at her before turning to me. "So, Addy girl, I bet you're happy to be back in civilization?"

"Sure," I drawl but don't meet his gaze. Civilization is the last place this girl wants to be. Our food arrives and Adam plucks a strand of spaghetti from my plate like we have gone backward twelve months and he and I are still sharing food, a bed, and whatever else. I slap his hand the way Louisa would.

"Oi!" he snaps.

"Get your own, Hervey."

"Oh, I see how it is. You go off getting all wild in the middle of nowhere and now I am just Hervey?"

Ruby's phone vibrates, wiggling across the table.

Reed.

My stomach plummets.

Then it pings.

Again.

And again.

Ping.

Ping.

Ping.

Ping.

Ping.

"Shit, sorry Adds, I have to answer him."

"Go ahead," I say. But inside I'm screaming, *Don't leave me here with Adam! Take me with you, Rubes!* I school my face to socially appropriate politeness and comment on the weather. Ruby takes off toward the front of the restaurant, and when her voice turns to an urgent whisper, she veers and disappears into the ladies' room.

I shove the spaghetti around my fork, trying to convince my stomach it's hungry. The food smells so good. The company leaves a little to be desired . . .

Adam leans back on his chair and lays an arm over the back of my chair.

I glance to the street, desperate to put my focus anywhere else than to where he sits. Shoulders hunched over, I slurp up a strand of spaghetti and look back out the window.

And then . . . On the other side of the restaurant window.

That white Stetson.

Blue eyes that swallow me whole.

His gorgeous face . . .

His gaze shifts to my left.

To Adam.

He turns back, heads for the door, but walks away, disappearing into the crowd on the sidewalk.

The breath in my lungs burns out.

No . . . No!

I push from the chair fast. It falls over, hitting the floor with a clatter. Skipping around Adam, who gives me a stunned, confused look, I push through the patrons in the restaurant entrance. "Sorry, sorry. Please, I have to get out."

I slam a hand onto the glass door and spill out onto the street. Air leaving my lungs laced with fire, tears burning my eyes, I spin side to side. Trying desperately to find that white Stetson in the sea of commuters and nightlife. My hands ball to fists by my sides. "Huddy," I rasp. Yellow catches my attention, poking up from the bin near the restaurant door.

I step over and glance in. A bunch of yellow daisies. The same as the ones he bought me when we went to the restaurant in Lewistown. Like the ones he scattered around the house the night of Louisa's party. I slap a hand to my mouth, stifling a moan.

"Hudson!?" I push through the crowd one way, then another. I have no idea where he would have gone to. "Hudson!"

Tears stream down my face. *Shit.*

Dammit.

I come to a stop, sobs bubbling from my throat. A hand touches my arm.

I spin back.

"I'm sorry, Adds." Ruby stands with Adam behind her.

"Hudson, he was—"

Adam scoffs. "What? The hick was here?"

"Shut up, Adam. Just stop it!"

"Why are you getting hung up over that small-town yokel?"

I stalk to where he stands. "I said, shut up." I shove him. But he chuckles.

"Come on, Addy girl. You know you and I are meant to be. I have forgiven you for your little fling. Come home."

"You forgive *me*?" I huff out an incredulous laugh. "Three years, Adam. Of you doing whatever you want and me letting you! We are *done*. We were done over six months ago. And I am *not* yours." The words growl from my lips. My fists shake by my sides.

Ruby waves to the crowd. "You heard her, Hervey. Fuck off." When she turns back her brows drop and her mouth twists. "Reed was trying to tell me Hudson was here. Guess he was a bit late?"

"I have to find him, Rubes." I grip my hair in my fists. "God, I can't believe the only time Hervey bothers to show up, it fucks everything up."

"Irony is funny like that." She grabs my hand. "Come on, let's go home. Reed gave him our address; maybe he went there."

We all but run the three blocks back to Ruby's place. But when we dash up the four flights of stairs, Hudson is nowhere to be found. Ruby unlocks the door, and we sink onto the couch. I stare numbly at the black TV screen. "You want Reed to find him for you?" Ruby asks. The messages and calls I tried to find Hudson with have gone unanswered.

"I—"

She pulls me into her side. "I'm sorry, Adds."

I have never cried so much in my entire life as I have in the past five days.

Ruby's phone pings again and she groans. "You want me to tell him to drop it?"

I don't answer. I can't.

"What the?" Ruby utters, moving away from me a little. "Message from Reed to the Captain?"

When I turn to her with wide eyes, hers light up. "You know what that means, don't you . . ."

I nod.

She glances down at her phone before looking back up.

"He says, 'Come home and sign the paperwork, Captain.'"

I gasp.

Ruby turns the phone around . . . A salute emoji from Reed.

I chuckle a strained laugh. I need to video call Harry. Right now.

Chapter Thirty-One

HUDSON

I've lost my mind. This is so much worse than last time, with Jemma. I thought I heard Addy's voice in Ma's study a few days ago. Heartbreak has gone straight to my head, 'cause she is gone, and I can still hear her. My heart shatters all over again.

Keep your hands busy, Huddo.

Solid advice from my little brother. Mack and Reed were here for my last heartbreak. I shouldn't have expected anything less. But unlike last time, there is no coming back from this. The way that Adam guy slung his arm over her chair . . . I never pegged Addy for a pushover, but he is familiar, and maybe she needed that. I don't believe it . . . At least, I don't want to.

Silver lining, I'm sure Charlie enjoyed his first and last road trip. Back to the task at hand, I measure for the fifth time and line the trim up to the proper angle before letting the blade drop. After a full day working with the colt and wrangling cattle, my body aches. But my mind won't quit, so I raise the blade and tug the trim from the deck.

Up the ladder, I hold it in place before nailing it between the wall and the ceiling with the pneumatic nail gun. The thwack echoes through this empty house, rattling through my heart with each nail I send into the trim. And by the time I reach the end, my hands tremble.

Charlie is curled up in front of the fire. The wind picks up outside. The chance of freezing rain or sleet is high. I grab the whiskey from the cabinet. At least it might take the edge off and warm me up. The sun is falling fast outside, and I grab a glass and pour a couple inches in the bottom. I toss it down and revel in the burn that sinks all the way to my gut.

Charlie's head pops up and he stares at the door for a moment before laying it on his paws again. But his beady eyes are stuck on the damn door. The way they have been for the past three days. I don't have the heart to tell him he's waiting for something that's not going to happen. Someone who's not coming.

I pour another inch into the glass and raise it to my lips. Charlie springs up and darts to the door, tail wagging. *What the hell?*

I place the glass down and am halfway to the door when I hear tires on gravel.

I halt in my tracks.

Hoping that it's Reed's truck.

Hoping it's not.

A car door opens and slams shut. Then another.

I walk to the front door and bend down to where Charlie is going nuts, desperate to be let out. "Who is it, boy?"

Thunder crackles overhead. Rain pelts down and the wind picks up as the house darkens inside. Charlie barks impatiently at me now. "Alright."

But my hand hesitates over the door handle.

When Charlie growls at me, I huff an incredulous laugh and open the door for him. "Alright, little man, you win."

The rain is heavy.

The Cherokee parked in my drive is covered in mud.

Charlie flies down the stairs.

Addy stands holding her bags in the pouring rain. She drops them the instant Charlie reaches her and drops to her knees. He jumps around her, lapping at her face. A rock slides into my throat. I walk across the porch and down the stairs until I am standing inches from her crouched form. Jaw clenched tight, I wait for her. And when she pushes to her feet, those gorgeous brown eyes find mine.

Hair, wet and messy, dangles around her shoulders. Her chest heaves and her mouth parts. "Huddy," she rasps, and her face crumples.

My hands find her face and I slam my mouth to hers.

She huffs a strangled laugh and sobs into my mouth. Tears burn down my cheeks and I pull her closer. She parts her mouth and I claim every inch of her.

Her hands wander into my soaked hair. My cock thickens with every touch as she pushes and pulls her way through my hair, down my neck, and to my collar. She grips the shirt with both hands and breaks from the kiss. "I heard there was a position available . . . Something about a vacancy for captain?"

She smiles.

So fucking beautiful.

I sweep her up into my arms and walk up the stairs. Charlie trots inside and heads back to the fireplace.

Addy shivers in my arms. "Need a hot shower, sweet girl?"

"Amongst other things." She pulls my mouth down to hers, and I fumble my way to the shower. When I have the water on, I set her down and she stares at me, her breathing fast, heavy. "Hudson?"

"Yeah?"

"You were never a choice for me. You're it . . . I love you."

I turn back and rip the shirt from my back. Her eyes follow the lines on my body. "Adeline Howard, I have loved you since the day Charlie killed that snake."

Her mouth drops open with the word "oh" before curling into a smile. Her hungry eyes follow me as I close the distance between us and I growl, "Arms up."

She raises her arms, eyes locked on mine as I peel the cold, wet clothes from her body. When they hit the floor with a wet slap, I slide my fingers into the waistband of her jeans. Her beautiful brown eyes burn into mine as I push them down and she steps out. I kick them to the side and kiss her mouth before tracking kisses down her neck. She runs her fingers into my hair and moans. "God, you have no idea how much I missed you, Hudson Rawlins."

"I have a pretty good idea, Adeline."

My cock throbs in my jeans.

"You have far too many clothes on, Huddy."

"Nope. We are going to take this so damn slow."

She huffs a small laugh and arches as my mouth finds her hard peaks. Steam fills the bathroom, and when I have sufficiently sucked and nibbled both nipples, I drop to my knees and kiss her stomach, sliding a thumb over her clit. She whimpers, and I spread her legs with my hands. "I have been driving for four days. Shower first, please."

I push to my feet and pick her up. Her legs wrap around my waist, and I walk into the stream of hot water, jeans and all. She devours my mouth with hers, and I let her down. Swiping the soap up, I lather her up, making sure to cover every inch of her body. When I stand back up after soaping her calves, she grabs the button of my fly and flicks it open and drags the zipper down. A heartbeat later, my cock springs free, and I press it into her stomach, covering her lips with mine.

I run a hand down her stomach and trace circles

around her clit. As she mutters something incoherent, I smile against her. Water running over those gorgeous breasts, her stomach, hips and ass, she is incredible. Shampoo appears in front of my face. "Wash my hair."

I take the bottle from her hand, and she drops to her knees. "You're not that tall, sweet girl."

"I know." Her mouth slips around the head of my cock, and my grip on the shampoo tightens. When I have some semblance of control, I squirt the liquid into my hand and start massaging it through her hair. She takes me deeper and I groan, fingers fisting in her hair. "Goddamn, Addy."

She swirls her tongue around the head, and it is all I can do to hold back from thrusting into her pretty mouth. I concentrate on the shampoo and making sure all of her hair is lathered up before grabbing her under the arms and spinning her to face the tile. "Your turn."

She glances over her shoulder at me and smiles.

My heart explodes.

And when she spreads her legs and tilts her ass toward me, I tug her closer and sweep the tip against her wet folds. "God above, Hudson. Please."

I push into her entrance. She moans with every inch I give her. It's too much. Not enough. I sweep her hair to one side and kiss her neck, finding her apex with my free hand. When her back curls further and her legs shake with every soft whimper, I thrust in hard. Sending her spiraling.

"Huddy! Oh god."

I follow her, falling like I never have before.

Knowing this is only the start of our always.

"Hudson . . . Huddy."

Something touches my face, light, feather soft, tracking down my jaw, down my neck. And when I crack my gaze open, beautiful, lit-up brown eyes are close in front of my face before soft lips cover mine. A man could get used to this.

My body responds to Addy's. Cock hard, fire pooling deep in my belly. The canopy bed that I picked because it reminded me of her in her tiny townhouse creaks a little as I flip her over, pinning her under me. She stretches, languid like a cat in the sun. Naked, her soft, perfect breasts move, calling my name. And like a man starved, I grunt and nip at the peaks, rousing giggles from this amazing woman in my bed.

In *our* bed.

'Cause I sure as hell won't be letting her go, ever again.

But first, I want to make this beautiful woman come undone. Every goddamn day from this moment forward.

Always.

By the time I track kisses to her belly button, she is writhing underneath me. Good.

And when I push her legs wider with my hands inside

her thighs, I lap up the wetness that is mine. I suckle her apex, and she arches off the bed like a damn goddess. Hands gripping the headboard, she whimpers as I slide two fingers inside her and sweep my tongue back and forth over her clit.

She unravels, riding my hand, and I can't help the smile that stretches my face, watching my Addy. Then this sweet girl comes around my fingers. Fucking perfect. And she's mine.

"More," she pants.

I shift to my knees and line her up with my hard cock. Her hands are over the headboard as I sink into her. Fuck me.

No amount of time with Addy is gonna be enough for me.

Never.

She decided I was worth her forever, and I will spend the rest of mine making damn sure I earn it. Even if it's one kiss at a time.

One milestone.

One hurdle.

Whatever comes our way.

And there is only one way this cowboy knows how to make sure that happens.

Chapter Thirty-Two

ADDY

Twelve months later . . .

I may be his captain, but Hudson is my anchor. The solid ground I walk on. And with that sentiment, I squeeze Sergeant forward. We trot up the hill on the far side of the vista. My dress, white, lacy, and studded with rhinestones, flows over the gelding's rump.

As we near the crest where our family and friends are seated, I imagine them in perfect rows of white chairs, yellow petals scattered as far as the Montana four winds care to take them. Of course, I wasn't allowed to see the actual setup. Ruby's rules, of which there are many. But this one she is ruthless about.

I glance at my wrist, where an identical bracelet to the one I gave Louisa jangles as I move with Sergeant. But unlike hers, mine has only one charm, the captain's wheel, and on the back engraved in script font is *Hudson*.

When Reed appears beside me on Magnet in dress jeans, jacket, tie, and black hat, the butterflies in my belly turn to full on eagles.

"Ready, Adds?"

"Of course."

He beams at me, and I lean forward in the saddle. Sergeant takes off up the hill. My hair flows around my shoulders. Crisp Montana mountain air hits my lungs. Sunshine warms my face, and for a heartbeat I let my eyes drift shut. There was a long, long period of my life that I thought I would never have this again. This freedom. The part of me that lights up my soul.

Reed lopes beside me, and when we crest the rise, the rows of seated people I love stand as one. Ruby has outdone herself this time. And I'm glad she did. Hudson deserves nothing less. The Rawlins deserve nothing less. Dad waits for me at the start of the aisle. I slow Sergeant to a walk, and Reed follows my lead.

Before we reach the gathering, I give him a *thank you* smile and he veers left, saluting with two fingers to his forehead, the widest grin stretching his face.

Sergeant slows to a halt, and I look down to Dad. His hands on the reins steady the gelding before he offers me a lift down.

"I got it, Daddy."

"Yes, you do, baby."

Shifting the dress to my left, I swing out of the saddle, feet landing on the grassy hilltop. Mack takes Sergeant and leads him away to where Reed is handing over Magnet to a young boy. They walk toward the front of the aisle. I adjust my skirts, tidy my hair, and lift the front of the dress a little to walk to where the aisle begins. Dad loops his arm through mine, dotting a kiss to my head. "Don't keep the man waiting, Addy."

"Never."

The music starts. A six-piece string ensemble with an acoustic guitar. A rendition of "Oh Love" by Brad Paisley and Carrie Underwood starts. Ma sits with Ruby to the right, up the front.

Standing at the end of the aisle, hands clasped in front of him, is my Huddy. In dress jeans, a white shirt, jacket, and tie, with his trusty Stetson hat over those blue eyes. And the biggest smile I have ever seen on that gorgeous face. A single yellow daisy is pinned to his lapel. And then I see him . . .

Charlie.

Sitting by Hudson's side, calm as a cat in the sun. Small black bow tie, and all clean. No growls at the guests. No barking at the boys or Harry. Dad nudges me, and we walk down the aisle as the song reaches a crescendo. Louisa is all tears. Harry's crinkled eyes meet mine and his jaw feathers. Fancy that—never thought I'd live to see the day Harry Rawlins gets emotional.

When Dad releases me, I step to where Hudson stands.

His warm hands wrap around mine. "Hey, sweet girl." His voice is soft, a little wobbly.

My heart skips a beat or two and I steady my galloping breath. "Hello, Huddy."

The preacher leans in. "Okay if I start, you two?"

We nod and he chuckles. Charlie barks, as if to say *come on, already.* Hudson throws him a *calm down, buddy* look. Mack and Lawson smile at me and Reed beams, all of them with their hands clasped in front like their brother's were moments ago. The preacher clears his throat.

"We are gathered here today . . ."

"Put me down, Hudson." I chuckle.

"Nope, not a chance." He kicks the front door open and carries me across the threshold, and my dress trails behind us. I drag his mouth to mine with both hands. Charlie trots by his side, his paws clacking over the hardwood floor. The windows are open, and the cool night breeze rolls in from the mountains around us.

Yellow flowers are tossed over the floor of the entire house. Flames flicker in hurricane lanterns on every surface, lining the hallway. More yellow petals are strewn on every surface of our home. Ruby has been here, and

Reed, too, I bet. I pull the hat from Hudson's head and toss it onto the sofa by the fire.

"Welcome home, Mrs. Rawlins." His voice is gravel, raw.

"Why, thank you, Mr. Rawlins." I dot kisses along his jaw, and he strides toward our bedroom.

"As stunning as that dress is, it will still look better on the floor."

I nip his ear. "I one hundred percent agree."

He sinks his face into my hair, nuzzling until his mouth finds my neck. When I have worked him up into a frenzy, I wriggle to be put down. Reluctantly, Hudson releases his grip and my feet hit the floor. "One more thing before the rest of our lives start, Huddy."

I grab his hand and drag him down the hallway and out the back door. More hurricane lanterns dot the back porch, two flanking each step down to the backyard. "Where are you taking me?" he says with a chuckle.

"You'll see."

When we clear the last step, I spin back and put a hand over his eyes. He chuckles, his Adam's apple bobs, and his hand wraps around my free one. "You will never cease to amaze me, Adeline Rawlins."

Breath lodges in my throat. And I fight the urge to let him fold me into his arms, and instead pull him along beside me to the last weeping willow at the back of the yard. When we round the tree to where his wedding present sits, I turn him on the spot.

"Open your eyes, Hudson," I whisper as I drop my hand.

He stares at me before turning to face the swinging love seat set under the tree facing south. The one we talked about on that camping trip. Even in the dim candlelight, it's the perfect spot for our lives to start.

He swallows.

I study his face. "Welcome to the bridge, sailor."

He chuckles and sweeps me up. Wind hisses through the hanging branches that have us cocooned. When the back of his legs meet the swing, he smashes his mouth to mine. A heartbeat later the zipper swishes, the bodice loosens, and his mouth finds my peaks as I arch into him.

"I changed my mind, that dress will look perfect on the grass."

A moment later our clothes are a pile on the grass below the willow. I straddle his lap, exploring his face with my lips, and his hair, neck, and chest with my hands.

"Turn around, Addy."

I sink my knees on either side of him, and lean into him as he thrusts upward, filling every place that matters. I lay my head on his shoulder as he rolls my nipples through his fingers. I take up the rhythm between us, the four winds caressing every inch of my skin.

"Goddamn, how much I love you, sweet girl."

I moan as his pace gets rougher, faster. His thumb finds my apex and I open my eyes. Ragged breaths burn as I say, "Always, Hudson . . ."

Stars shimmer in the messy spaces between the waving long, thin branches overhead. The inky blanket that bursts with stars disappears as I close my eyes, climbing so high with Hudson wrapped around me. "Come for me, beautiful."

I let go and spiral, whimpering his name.

He follows.

My heart is full.

My Hudson. *Always.*

Epilogue

HUDSON

Hattie slips off her little pony at an awkward angle and slams into the dirt in a tangle of blonde curls, blue jeans, boots, and pink cowgirl hat. Head down and still prancing across the round yard, the tiny pony sure packs some attitude. She pushes to her feet and dusts off her jeans. Her face crumples, those beautiful big brown eyes crinkling with a swell of tears. And my heart ceases to move.

I resist the urge to run to where she stands. And when she bends down to swipe up her pink cowgirl hat, she releases a string of huffed curses. Addy's goin' to have my liver for breakfast if she hears our five-year-old daughter's workin' talk.

The Cherokee rolls down the driveway as I take the pony's reins and Hattie walks over. The instant she notices her mama's car, she races to the gate of the round yard. When Addy parks in front of the white gate to the homestead, Pa climbs out of the passenger's seat and walks over.

His gait a little slower these days, he has been riding along with Addy ever since we told my parents about the second baby. He claims it's for business purposes. We all know he is keeping an eye on Addy so she doesn't overdo it. Harry Rawlins will never stop caring about his family.

I open the gate for Hattie, and she shoots out to meet him. "Grandpa!"

When she reaches Pa, he swoops down and picks her up, sitting her high in his arms so her five years towers over his almost seventy. Then she leans in and nuzzles him with a harrumph.

"What's up, pumpkin; what's with the tears?"

"I fell off." She leans back up and looks to where I stand with her pony. "And Dada is giving me the *tough love*," she says, pushing out her bottom lip.

"Is that so? Well, you know what you gotta do when ya fall off your horse, little lady?" Harry asks, giving up a quizzical face.

She nods, slowly.

"That's right, you hop straight back on."

Addy rounds the car and pads to where Pa stands with Hattie. She thumbs the tears from our little girl's red cheeks. "Hello, Hattie girl, you been helping Dada?"

She nods furiously. "You fix them horses up good, Mama?"

"Sure did, baby girl. You two have been busy." Addy nods toward the pony.

"Yeah, but I not sure I wanna anymore."

Pa lets her down, and she huffs her way back to the round yard.

"Alright, baby, what's the plan?" I ask.

She stomps her foot, sinking her hands onto her hips.

"Harriette Elouise Rawlins, you poutin' girl?" I lean on the rail, one foot up on the last rung, and lift the Stetson to look at her. Sighing, she stares at the pony, then walks over to me and lifts her face, little mouth still pouting.

"This cowgirl is gettin' back on the horse." Glancing to Harry, she moves closer, and I lean down. "Grandpa said so," she whispers.

I chuckle as Addy comes to my side. I kiss her, laying a hand on her six-month belly. A boy. *Her little man*, she says.

Hattie walks over to her pony and takes the reins. She sticks her foot into the stirrup iron but stills. "No, Dada. I can't."

Tears run down her little face and my heart wrings out. I crouch down and take her hands in mine. "I know it hurts, baby. But you have to get back on, sweetheart. Mama did."

"I don't think I am as brave as Mama." Her little chin wobbles as she dips her head. Blonde curls fall around her shoulders. Her brown eyes swell with tears.

"You know what, you and Mama are both strong girls, you can do anything. *Anything* you put your minds to."

She stares at the pony, then turns back. "Anything, Dada?"

"Yeah baby, anythin' you want."

She climbs up. When she pushes the pony into a trot around the yard, Harry and Addy salute her. She giggles, throwing her head back.

Happiness is the freedom a good horse brings.

And the woman who found her way to Montana because she was chasing hers.

Always . . .

That, I know for sure, will never change.

Need more Addy & Hudson?
Grab the BONUS SCENE now!
https://BookHip.com/TGFQJTR

Continue the Rosewood Ranch series with
Reed & Ruby's story,
Heart & Hope*!*

Sign up to the newsletter to make sure you never miss an Alexandra Banks book!!

ALEXANDRA
Banks
CONTEMPORARY ROMANCE
AVAILABLE NOW!!

TOUGH LOVE *playlist*

HARD TO LOVE Bryce Lee	3:44
TICKS Brad Paisley	4:33
NOTHING ON BUT THE RADIO Gary Allan	3:33
I COULD FLY Keith Urban	5:19
I'LL BE YOUR SMALL TOWN Cole Swindell	3:15
HER Cole Swindell	3:31
FOREVER AFTER ALL Luke Combs	3:52
ANY OL' BARSTOOL Jason Aldean	3:23
DON'T MENTION MEMPHIS Tim McGraw	3:00
RIGHT WHERE I NEED TO BE Gary Allan	3:02
OH LOVE Brad Paisley & Carrie Underwood	4:09
THEN Brad Paisley	4:20

ROSEWOOD RANCH SERIES

HEART
&
HOPE
ALEXANDRA
BANKS

Acknowledgments

A love story like this one is all consuming to write and it is my hope that readers find themselves immersed.

As always, thanks to my editors, Lindsey and Zainab. Your input and guidance is always wanted and appreciated.

To every ARC reader who volunteered to read this book, thank you!!

And lastly, but most certainly not least, my family for putting up with the endless country music playlist that I made them endure during the writing process to get into the zone. Sorry... ;)

Alex xx

Alexandra Banks is a romantic at heart, and an optimist down to her very bones. Her love for everything romance sees her writing HEAs all day long.

But don't be fooled, there will be angst along the way, possibly heartbreak. But her fierce heroines can handle just about anything!

For more heartwarming reads, follow her on socials and join the mailing list so you never miss another heart throb!